"You've probably spent most of your life moving from one place to another. So perhaps you can't understand why a child who's lost her mother and father would want to stay in a familiar place around people she's used to."

"I understand better than you suppose, Miss Murray." Captain Radcliffe spoke so softly, Marian wondered if she had only imagined his words.

"You do?"

He replied with a slow nod, a distant gaze and a pensive murmur that seemed to come from some well-hidden place inside him. "I was ten years old when I was set to sea after my mother died."

The wistful hush of his voice slid beneath Marian's bristling defenses. Her heart went out to that wee boy.

"I shall delay contacting Lady Villiers until January." Captain Radcliffe sounded resigned to his decision. "That will allow the children to spend Christmas in the country. After that, the New Year is a time for new beginnings."

"Thank you, sir."

As she hurried back to the nursery, Marian thanked God, too, for granting this reprieve. Perhaps her earlier prayers had been heard after all.

Books by Deborah Hale

Love Inspired Historical

The Wedding Season
  "Much Ado About Nuptials"
*The Captain's Christmas Family

*Glass Slipper Brides

DEBORAH HALE

After a decade of tracing her ancestors to their roots in Georgian-era Britain, Golden Heart winner Deborah Hale turned to historical romance writing as a way to blend her love of the past with her desire to spin a good love story. Deborah lives in Nova Scotia, Canada, between the historic British garrison town of Halifax and the romantic Annapolis Valley of Longfellow's *Evangeline*. With four children (including twins), Deborah calls writing her "sanity retention mechanism." On good days, she likes to think it's working.

Deborah invites you to visit her personal website at www.deborahhale.com, or find out more about her at www.Harlequin.com.

The Captain's Christmas Family

DEBORAH HALE

Love Inspired

LOVE INSPIRED BOOKS

Recycling programs
for this product may
not exist in your area.

ISBN-13: 978-0-373-82896-8

THE CAPTAIN'S CHRISTMAS FAMILY

Copyright © 2011 by Deborah M. Hale

www.LoveInspiredBooks.com

Printed in U.S.A.

Thy will be done...
—*Matthew* 6:10

For Gloria Jackson
and in memory of Rev. David Jackson,
who both made worship the kind of joyful,
uplifting experience it was meant to be.

Chapter One

Nottinghamshire, England
1814

"He's coming, Miss Murray!" A breathless housemaid burst into the nursery without even a knock of warning.

The book Marian Murray had been reading to her two young pupils slid from her slack fingers and down her skirts to land on the carpet with a soft *thud*. A tingling chill crept down her back that had nothing to do with the gray drizzle outside. The moment she'd been dreading for weeks had arrived at last…in spite of her prayers.

A new prayer formed in her thoughts now, as she strove to compose herself for the children's sake. She hoped it would do better at gaining divine attention. *Please, Lord, don't let him be as bad as I fear and don't let him send the girls away!*

Unaware of her governess's distress, Dolly Radcliffe leapt up, her plump young features alight with excitement. "Who's coming, Martha? Are we to have company?"

The housemaid shook her head. "Not company, miss. It's the new master—Captain Radcliffe. Mr. Culpepper sent me to fetch ye so we can give him a proper welcome to Knightley Park."

"Tell Mr. Culpepper the girls and I will be down directly," Marian replied in a Scottish burr that all her years in England had done little to soften.

Forcing her limbs to cooperate, she rose from the settee and scooped up the fallen book, smoothing its wrinkled pages.

"New master?" Dolly's small nose wrinkled. "I thought Mr. Culpepper was master of the house now."

"Don't be silly." Cissy Radcliffe rolled her wide blue-gray eyes at her younger sister's ignorance. "Mr. Culpepper is only a servant. Knightley Park belongs to Captain Radcliffe now by en...en... Oh, what's that word again, Miss Marian?"

"*Entail,* dear." Marian plumped the bow of Cissy's blue satin sash, wishing she had time to control Dolly's baby-fine fair hair with a liberal application of sugar water. "Come along now, we don't want to keep the captain waiting."

Likely the new master would insist on the sort of strict order and discipline he'd kept aboard his ship. It would not do for her and the girls to make a bad impression by being tardy.

"What is entail?" asked Dolly, as Marian took both girls by the hands and led them out into the east wing hallway.

Marian stifled an impatient sigh. Ordinarily, she encouraged the children's endless questions, but at the moment she did not feel equal to explaining the legalities of inheritance to a curious six-year-old.

Cissy had no such qualms. "It's when an estate must pass to the nearest male relative. If I were a boy, I would be master of Knightley Park now. Or if little Henry had lived, he would be. But since there's only us, and we're girls, the estate belongs to Papa's cousin, Captain Radcliffe."

After a brief pause to digest the information, Dolly had another question. "Do you suppose the captain will look like Papa, since they're cousins?"

"*Were* cousins," Cissy corrected her sister. The child's slender fingers felt like ice as she clung to Marian's hand.

Dolly's forehead puckered. "Do people stop being relations after they go to heaven? That doesn't seem right."

"You'll find out soon enough whether Captain Radcliffe bears any family resemblance," said Marian as they reached the bottom of the great winding staircase and joined a stream of servants pouring out the front door.

Exchanging furtive whispers, the maids smoothed down their aprons, and the footmen straightened their neck linen. They seemed curious and apprehensive about the arrival of their new master. Marian shared their qualms.

Outside, under the pillared portico, Knightley Park's aging butler struggled to marshal his staff into decent order to greet Captain Radcliffe. Shaken by the sudden death of Cissy and Dolly's father, Culpepper had let household discipline slip recently. Now he was paying the price, poor fellow.

Marian had too many worries of her own to spare him more than a passing flicker of sympathy.

"This way, girls." She tugged them along behind the shifting line of servants to stand at the far end of the colonnade, a little apart from the others.

By rights, they probably should have taken a place up beside Mr. Culpepper and Mrs. Wheaton, the cook. Cissy and Dolly were the ladies of the house, in a way. At least, they had been until today. What they would be from now on, and where they would go, depended upon the man presently driving up the long, elm-lined lane toward them. Marian wanted to delay that meeting for as long as possible.

When the carriage came to a halt in front of the house, she could not stifle a shiver.

Dolly must have felt it for she edged closer. "Are you cold, Miss Marian?"

"A little," Marian whispered back, conscious of a breathless silence that had gripped the other servants. "Drizzle like this can make midsummer seem cool, let alone October. Now, remember, bright smiles and graceful curtsies to welcome the captain."

The carriage door swung open, and a tall, rangy figure emerged, clad in black from head to toe, relieved only by a glimpse of stark white shirt cuffs and neck linen. Marian felt a mild pang of disappointment that Captain Radcliffe had not worn his naval uniform. But, of course, he wouldn't, under the circumstances. From rumors in the newspapers, Marian had gleaned that the captain was on leave from his command under a cloud of suspicion.

As Captain Radcliffe removed his hat, a breath of wind stirred his brown hair strewn with threads of gold. Tucking the hat under his arm, he strode slowly past the line of servants while Mr. Culpepper introduced each one. The movement of their bows and curtsies rippled down the line like an ominous wave rolling toward Marian and her young charges. Resisting an urge to draw the girls into a protective embrace, she took a step backward so they would have room to make their curtsies.

At that moment, Captain Radcliffe loomed in front of them, looking even taller than he had from a distance. His face was too long and angular to be called handsome. But it was quite striking, with a jutting nose, firm mouth and deep set, gray eyes beneath sharply arched brows.

Those brows slanted together at a fierce angle as he stared at Cissy and Dolly with a look of the most intense severity Marian had ever seen. Beneath his relentless scrutiny, Cissy lost her nerve. Her curtsy wobbled, and her squeaks of greeting sounded more terrified than welcoming. Dolly forgot to curtsy at all but stared boldly up at the captain.

Mr. Culpepper seemed not to notice as he continued his introductions. "Sir, these are the daughters of your late cousin, Miss Celia Radcliffe and Miss Dorothy. Behind them is their governess, Miss Murray."

A clammy knot of dread bunched in the pit of Marian's stomach as she waited for Captain Radcliffe to speak. It was the same sensation that always gripped her between a dangerous flash of lightning and the alarming crack of thunder that followed.

"Children?" His voice did sound like the rolling rumble of distant thunder, or the pounding of the sea upon a lonely, rock strewn coast. "No one said anything about children."

The man was every bit as bad as she'd feared, if not worse. Besides all the other feelings roiling inside her, Marian felt a twinge of disappointment at the thought of another prayer unanswered. Once again, it appeared she would have to fight her own battles in defense of those she cared for. Some tiny part of her even stirred at the prospect—perhaps the blood of her warlike ancestors.

Or was it something about the captain's presence that stirred her? Surely not!

When Cissy backed away from her formidable cousin, Marian wrapped a reassuring arm around her shoulders and reached out to tug Dolly back, as well. "Perhaps we can discuss the girls and their situation this evening after I've put them to bed?"

The captain seemed to take notice of her for the first time, looking her over carefully as if to assess the strength of an adversary. His scrutiny ignited a blistering blush in Marian's cheeks. For an instant, the children and all the other servants seemed to melt away, leaving her all alone with Captain Radcliffe.

Perhaps the captain felt it, too, for he gave his head a brisk shake, collecting himself from a moment of abstraction. "Very well. Report to the bridge at eight bells of the last dog watch. That is…the Chinese drawing room at eight o'clock."

"Yes, sir." Marian dropped a curtsy, wondering if he expected her to salute. "Now I will take the children back indoors before they catch a chill...with your permission, of course."

"By all means, attend to your duties." The captain looked as if he could hardly wait for Cissy and Dolly to be out of his sight.

Marian was only too eager to obey his curt order.

"Come along, girls." She shepherded them into the house, resisting the perverse urge to glance back at him.

Neither of the children spoke until they were halfway up the broad spiral staircase.

"The captain doesn't look much like Papa." Dolly sounded disappointed.

"He isn't *anything* like Papa!" Cissy muttered fiercely.

"I don't think he likes us very much." Dolly sighed.

"I'm certain the captain doesn't dislike you, dear." Marian strove to convince herself as much as the children. "He was...surprised to find you here, that's all."

As they slipped back into the comforting familiarity of the nursery, Dolly's grip tightened with such sudden force that it made Marian wince. "The captain won't send us away, will he?"

"Of course not!" Marian stooped to gather her beloved young pupils into a comforting embrace.

They had been through so much in the two short years since she'd come to be their governess—first losing their mother and infant brother, then their father. She had done all she could to make them feel secure and loved, to protect them from the kind of harsh childhood she'd endured.

To herself she vowed, *That man won't send you away if there is anything I can do to prevent it!*

As he waited for the mantel clock to chime eight, Gideon Radcliffe paced the rounded bay end of the Chinese drawing room, peering out each of its tall, slender windows in turn.

Even in the misty dusk, they afforded a fine view down a gently sloping knoll to the lake, which wrapped around a small, green island. Gideon had pleasant memories of boating on that lake from long-ago visits to Knightley Park when his grandfather was master. At the time, he'd enjoyed an even better view from the room directly above this one—the nursery.

That thought reminded him of his cousin's children. He would rather have been ambushed by the combined French and Spanish fleets than by those two small girls. They could not have been more alien to his experience if they'd been a pair of mermaids. He had no idea what they might need, except to sense that he was entirely unequipped to provide it.

More than ever he felt the urgent necessity to restore his reputation, regain his command and get back to sea. He was confident he possessed the skill, experience and temperament to serve his country well in that capacity. After all these years of service, it was the only life he knew. Losing it would be worse than losing a limb—it would be like losing his very identity.

"I beg your pardon, sir." The soft lilt of a woman's voice intruded upon Gideon's most private thoughts. "You told me to report here at eight. Did you not hear me knock?"

"I...didn't." Gideon withdrew into himself, like a sea creature retreating into the shelter of its tough, rigid shell. "But do come in. I wanted to talk to you about the...children."

"As did I, sir." She approached with deliberate steps, halting some distance away, behind an ornate armchair.

During their first meeting, Gideon had been so taken aback by the sight of his young cousins that he'd paid little heed to their governess, beyond her hostile glare. No doubt she had read all the scurrilous gossip about him in the papers and judged him guilty of the false accusations against him. So much for his hope of finding a sanctuary at Knightley Park to escape public condemnation!

Now he forced himself to take stock of his potential adversary. Marian Murray was small and slender, her dark brown hair pinned back with strict severity. Only a single wisp had escaped to curl in a softening tendril over her left temple. With high cheekbones and a fresh complexion, her face might have been quite pleasant to look at if she ventured to smile occasionally. At the moment, her brown eyes were narrowed and her full lips compressed in an expression of barely concealed hostility, if not outright contempt.

Though Gideon told himself her opinion was not of the slightest consequence, he could not deny the sting. "Yes. Well...about the children. I hope the entail of the estate did not leave them unprovided for."

If that were the case, he would take responsibility for their maintenance. It might ease the unreasonable guilt he felt for displacing them from their home.

"No, sir." The governess seemed surprised by his

question, as if she had not expected him to care. "The girls each have a comfortable little fortune from their mother."

"I am relieved to hear it." Gideon nodded his approval. "Pray who is their guardian and why have they been left alone here?"

Surely he would have been informed if Cousin Daniel had named him in that capacity. And surely Daniel would have known better than to entrust his young daughters to the care of a distant relation who was apt to be away at sea for years on end.

"The girls have not been alone," Miss Murray corrected him. "They have had an entire household to care for them. Their mother's younger sister, Lady Villiers, is their godmother. She is to be their guardian."

"Capital!" Tension released its grip on his clenched muscles so swiftly Gideon feared he might crumple to the floor. "I mean to say...how fortunate...for the children. Will Lady Villiers be coming to fetch them soon or should they be sent to her?"

The look on Miss Murray's face grew even grimmer. A passing thought pricked Gideon's conscience. Was she too strict a person to have charge of two sensitive children? Perhaps he should suggest Lady Villiers hire a more amiable governess for his young cousins.

Captain Radcliffe didn't like her. That much was evident to Marian. Not that she minded—quite the contrary. Besides, it set them even.

She resented his obvious eagerness to palm off responsibility for Cissy and Dolly on someone else, without asking or caring whether that person might be the least bit suitable. In Marian's opinion, Lady Villiers was not.

"Her ladyship has been abroad since before Mr. Radcliffe's death. The family's solicitor has not been able to contact her. She was in Florence the last we heard, but she may have gone on to Paris."

"It does seem to be a fashionable destination since Napoleon's defeat." Captain Radcliffe sounded disappointed that Lady Villiers would not be taking the girls off his hands immediately. "I know someone in France who might be able to get a message to her."

A message to come at once and take the girls away? The prospect made Marian queasy. But would Cissy and Dolly be any better off with this glacial man about whom she'd heard disturbing rumors?

Her gaze flitted around the elegant, exotic room. At least this house was familiar to the girls. And if the new master had no fondness for them, she and the other servants did. Besides, unlike their aunt, Captain Radcliffe had no reason to harbor designs on the girls' fortunes. "Could you delay sending that message for just a bit, sir?"

"Why on earth…?"

"Knightley Park is the children's home—the only one they've ever known. If they must leave it, I would like some time to get them used to the idea, if that's all right?"

It wasn't all right. That much was clear from his taut, forbidding scowl.

"Please," she added, though she doubted any amount of begging would budge a man like him. "You've probably spent most of your life moving from one place to another. So perhaps you can't understand why a child who's lost her mother and father would want to stay in a familiar place around people she's used to."

It was not her place to speak to the new master in such a tone. Marian could imagine Mr. Culpepper's look of horror if he heard her.

"I understand better than you suppose, Miss Murray." Captain Radcliffe spoke so softly, Marian wondered if she had only imagined his words.

"You do?"

He replied with a slow nod, a distant gaze and a pensive murmur that seemed to come from some well-hidden place inside him. "I was ten years old when I was sent to sea after my mother died."

The wistful hush of his voice slid beneath Marian's bristling defenses. Her heart went out to that wee boy. A navy ship must have been an even harsher place to grow up than the Pendergast Charity School, where she had been sent. She wondered if young Gideon Radcliffe had been blessed with good friends and strong faith to help him bear it.

But she had no right to ask such questions of a man like him. Besides, the girls were her first priority.

Perhaps she could appeal to the part of him that remembered the loss and displacement he'd suffered. "Cissy is only nine and Dolly hasn't turned seven yet. I know you don't mean to send them off to sea, Captain. But *away-from-home* is all the same, no matter where, don't you think?"

His brows rose and his lower lip thrust out in a downward curve. "I see your point."

Marian sensed this was as receptive as he was likely

to get. "I'm not asking anything of you, Captain, except to provide us with food and houseroom until Lady Villiers returns. This place has plenty of both to spare. I will see to the girls, entirely, just the way I have since their father died. I'll make certain they don't disturb you."

For a moment Captain Radcliffe stared down at the finely woven carpet. Then suddenly he lifted his head to fix her with a gaze that *did* see her—too clearly for her comfort. "Very well, Miss Murray. I am not such an ogre as you may suppose. I know this is *their* home and would have remained so if they'd had a brother."

"I never thought you were an—"

Before she could blurt out that bald lie, the captain raised his hand to bid her not interrupt him. "Until the New Year then."

"I beg your pardon, sir?"

"I shall delay contacting Lady Villiers until January." Captain Radcliffe sounded resigned to his decision. "That will allow the children to spend Christmas in the country. After that, the New Year is a time for new beginnings."

"Perhaps so." That sounded ungrateful. Captain Radcliffe was under no obligation to let them stay for any length of time, let alone the whole winter. "What I meant to say was…thank you, sir."

As she hurried back to the nursery, Marian thanked God, too, for granting this reprieve. Perhaps her earlier prayers had been heard after all.

Chapter Two

After his first night in his new home, Gideon woke much later than usual. He'd slept badly—the place was far too quiet. He missed the soothing lap of the waves against the hull of his ship, the flap of sails in the wind and the mournful cries of seagulls. When he had drifted off, the face of that young midshipman had appeared to trouble him. Though the charges brought against him were entirely unfounded—of causing the death of one member of his crew and threatening others—that did not mean his conscience was clear.

An iron band of pain tightened around Gideon's forehead when he crawled out of bed. He staggered when the floor stayed level and still beneath his feet. It had taken him a while to gain his sea legs when he'd joined his first crew, all those years ago. Now the roll of a deck was so familiar he wondered if he would ever feel comfortable on dry land. Nottinghamshire had some of the driest land in the kingdom, many miles from the ocean in any direction. Coming here had given Gideon a far more intimate understanding of what it meant to be "a fish out of water."

Perhaps some coffee and breakfast would help. Though he'd lived on ship's rations for more than two-thirds of his life, he could not claim they were superior to the fare available at Knightley Park.

As he washed, shaved and dressed for the day, Gideon's thoughts turned back to his unsettling interview with Miss Murray the previous evening. The woman reminded him of a terrier—small and rather appealing, yet possessed of fierce tenacity in getting what she wanted. What in blazes had possessed him to tell her about being sent to sea after his mother's death?

He seldom talked to anyone about his past and never about that unhappy time. Perhaps it was what she'd said about a bereaved child needing the comfort of familiar surroundings. It had struck a chord deep within him—far too deep for his liking. Before he could stop himself, the words had poured out. For an instant after he'd spoken, Gideon thought he sensed a thawing in her obvious aversion to him. Then she had turned and used that unintentional revelation as leverage to wring from him a concession he'd been reluctant to grant.

He counted himself fortunate that he had not come up against many enemy captains who were such formidable opponents as this simple Scottish governess.

It wasn't that he begrudged his young cousins' houseroom—quite the contrary. They had been born and lived their whole lives at Knightley Park, while he had only visited the place at Christmastime and in the summer. Though it belonged to him by law, he could not escape the conviction that they had a far stronger claim to it.

While they remained here, he would be reluctant to make many changes in the domestic arrangements they were accustomed to…no matter how sorely needed. He would always feel like an interloper in his own home, prevented from claiming the solitude and privacy he'd hoped to find at Knightley Park.

That was not his only objection to the arrangement, Gideon reminded himself as he headed off in search of breakfast. What if his young cousins needed something beyond the authority of their governess to provide? What if some harm befell them and he was held accountable? He, who had been charged with the welfare of an entire ship's crew, shrank from the responsibility for two small girls. It vexed Gideon that he had not thought to raise some of these objections with Miss Murray last night.

It was too late now, though. He had given his word. He only hoped he would not come to regret that decision as much as he regretted some others he'd made of late.

"Dolly!" That soft but urgent cry, and the light, fleet patter of approaching footsteps jarred Gideon from his thoughts; but too late to take proper evasive action.

An instant later, the child came racing around the corner and barreled straight into him. Her head struck him in the belly, like a small blond cannonball, knocking the breath out of him. Meanwhile the collision sent her tumbling backward onto her bottom. It could not have winded her as it had Gideon, for her mouth fell open to emit an earsplitting wail that made his aching head throb. Her eyes screwed up and commenced to gush tears at a most alarming rate. The sight unnerved Gideon like nothing in his eventful naval career…with one recent exception.

Before he could catch his breath or rally his shattered composure, Marian Murray charged around the corner and swooped down to enfold her young charge. "Wist ye now, Dolly!"

She looked up at Gideon, her eyes blazing with fierce protectiveness. "What did you do to her?"

"What…?" Gideon gasped. "I…?"

That was one unjust accusation too many. Somehow he managed to suck in enough air to fuel his reply. "I did…*nothing* to her! That little imp ploughed into me. A few inches taller and she'd have stove in my ribs."

Anger over a great many things that had nothing to do with the present situation came boiling out of him. "What was she doing tearing through the halls like a wild thing? Someone could have been hurt much worse."

Now he'd done it. No doubt his rebuke would make the child howl even louder, if that were possible. Less than twenty-four hours had passed, and already he'd begun to regret his hasty decision to let the children stay.

To his amazement, Gideon realized the child was not weeping harder. Indeed, she seemed to have stopped. Her sobs had somehow turned to chuckles.

"Wild thing." She repeated his words as if they were a most amusing compliment, then chuckled again.

"You needn't sound so pleased with yourself." Miss Murray helped the child to her feet and dusted her off.

"Captain Radcliffe is right. You could have been hurt a good deal worse. Now tell him you're sorry and promise it won't happen again."

The little scamp broke into a broad grin that was strangely infectious. "I'm sorry I bumped into you, Captain. I hope I didn't hurt you too much. I promise I won't run so fast around corners after this."

"I'm not certain that running indoors at all is a good idea." Gideon struggled to keep the corners of his mouth from curling up, as they itched to do. "You are not a filly, after all, and this is not Newmarket race-course."

If Miss Murray found his remark at all amusing, she certainly gave no sign. "I apologize, as well, Captain. This is all my fault. I will keep Dolly under much closer supervision from now on."

Gideon found himself torn between a strange desire to linger there in the hallway with them and an urgent need to get away. Since the latter made far more sense, he gave a stiff nod to acknowledge her assurance and strode away in search of a strong cup of coffee to restore his composure.

"Dorothy Ann Radcliffe," Marian muttered as she marched her young pupil back to the nursery, "you won't be content until you make my hair turn white, will you?"

"Could I really do that, Miss Marian?" Dolly sounded far more intrigued by the possibility than chastened.

"I don't care to find out, thank you very much." Marian pointed to a low, three-legged stool in the corner, with which Dolly's bottom was quite familiar. "Go sit for ten minutes and think about what you've done."

"Why must *I* sit in the corner?" demanded the child. "When you told the Captain it was all your fault?"

"Impudence, for a start." Marian fixed her with a stern look. "I warn you, I am not in the mood to tolerate any more of your foolishness, just now."

Though Dolly deserved her punishment, Marian could not deny her own responsibility for what had happened. Since their father's death, she had encouraged Dolly's high spirits, in the hope of lifting her sister's.

"What happened?" asked Cissy, who sat at the nursery table, an untouched bowl of porridge in front of her. "I heard shouting and bawling."

Before Marian could get a word out, Dolly announced, "I bumped into the captain and fell down."

Walking toward the corner stool, she rubbed her bottom. "He called me a wild thing and said the house isn't a racecourse. I think he's funny."

Captain Radcliffe was anything but amusing. A little shudder ran through Marian as she recalled his dark scowl, which seemed to threaten he would send the girls away if another such mishap occurred. "That's quite enough out of you, miss. I don't want to hear another word for ten minutes or I'll add ten more. Is that understood?"

Dolly opened her mouth to reply, then shut it again and nodded as she sank onto the stool.

Marian returned to her rapidly cooling breakfast but found she had no appetite for it now.

"What did he say, Miss Marian?" Cissy asked in an anxious tone.

"He wasn't happy about being rammed into on his first morning here, of course." Marian cast a reproachful look toward the corner stool. "I can't say I blame him."

Now that she thought back on it, the captain had seemed more vexed by her tactless assumption that he'd done something to hurt Dolly, rather than the other way around. She couldn't blame him for that, either. No one liked to be unjustly accused, especially when *they* were the injured party. But what else was she to think, after the experiences of her past and the things she'd read about him in the newspapers? There had been reports of severe cruelty to the younger members of his crew, resulting in at least one death,

"I don't mean what the captain said just now." Cissy pushed her porridge around the bowl with her spoon. "What did he say last night when you went to talk to him…at *eight* bells?"

"Oh, that." He'd told her about being sent away to sea when he was only a little older than Cissy, though Marian sensed he hadn't intended to. "He said you and Dolly are welcome to stay at Knightley Park until your aunt comes back from abroad. That was kind of him, wasn't it?"

So it was, Marian reminded herself, though she still resented his obvious reluctance.

Cissy ignored the question. "I wish Aunt Lavinia would come tomorrow and take us away with her."

"I don't!" cried Dolly, undeterred by the prospect

of ten more minutes in the corner. "I want to stay at Knightley Park as long as we can."

That was what Marian wanted for the girls, too. She feared what might become of Cissy and Dolly once Lady Villiers took charge of them. Her best hope was that she would be allowed to remain as their governess. Though she disliked the idea of having no fixed home, flitting from one fashionable destination to another, at least she would be able to shield the children from the worst excesses of their aunt's way of life.

But what if Lady Villiers decided that traveling with her two young nieces and their governess in tow would be too inconvenient? What if she dismissed Marian and placed the girls in a boarding school, while she used their money to stave off her creditors?

Worrying down a spoonful of cold porridge as an example to the girls, Marian tried to push those fears to the back of her mind. She had enough to be getting on with just now—she didn't need to borrow trouble. If she could not keep the children from disturbing Captain Radcliffe, she feared he might turn them out long before Lady Villiers arrived to collect her nieces.

Gideon had intended to catch a few days' rest before plunging into his new duties as master of Knightley Park. But after the collision with his young cousin on his way to breakfast, he decided a dignified retreat might be in order. If Miss Murray could not keep the children out of his way, then he must take care to keep out of theirs.

His belly was still a little tender where the child's sturdy head had butted it. That did not smart half as much as the memory of Miss Murray's accusation. Her tone and look made it abundantly clear her opinion had been turned against him before he ever set foot in Knightley Park. Was that the case with all the servants? He'd hoped the vile gossip about him might not have spread this far into the countryside. Apparently, that had been wishful thinking.

Such thoughts continued to plague him as he rode around the estate, investigating its operation. What he discovered provided a distraction, though not the kind he'd hoped for. Everywhere he looked, he encountered evidence of idleness, waste and mismanagement. By late that afternoon, his bones ached from the unaccustomed effort of sitting a horse for so many hours. His patience had worn dangerously thin by the time he tracked down the steward of Knightley Park.

"Pray how long have you been employed in your present position, Mr. Dutton?" Hands clasped behind his back, Gideon fixed the steward with his sternest quarterdeck stare.

Unlike every midshipman who'd ever served under him, this landlubber seemed not to grasp the significance of that look.

The steward was a solid man of middling height with bristling ginger side-whiskers and a confident air. "Been here nigh on ten years, sir. Not long after the late master's marriage, God rest both their souls. In all that time, Mr. Radcliffe never had a fault to find with my service."

"Indeed?" Gideon's voice grew quieter, a sign his crew would have known to heed as a warning. "You must have found my late cousin a very satisfactory em-

ployer, then—easygoing, content to leave the oversight
of the estate in your hands with a minimum of interfer-
ence."

"Just so, sir." Dutton seemed to imply the new
master would do well to follow his cousin's example.
"I didn't presume to tell him how to hunt his foxes and
he didn't tell me how to carry out my duties."

The man was drifting into heavy weather, yet he
appeared altogether oblivious. "But there is a difference between those two circumstances, is there not?
My cousin's hunting was none of your affair, while your
management of this estate was very much his. Now it
is mine and I have never shirked my duty."

At last the steward seemed to sense which way the
wind was blowing. He stood up straighter, and his
tone became a good deal more respectful. "Yes, sir. I
mean...no, sir."

From his coat pocket, Gideon withdrew a folded
sheet of paper on which he had penciled some notes
in the tight, precise script he used for his log entries.
"From what I have observed today, Mr. Dutton, you
have not been over*seeing* this estate so much as over-
looking waste and sloth. I fear you have left me with
no alternative but to replace you."

"You can't do that, sir!"

With a raised eyebrow, Gideon inquired what prevented him.

"What I mean to say is, I've got a wife and family
and I'm not as young as I used to be." Dutton's former
bluster disappeared, replaced by fear of reaping the bad
harvest he had sown. "If word gets out that I've been
dismissed..."

"I have no intention of broadcasting the information," replied Gideon. "Though I could not, in good conscience, provide you with a reference."

"Please, sir. Perhaps I have let things slide around here of late." The man looked a proper picture of repentance. "But if you give me another chance, I'll lick the estate into shape. So help me, I will."

Though he knew the importance of decisiveness in maintaining command, Gideon hesitated. Granting second chances had not worked well for him in the past. One might argue that it had contributed to his present predicament. Too often, offenders looked on such a reprieve as a sign of weakness to be further exploited. And yet, there was Dutton's family to consider. His wife and children had done nothing wrong, but they would suffer for his conduct, perhaps more than he.

"A fortnight." Gideon fixed the man with his sternest scowl, so Dutton would be in no doubt this was an undeserved opportunity he had better not abuse. "I will give you that long to persuade me you are worth keeping."

Ignoring the man's effusive thanks, Gideon turned on his heel and strode away. He hoped this decision would not prove as much a mistake as his last one.

Making certain Cissy and Dolly did not disturb Captain Radcliffe was proving a great deal harder than she had expected. Marian reflected on that difficulty as she put the girls to bed one evening, a week after his arrival at Knightley Park.

Part of the problem was the captain's unpredictable comings and goings. She could never tell when he might be spending time in the house, out roaming the grounds or riding off around the estate. If she knew, perhaps she could have adjusted the children's schedule of lessons to take advantage of his absences. As it was, she could not take the chance of encountering him out in the garden or on their way down to the music room.

Since their disastrous run-in, Dolly had taken an unaccountable fancy to the captain and would no doubt pester him for attention if they met again. Cissy clearly resented his presence and might offend him with a rude remark.

Neither of the girls took kindly to being confined to the nursery after enjoying the run of the house during their father's time. Just that morning, the governess had overheard Cissy muttering about being "kept prisoner."

Marian found it difficult to discourage such an attitude, since it mirrored her own far too closely. In all her time at Knightley Park, and especially after Mr. Radcliffe's death, she'd felt at liberty to come and go as she pleased, even free to borrow books from the well stocked library. Wistfully, she recalled the master's hospitable answer when she'd first asked if she could.

"By all means, Miss Murray! Those books might as well serve some better purpose than giving the maids more things to dust."

Since Captain Radcliffe's arrival, she had not even dared return the last volume she'd borrowed for fear of meeting up with him. Considering the captain's reluctance to have his young cousins around, Marian doubted he would tolerate a servant making use of *his* library. She knew she must soon put it back, before he noticed its absence and blamed someone else.

Perhaps now would be a good time, with the girls off to bed and the captain occupied with his dinner.

"I won't be long, Martha," she informed the nursery maid, who sat by the fire darning one of Dolly's stockings. "Just a quick errand I have to run."

And run she did—first to her own room to fetch the book, then down the back stairs. She was in such a hurry that she nearly collided with the butler on the landing.

Poor Mr. Culpepper seemed more agitated than ever. "Miss Murray, have you heard? Mr. Dutton has been threatened with dismissal! I fear I shall be put on notice next."

The news about the steward did not come as a great surprise to Marian. Though she was working hard to make sure Captain Radcliffe was not conscious of the girls' presence in the house, she found herself constantly aware of his. It was as if a salty ocean breeze had blown all the way into the landlocked heart of England, bearing with it a host of unwelcome changes.

"These naval men have most exacting standards." Mr. Culpepper wrung his hands. "At my age, where should I go if I am turned out of Knightley Park?"

Marian bristled at the thought of such a good and faithful servant treated so shabbily. "Has Captain Radcliffe complained about the running of the house?"

The butler shook his head. "Not in so many words. But he is so very quiet and solemn, just the way he was as a boy. Who knows what plans he may be making? He is so little like his cousin, one would scarcely believe they could be of the same blood."

That was true enough. The girls' jovial, generous

father had been a down-to-earth country squire devoted
to his children, his horses and his dogs. His cousin
seemed distinctly uncomfortable with all three.

"Don't fret yourself, Mr. Culpepper. I'm sure the
captain would tell you soon enough if the housekeeping
was not up to his standards. He seems the type that's
quick to find fault. Silence is as close to praise as you
can hope for from him."

The furrows of worry in the butler's forehead relaxed
a trifle. "I hope you are right, Miss Murray. I will en-
deavor to remain calm and go about my duties."

"Good." Marian flashed him an encouraging smile,
pleased that she had been able to ease his fears a little.
"That's all any of us can do, I reckon."

As she continued on down the stairs, Marian strove
to heed her own advice, though it wasn't easy. She
would have feared the captain's disapproval less if her
position was the only thing at stake. But with the children's welfare hanging in the balance, she could not
afford to put a foot wrong.

As she tiptoed past the dining room, the muted clink
of silverware on china assured her the captain was busy
eating his dinner. A few moments later, as she hurried
back from the library, a sudden crash from inside the
dining room made her start violently. It sounded as if a
piece of china had been hurled to the floor and smashed
into a hundred pieces. The noise was immediately followed by a wail of distress from Bessie, a nervous, and
often clumsy, housemaid. What had the captain done
to make the poor lass take on so?

Marian marched toward the dining room, not certain

how she meant to intervene but compelled to do what she could to defend the girl.

She was about to fling open the door when she heard Bessie sob, "I'm s-sorry, s-s-ir! Have I burnt ye with that tea? I told Mr. Culpepper I'm too ham-fisted to be waiting table. Now ye'll send me packing and I wouldn't blame ye!"

So it was Bessie who had fumbled a teacup. A qualm of shame gripped Marian's stomach as she realized she had once again jumped to a most uncharitable conclusion about Captain Radcliffe.

His reply to Bessie made Marian feel even worse. "Don't trouble yourself. If Mr. Culpepper asks, you must tell him it was my fault. I am not accustomed to handling such delicate china. Now dry your eyes, sweep up the mess and think no more of it."

As Marian fled back to the nursery, her conscience chided her for all the harsh things she'd thought and said about Captain Radcliffe since his arrival. She should have been grateful to him for allowing Cissy and Dolly to stay at Knightley Park when he'd been under no obligation to keep them here. Instead, she'd compared him unfavorably with his cousin and held those differences against him. She'd resented the loss of a few petty privileges, as if they'd been hers by right rather than by favor. Worst of all, she had allowed mean-spirited rumors to poison her opinion of the man without giving him a fair opportunity to prove his worth.

Clearly she needed to pay greater heed to her Bible, especially the part that counseled "judge not, lest ye be judged." It might be that, in the eyes of God, Captain Radcliffe had a great deal less to answer for than she.

Chapter Three

Coming to Knightley Park had clearly been a huge mistake. As Gideon returned to the house after several frustrating hours reviewing the steward's progress, he reflected on his folly.

He had come to Nottinghamshire expecting to escape his recent troubles by revisiting simpler times past. But Knightley Park was no longer the calm, well run estate it had been in his grandfather's day. And he was no longer the solitary child, made welcome by one and all.

The seeds of gossip had followed him here and found fertile soil in which to breed a crop of noxious weeds. Young footmen turned pale and fled when he approached. Tenants eyed him with wary, resentful servility. Housemaids trembled when he cast the briefest glance in their direction. His cousins' governess sprang to her young charges' defense like a tigress protecting her cubs.

Gideon had to admit he preferred Miss Murray's open antagonism to the sullen aversion and dread of the others. And he could not fault her willingness to shield the children, even if there had been no need. Unfortunately, his flicker of grudging admiration for Miss Murray only made her suspicion and wariness of him sting all the worse.

As he entered the house quietly by a side door, Gideon could no longer ignore a vexing question. How could he possibly expect the Admiralty's board of inquiry to believe in his innocence when his own servants and tenants clearly judged him guilty?

Passing the foot of the servants' stairs, he heard the voices of two footmen drift down from the landing. He did not mean to eavesdrop, but their furtive, petulant tone left Gideon in no doubt they were talking about him.

"How long do you reckon we'll have to put up with him?" asked one.

The other snorted. "Too long to suit either of us, I can tell you that. With old Boney beaten at last, I'll wager the navy won't want him back."

Gideon told himself to keep walking and pay no heed to servants' tattle. He knew this was the sort of talk that must be going on behind his back all the time. The last thing he needed was to have their exact words echoing in his thoughts, taunting and shaming him. But his steps slowed in spite of himself, and his ears strained to catch every word.

Did part of him feel he deserved it?

One of the footmen heaved a sigh. "So he'll stay here to make our lives a misery instead of his crew's. It's not right."

"When did right ever come into it?" grumbled the other.

Gideon had almost managed to edge himself out of earshot when a third voice joined the others—a woman's voice he recognized as belonging to Miss Murray.

"Wilbert, Frederick, have you no duties to be getting on with?" she inquired in a disapproving tone, as if they were a pair of naughty little boys in the nursery.

"We just stopped for a quick word, miss. We've been run off our feet since the new master arrived." They were obviously counting on the governess to sympathize with their disgruntled feelings.

By now Gideon had given up trying to walk away. He braced to hear the governess join in abusing him.

"Perhaps if you'd kept up with your duties during the past few months," she reminded the young footmen instead, "you might not have to work quite so hard now to get the house back in decent order."

"Why should we run ourselves ragged for a master who's done the things he has? They say he did away with a young sailor. If he wasn't the captain of the ship they'd have called it plain murder."

As he waited for Miss Murray's reply, Gideon wondered if he'd been wrong to assume her opinion of him had been tainted by the kind of gossip she was hearing now. Surely, she would not have wanted her young pupils to remain in the same house as a rumored killer. Perhaps this was the first time she'd heard the worst of the accusations being whispered against him.

Though he tried to tell himself one unfavorable judgment more or less did not matter, Gideon shrank from the prospect of Miss Murray thinking even less of him.

"I am sorely disappointed." The gentle regret in her tone troubled Gideon worse than the harsher censure he'd expected. "I thought better of you both than to condemn your master on the basis of malicious rumors."

Had he heard her correctly? Gideon shook his head.

The young footmen sputtered in protest, but Miss Murray refused to back down. "Has the captain mistreated either of you in any way since he arrived at Knightley Park?"

"No...but he is very haughty and ill-humored. You must grant that, miss."

"And did you hear he threatened to give Mr. Dutton the sack?"

"I have heard such a rumor, though that does not guarantee it is true. Besides, Wilbert, I have often heard you complain what a poor job Mr. Dutton has been doing of late. If you were in the captain's place, would you have kept him on?"

After an awkward pause, Wilbert muttered, "I reckon not, miss."

"And you, Frederick, would you be jovial and talkative in a place where you were made to feel as unwelcome as I fear we have made Captain Radcliffe?"

Gideon did not catch the young footman's muffled reply, but that scarcely mattered. What did matter was that someone had defended him against the whispered slurs he could not bring himself to acknowledge, let alone refute. What astonished him even more was to find a champion in Marian Murray, a woman he could have sworn detested him.

And not altogether without reason, he was forced to admit. None of their encounters since his arrival had been particularly cordial. And his reaction to the children's presence might have given her cause to regard him as a very hard man indeed. Yet there she was, taking his part against the prevailing opinion of the other servants. He did not know what to make of it.

To be championed in such a way when he neither expected nor deserved it stirred a flicker of welcome warmth deep within his fallow heart.

The hangdog looks of the two young footmen reproached Marian. What was she doing?

For as long as she could recall, she had felt compelled need to stand up for anyone who was the victim of mistreatment. The stronger the forces against them, the more fiercely she felt called to intervene.

It had not occurred to her that a man of strength and authority like Captain Radcliffe might need *anyone* to defend him, let alone her. But when she'd heard Wilbert and Frederick exchanging backstairs gossip about the captain, she had suddenly seen the matter in a whole new light. A sense of shame for the unfair things she'd thought about the man and her manner toward him had made her leap to his defense all the more fiercely.

Now she realized that that was not fair either. "I beg your pardon. I have no right to reproach you when I have behaved just as uncharitably toward Captain Radcliffe."

Her rueful admission seemed to have better effect on the young men than her rebuke.

"That's all right, miss." Wilbert hung his head. "I reckon we may have been too hard on the master."

Frederick nodded. "It's true enough what you said,

miss. The captain hasn't done us any harm. We'll mind our tongues after this."

"We should get back to work," Wilbert added, "before Mr. Culpepper comes looking for us."

After brief bows, the pair hurried off below stairs, leaving Marian to follow as far as the ground floor. Lost in thought about her encounter with the footmen and the sudden reversal of her opinion toward Captain Radcliffe, she rounded the corner and nearly collided with him.

"I beg your pardon, sir!" She started back, frantically wondering whether he'd heard what had just passed in the stairwell. "I didn't expect to find you home at this hour."

The captain seemed every bit as rattled by their sudden meeting as she. "I...er...just got in. I'm sorry if I startled you."

Caught off guard, his whole appearance was far less severe than Marian had yet seen it. The austere contours of his face seemed somehow softened. The sweeping arch of his brow looked less forbidding. His steely gray eyes held a tentative glimmer of warmth. Had he changed so much or was it her perception that had altered?

"No, indeed," she sputtered, painfully aware that she owed him an apology for offenses she dared not confess. "I should have minded the warning I gave Dolly about charging around corners."

"Ah, yes." A half smile crinkled one corner of the captain's resolute mouth. "I hope the child has recovered from our collision."

"Entirely." Marian nodded, relieved at this turn in

the conversation. Perhaps the captain had not overheard anything between her and the footmen after all. "I believe you took greater injury from it than she did."

His unexpected query about Dolly's well-being emboldened her to continue. "I believe she would be less apt to run in the house if she could use up some of that energy running and playing out of doors."

"I agree." The captain raised an eyebrow. "What prevents the children from going out? Are they ill? Do they not have warm enough clothes?"

A fresh qualm of remorse gripped Marian. Not only had she misjudged Captain Radcliffe, she had allowed her prejudice against him to make life less agreeable for her pupils. In doing so, she might have provoked Cissy's aversion to the captain.

"The girls are quite well," she replied, "and they do not lack for warm garments."

"Then what is the difficulty?"

She might as well confess and hope the captain would be as forgiving with her as he had of the clumsy serving maid. Marian inhaled a deep breath and forged ahead. "I'm afraid I thought, sir…that is…I presumed… You did tell me I should keep the girls from disturbing you. I was afraid we might disrupt one of your walks, or their noise from outdoors might bother you while you were trying to rest or read."

"I see." He flinched slightly, as if she had injured an unhealed wound but he was determined not to let her see the pain it caused. "I suppose my reputation made you fear I would have them flogged for it."

He must have overheard her talking to the footmen. Marian scrambled to recall exactly what she'd said. If the captain had heard only part of their exchange, might he think she was spreading malicious gossip about him?

"Nothing like that, sir!" she cried, though her stricken conscience forced her to confess, "Though I was worried you might send the girls away from Knightley Park."

Captain Radcliffe gave a rueful nod that seemed to excuse her suspicions. "I fear you and I have gotten off on the wrong foot, Miss Murray. For that I take full responsibility. In future, feel free to do with the children whatever you were accustomed to before I arrived. Proceed as if I am not here. All I ask is that you not seek me out. I have no experience with children and, as you have seen, no knack for getting on with them."

Perhaps not, but in spite of that he had managed to catch Dolly's fancy. In her forthright innocence, the child must have responded to something in him that had eluded Marian.

"Does that include the music room, sir?" she asked. "It can be irksome to hear a great many wrong notes struck on the pianoforte."

After only a slight hesitation the captain nodded gamely. "It is difficult to learn anything of value without making mistakes."

His assurance made Marian more conscious than ever what a grave error she had committed in her judgment of him.

"Thank you, Captain." She dropped him a curtsy that she hoped would convey an apology as well as gratitude. "I'm sure the girls will be very pleased to enjoy greater liberty."

He replied with a stiff bow. "I am only sorry they were ever deprived of it."

The captain made it sound as if that were his fault, yet Marian knew which of them was more to blame. Perhaps it was the burden of her misjudgment that made her more self-conscious than ever in Captain Radcliffe's presence. A blush seemed to hide in the flesh of her cheeks, ready to flame out at any second.

"I was just on my way to the music room to fetch a song book. If you will excuse me, I must finish my errand and get back to the nursery before the girls wonder what has become of me."

"By all means," he replied. "Do not let me detain you."

Marian made another curtsy, then hurried away, torn between eagerness to escape his presence and a strange inclination to linger.

"Miss Murray."

The sound of her name on his lips made her turn back swiftly, as if some part of her had anticipated the summons. "Sir?"

He hesitated for an instant, making her wonder if he had not intended to call out. "Thank you for speaking up on my behalf to those young men. I only hope I will have as able an advocate to defend me when the Admiralty convenes its inquiry."

The blush that had been lying in wait now flared in Marian's cheeks. "I don't deserve your gratitude. I wish I could claim I have kept an open mind about you and not let my opinion be influenced by reports I've heard…or read. But I'm afraid that would not be true."

Captain Radcliffe gave a rueful nod, as if her confession grieved him a little but did not surprise him. "If your mind was not fully open, neither was it altogether closed. May I ask what altered your opinion of me?"

His question flustered Marian even more. She could not bring herself to admit eavesdropping on his exchange with Bessie over the broken china. "I...I'm not certain, Captain. Perhaps it was hearing Frederick and Wilbert talking that made me realize I hadn't given you a fair chance. I reckon it's easier to see our own faults in others."

"Perhaps so, but it is not so easy to admit those faults and alter our conduct accordingly." A note of approval warmed his words and went a long way toward absolving Marian's shame over her earlier actions.

She was about to thank him for understanding and head away again when Captain Radcliffe continued, "I can assure you the nonsense being written about me in the newspapers is entirely without foundation. I never laid a hand on that poor lad, nor did I drive him to do away with himself on account of my harsh treatment."

What made her believe him so immediately and completely? Marian could not be certain. Was it only guilt over her prior misjudgment of him or was it something more? Even at first, when she'd thought him a strict, uncaring tyrant, she had not been able to deny his air of integrity.

"I believe you, Captain." She strove to infuse her words with sincere faith.

She recalled how it felt to be unfairly accused and disbelieved, and how much it had helped to have even one person take her side. The image of her loyal friend, Rebecca Beaton, rose in Marian's mind, unleashing a flood of gratitude, affection and longing. Rebecca now lived in the Cotswolds, more than a hundred miles to the south. Though the two corresponded as often as they could afford, they had not seen one another since going their separate ways after they'd left school.

Captain Radcliffe's voice broke in on her wistful thoughts. "I appreciate your loyalty, Miss Murray, considering how little I have done to earn it. I hope the board of inquiry will render a decision to justify your faith in me."

"When will this board hear your case, sir?" Though duty urged her to cut their conversation short and return to the nursery at once, Marian could not quell her curiosity.

The captain replied with a shrug and a sigh of frustration. "Not soon enough to suit me, of that you can be sure. Probably not until after the New Year at this rate. In the meantime, I am forbidden to speak publicly about the matter. I must remain silent while the newspapers make me out to be some sort of heartless monster. All I want is the opportunity to prove my innocence so I can return to active duty."

"I'll pray for you, Captain." Marian wished there was more she could do. "That the inquiry be called soon and that your name will be cleared once and for all."

"Why…er…thank you, Miss Murray," he replied with the air of someone reluctantly accepting an unwelcome gift. "Though I doubt your prayers will avail much."

His reaction surprised and rather dismayed her. "Do you not believe in God then?"

How could that be? He had treated her more charitably than many people who'd claimed to be pious Christians.

Captain Radcliffe considered her question a moment, then replied with quiet solemnity. "One cannot spend as much time as I have at sea and not come to believe in a powerful force that created the universe."

Scarcely realizing what she was doing, Marian exhaled a faint breath of relief. Why in the world should it matter to her what the man believed? "But you just said…"

"It is not so much a contradiction as you suppose." The corner of his straight, firm mouth arched ever so slightly. Yet that one small alteration quite transformed his face, warming and softening its stern, rugged contours. "What I cannot imagine is that such a being knows or cares about my trivial concerns any more than the vast ocean cares for one insignificant ship that floats upon it."

No wonder the captain seemed so profoundly solitary, Marian reflected, if he did not believe anyone cared about him…not even his Maker.

"Your concerns are not trivial," she insisted. "You want to see justice done and your reputation restored so you can continue to defend this land. Even I can sympathize with them, and I could not begin to know your heart as deeply as the Lord does."

"You sound very sincere and certain, Miss Murray." He did not seem to think less of her for it, as Marian had feared he might. "Why is that, if you don't mind my asking?"

She was not in the habit of discussing her beliefs, especially with a man she scarcely knew and hadn't much liked at first. Yet there was a kind of openness in the way he regarded her that assured Marian of his honest desire to understand.

"Cannot a God who is infinitely large also be infinitely small and infinitely close?" she ventured, trying to put complex, profound ideas into words that seemed inadequate to the task. "Just as the salt water that makes up the great ocean is not so different from our sweat and tears?"

This whole conversation was becoming altogether too intimate for her comfort. And yet she felt compelled to disclose one final confidence. "Perhaps that sounds foolish to you, but I have felt the loving closeness of God in my life. Never so powerfully as when I needed His presence the most."

What had made her tell him such a thing? Marian regretted it the moment the words were out of her mouth. She had never liked talking about her past, particularly that part of it. In all the time she'd known Cissy and Dolly's father, she had hardly told him anything about herself. Yet here she was blurting out all this to Captain Radcliffe, whom she'd met only a fortnight ago.

A spark of curiosity glinted in the depths of his granite-gray eyes. If she did not cut this conversation short and make her escape, she feared the captain might ask her how she'd come to be so alone and in need of Divine comfort. If he did, she was very much afraid the whole painful story might come pouring out. That was the last thing she wanted.

"I really must go now." Lowering her gaze, she bobbed the captain a hasty curtsy. "Cissy will be worried what's become of me and Dolly will be driving poor Martha to distraction with her mischief."

Before Captain Radcliffe could say anything that might detain her a moment longer, she rushed off to seek sanctuary in the music room. Only when she was quite certain the captain had gone elsewhere did she venture out and fly back up the servants' stairs to the nursery. Yet even as she took care to avoid him, an idea concerning Captain Radcliffe began to take shape in her mind.

Though the captain denied the power of prayer, Marian wondered if he might not be the answer to hers. A man like him would make an ideal guardian for Cissy and Dolly—far better than their profligate aunt. Once that inquiry was over and he returned to his ship, she would be left to care for the girls in familiar surroundings.

All day she mulled the notion over as she and the children relished their renewed liberty in the house and gardens. The more she considered her idea, the more certain she became that it would be an ideal solution.

That night when she knelt by her bed, Marian prayed fervently. "Lord, forgive me for misjudging Captain Radcliffe. I see now that he is a good man. Please let him be absolved of all the charges against him and permitted to return to active duty on his ship...but not before I can persuade him to challenge Lady Villiers for guardianship of Cissy and Dolly."

How exactly was she going to persuade him of that, Marian asked herself as she climbed into bed, when the captain did not want to have anything to do with the girls? Perhaps she could pray for him to come up with the idea on his own, but this was too important a task to leave up to the power of prayer alone.

Chapter Four

What had Miss Murray meant about having been alone with no one to whom she could turn to but God?

While Gideon ate his solitary dinner that Saturday evening, he reflected on his last conversation with her and the unexpected turn it had taken. How had his thanks for her defense of him led to an examination of his spiritual beliefs? Never before had he confided in another person his doubts about the value of prayer.

As captain of his ship, he had often been required to lead his crew in Sunday worship. Though he'd read many prayers aloud, and knew the Our Father by heart as well as any man, he had not uttered those sacred words with any particular expectation that his Creator was listening. The last time he'd truly prayed from his heart, he'd been a child imploring the Almighty to spare the life of his beloved, ailing mother. Of course his pleas had fallen on deaf ears.

Uncomforted by the words of the funeral liturgy, he'd watched them bury her poor, wasted body. Then he'd been wrenched away from everyone and everything familiar and sent to sea. The harsh conditions and the gnawing ache of loneliness had been almost more than he could bear. But somehow he had borne them, and the experience had made a man of him. Gradually he'd come to know and love the sea. In the end he'd dedicated his life to it and to the defense of his country. Those things had helped to fill the emptiness in his heart and give him a sense of purpose.

Was it possible *that* had been an answer to his unspoken prayer? Gideon dismissed the thought.

"What's for pudding, then?" he asked the young footman who collected his empty dinner plate.

"Plum duff, Captain. It's one of Mrs. Wheaton's specialties."

"And one of my favorites," Gideon replied.

Since the lecture they'd received from Miss Murray, the two footmen seemed a good deal less sullen. What she'd said must have made an impression. Could it have been gratitude for her unexpected defense of him that had made him let down his guard with her? Or had he somehow sensed a connection between them based on a common experience of loss?

As the footman set a generous serving of pudding in front of Gideon, a series of soft but determined taps sounded on the dining room door.

"Come through," he called as if he were back in the great cabin aboard HMS *Integrity.*

In response to his summons, the door swung open, and Miss Murray entered. "Pardon me for disturbing your dinner, Captain, but I wanted a word with you concerning the girls, if I might."

He did not care for the sound of that. *She* was supposed

to be tending to the children's needs, not pestering him with them.

Yet Gideon found himself strangely pleased to see her all the same. "Very well, Miss Murray. I was just about to sample Mrs. Wheaton's plum duff. Would you care to join me?"

His request seemed to throw her into confusion. "I couldn't...that is, I already had some when I gave the girls their supper. It was very good. I have no doubt you'll enjoy it."

"Surely you could manage a little more." Gideon was not certain what made him so eager to have her join him. Perhaps because it would be awkward to converse with her standing there while he tried to eat.

Sensing she was about to protest more strenuously, he decided to try another tack. "I'd be grateful if you would oblige me, Miss Murray. It can be tiresome to dine night after night with only my own company."

His appeal seemed to catch her as much by surprise as his original invitation. She glanced from him to the footman and back again. "Very well then, Captain, if that is what you wish."

At a nod from Gideon, the footman pulled out a chair for Miss Murray, to the right of his place at the head of the table.

"Only a very small helping for me, please," she murmured as she slipped into the chair.

Acknowledging her request with a mute nod, the footman headed off to the kitchen.

"Now then," said Gideon. "What was this matter you wished to discuss with me?"

Miss Murray inhaled a deep breath and squared her

shoulders. "Well, sir, tomorrow is Sunday, and I hoped you might accompany the girls and me to church in the village."

Gideon's eyebrows rose. "In light of what you know about my attitudes toward children and religion, that strikes me as a rather improbable hope, Miss Murray. I doubt the Creator of the Universe cares whether or not I attend services."

"That is not why I go to church!" The words burst out of her. "I go for my own sake, to...nourish...my soul."

She pushed back her chair and started to rise. "I suppose you think that is all rubbish, too."

Before Gideon had time to consider what he was doing, his hand seemed to move of its own accord and come to rest upon one of hers. "On the contrary, Miss Murray. Just because our beliefs differ does not mean I scoff at yours. I hope you will accord mine the same respect."

Her hand felt cool and delicate beneath his, calling forth feelings of warmth and protectiveness Gideon hadn't realized he possessed. But once discretion caught up with him, he knew he must not prolong such contact between them. The sound of the young footman's returning steps spurred him to withdraw his hand, leaving Miss Murray free to go or stay as she wished.

To his surprise, she stayed, dropping back into her chair and pulling her hands off the table to rest upon her lap. Gideon wondered if it was only the footman's return that had kept her from rushing away.

An awkward silence fell between them as the servant entered and placed a saucer of pudding in front of Miss Murray.

"Will there be anything else, sir?" he asked.

Gideon shook his head. "That will be all, thank you. You may go."

He didn't care to have his views on spiritual matters aired before the servants to fuel more gossip about him.

As the young footman withdrew, Miss Murray took a spoonful of custard from the dainty china bowl between them and dribbled it over her plum duff. In perfect unison, she and Gideon each took a bite.

"A sailor's pudding is that," he observed. "Though Mrs. Wheaton's is far superior to any I ever tasted while at sea."

If he'd hoped to draw Miss Murray into a conversation about food that would make her forget her original request, he was soon disappointed. "Let me assure you, Captain, I did not ask you to accompany us to church as a means of...converting you, but for the children's sake."

Gideon took another bite of pudding and chewed on it thoughtfully. What on earth did it matter to his young cousins how, or if, he observed the Sabbath?

Miss Murray seemed to sense his unasked question. "For Dolly's sake, actually. She has begun to balk at going to church. I know it can be a long while for a child her age to sit still, but I believe it is important for children to be raised in faith. Otherwise they're like ships without anchors."

The nautical comparison appealed to Gideon. "I agree. If nothing else, it is a sound foundation for their moral development. But what does that have to do with me?"

Miss Murray sighed. "Dolly says it isn't fair that she must to go to church when you do not. I didn't know what to tell her, Captain."

It was a valid point, Gideon reluctantly acknowledged. He was not certain how he would respond to the child's argument. "The matter of my beliefs aside, I cannot say I am eager to venture out in public. I know very well the sort of gossip that must be circulating about me. I have no desire to be gawked at and whispered about."

Miss Murray worried down another mouthful of pudding as if it were as tough as whale hide rather than a rich, moist confection that fairly melted on the tongue. "I understand your reluctance. But surely church is one place where you are less apt to be judged unfairly."

"It *should* be." Gideon placed skeptical emphasis on that middle word. "But can you assure me this particular church *will* be?"

She could not disguise her doubt. "I wish I could promise that, sir. But how can I expect others to behave more charitably toward you than I have? All I can say with confidence is that I believe once the local people meet you for themselves, they will be far less disposed to believe any false rumors about you."

It was hardly a ringing endorsement, but Gideon appreciated her honesty. Though accompanying his young cousins to church went against his original bargain with their governess, he found it difficult to resist her appealing gaze.

Miss Murray seemed to sense his indecision. "If

people see you going about your business openly, they'll realize you have nothing to hide."

That was true, Gideon had to admit. He wondered if his reclusiveness had fostered any mistrust the local people might have had of him. He could not let that continue. Besides, he felt responsible to set a good example for the children. At least *that* was one of their needs he was capable of meeting.

Having consumed the last morsel of pudding, he set down his spoon and carefully wiped his mouth with his napkin. "Very well, Miss Murray, I accept your invitation. You may tell Miss Dolly she will not be able to use me as an excuse to shirk attendance at church."

Gideon hoped this was not another decision he would come to regret.

"Thank you, Captain!" The governess surged out of her chair and dropped a curtsy. "I am very grateful for your assistance."

The smile that illuminated her features lent them an air of unexpected beauty. It sent a rush of happiness through Gideon unlike any he'd felt in a great while.

"There you go, Dolly." Marian smiled to herself as she tied on the child's bonnet the next morning. "Now please try not to get mussed up before church."

Since last evening, she had been more indulgent than usual with her headstrong little pupil. After all, it had been Dolly's complaints about going to church that had inspired her to invite Captain Radcliffe to join them. Stumbling upon such a fine way to bring him and the girls together had given her hope that God might endorse her plan to have the captain seek guardianship of Cissy and Dolly.

Now if only she could get her pupils to play their parts properly.

"I trust you will be polite to the captain this morning." She looked Cissy over and gave a nod of approval at her appearance. The ribbons on her straw bonnet matched the green velvet spencer she wore over her white muslin dress. The color looked well with her rich brown hair. "Remember, it is not his fault we were confined to the nursery this past while. It was mine for misunderstanding and rushing to judgment."

"I promise I will remember my manners, Miss Marian," the child replied demurely. Yet a subtle stiffness in her bearing suggested her behavior would be correct but not cordial.

Perhaps when Cissy got to know Captain Radcliffe a little better, that coolness would thaw. Marian hoped so.

"And you, Dolly." She heaved an exasperated sigh when she turned to find the younger girl kneeling on the floor to recover her sixpence offering that had somehow rolled under the bed. "Please try not to be too forward. Otherwise, Captain Radcliffe may not want to come to church with us again."

Clutching the tiny silver coin between her fingers, Dolly scrambled to her feet. "Why not?"

"Because…" Marian bent down to brush off a bit of dirt the child's skirt had picked up from the floor. "Captain Radcliffe has lived on his ship for a very long time. He isn't accustomed to the company of…young ladies."

"Why can girls not sail ships?" Dolly demanded. "I like rowing on the pond in the summertime."

Marian, too, had fond memories of their excursions to the little island in the middle of the ornamental lake. If her plan succeeded, it would mean she and the girls would still be at Knightley Park next summer to enjoy more of the same.

A glance at the mantel clock made her start with dismay. "We'll talk about that later. Now, we mustn't keep the captain waiting. Come along, girls."

Seizing them by the hands, she hurried out of the nursery and down the main staircase.

They found Captain Radcliffe waiting in the entry hall, looking rather severe. At first Marian feared he was vexed with them for being tardy. But a second look made her wonder if he might only be nervous. Recalling what he'd said about not wanting to be stared at and whispered about, she hoped the people at church would treat the captain with more Christian charity than she'd first shown him.

"Good morning, sir." She offered him an encouraging smile and was gratified when his expression relaxed a little. "The girls and I are very pleased to have you join us this morning."

"Indeed." He glanced from solemn-faced Cissy to her grinning little sister with a flicker of mild alarm in his gray eyes. "The carriage is waiting."

Opening the great front door, he held it for Marian to usher her pupils outside.

The grounds of Knightley Park glittered with frost on this crisp, sunny November morning as the girls climbed into the carriage. When Marian followed them, her stomach sank abruptly.

She found Cissy and Dolly perched side by side in the carriage box, leaving the opposite seat empty. If Marian sat there, Captain Radcliffe would be obliged to sit beside her. The thought of being so close to him set her insides aflutter.

"Girls, budge up, please." She tried to squeeze in beside them.

"You're squashing me!" Dolly protested. "Why can't you sit over there?"

"Hush!" Marian whispered. "Cissy, will you kindly move to the other seat?"

The child's eyes widened. She shook her head.

"Then, I will," said Dolly.

Before Marian could prevent her, the child wriggled out from between her and Cissy and bounced over to the opposite seat just as Captain Radcliffe climbed into the carriage. "It's better than being squashed."

The captain settled next to Dolly, with an air of reluctance similar to the one Cissy had displayed when asked to sit beside him.

One of the footmen closed the door behind them. Then, with a rattle, a lurch and the clatter of horses' hooves, they were on their way.

Silence settled inside of the carriage box, as brittle as the thin sheet of ice on the surface of Knightley Park's ornamental lake. Marian searched for something to say that might thaw it.

Before she could think of a suitable topic of conversation, Dolly turned toward the captain. "How do you go to church when you're on your ship?"

"Dolly…" Marian addressed the child in a warning tone. Though Captain Radcliffe might not be the sort of seagoing tyrant she had mistakenly believed him, he probably expected the younger members of his crew to speak only when spoken to.

At first he appeared taken aback by the child's forthright curiosity. But after a moment's consideration he seemed to decide he might do worse than answer her question. "At sea it is not possible to go to a church building, as we are doing now. But most ships in the Royal Navy have chaplains who conduct Sunday services on deck when the weather permits or in the wardroom when it does not."

"What's a wardroom?"

A sterner warning rose to Marian's lips, but before she could utter it, the captain replied, "That is what we call the officers' mess on a ship, a sort of dining room and drawing room combined."

Dolly digested all this new information with a look of intense concentration that Marian wished she would apply to her studies. "Your ship must be a great deal bigger than the boat we row on the lake. How many rooms does it have?"

By now Marian thought better of trying to restrain the child, for Dolly had clearly discovered one subject certain to set the captain at ease. To his credit, he did not seem to mind being bombarded with questions about all matters nautical. Marian was also favorably impressed with his answers, which were couched in simple enough terms for the children to understand without insulting their intelligence.

His discourse proved so informative that Marian

found herself listening with rapt attention. It was not only what he said that engaged her interest, but the mellow resonance of his voice that made it a pleasure to listen to.

Almost before she realized it, the carriage came to a halt in front of the village church.

In the middle of an intriguing explanation of sails and rigging, the captain grew suddenly quiet again. "I can tell you more about it on the ride home, if you like."

His features and bearing tensed as he gazed toward the other parishioners making their way into the church.

A qualm of doubt rippled through Marian's stomach as she speculated what sort of reception awaited them. She hoped the villagers would not be as quick to misjudge Captain Radcliffe as she'd been. Otherwise, he might refuse to accompany them to church again. That would be a great calamity because she could not conceive of any other way to bring the captain and his young cousins together without deliberately disobeying his orders.

As the footman pulled open the carriage door, Captain Radcliffe seemed to steel himself for the ordeal ahead. Once the steps had been unfolded, he climbed out. Dolly bounded after him, eagerly seizing the hand he offered to help her.

Marian nodded to Cissy, who followed her sister with a reluctant air. When Marian emerged a moment later, Captain Radcliffe assisted her with thoughtful courtesy. For the fleeting instant his gloved hand clasped hers, she could not suppress a sensation of warmth that quivered up her arm. It reminded her of the previous evening when he had grasped her hand to keep her from rushing away. For hours afterward, she could not stop thinking about that brief contact between them.

"Come, girls." Marian chided herself for succumbing to such a foolish distraction at that moment. She needed to keep her wits about her to divert the captain, if necessary, from any unpleasant reception he might receive.

She cast a swift glance around the churchyard, troubled to see a few people staring rudely in their direction. But others offered welcoming smiles.

Dolly ignored Marian's summons. Instead she seized the captain's hand and announced, "I'll show you the way to our pew."

Cissy shook her head and frowned at her governess as if to ask why she wasn't scolding Dolly for her forwardness. But Marian had no intention of doing any such thing. Instinctively, Dolly had managed to provide the captain with the diversion he required.

Perhaps he recognized it, too, for he showed no offense at the child's behavior. Indeed, her impudent grin provoked an answering flicker of a smile. "I appreciate your assistance. I have attended services at this church, but not for a very long time. I could not have been much older than you are now."

"My gracious," Dolly replied with her accustomed bluntness, "that *was* a long time ago!"

Marian was aghast. "Dorothy Ann Radcliffe, mind your manners!"

But the captain greeted the child's tactless remark with an indulgent chuckle. "Do not fret, Miss Murray. I find my young cousin's honesty refreshing. When I was her age, I remember thinking any person above five-and-twenty was hopelessly ancient."

The man had a sense of humor, Marian noted with approval, wishing she'd perceived it earlier. It was a most desirable trait in a person responsible for bringing up children.

"Please don't encourage her, Captain," she murmured as they entered the vestibule. "Or I fear she may take advantage of your good nature."

"Hush, Miss Marian." The child raised her forefinger to her lips. "You always tell me not to make noise in church."

Marian exchanged a glance with Captain Radcliffe that communicated exasperation on her part and barely suppressed amusement on his. Somehow that look made her feel as if she had accidentally wandered into a cozy room with a cheery fire blazing in the hearth.

They made their way into the sanctuary of golden-brown stone, bathed in the glow of sunshine filtered through the stained glass windows. Dolly led the captain up the aisle to the Radcliffe family pew, where he stood back to let "the ladies" enter first. Cissy scooted in at once and Marian followed. Dolly hung back, no doubt to claim her place beside the captain.

Later in the service, when it came time for prayers of thanksgiving, Marian offered a silent one to the Lord for answering her earlier plea.

His reluctant attendance at church had not turned out to be the ordeal he'd feared. Gideon reflected on it the following evening as he consumed his solitary dinner.

He'd been aware of a few hard looks, but most of

the parishioners were more welcoming. That reception gave him greater hope that he might be able to get a fair hearing at the inquiry after all. During the service itself, a curious sense of peace had stolen over him as he'd listened to the familiar readings and joined in the hymns and prayers. It had scarcely seemed to matter whether or not God was listening. Surely, there was something worthwhile in a person expressing gratitude for his good fortune and identifying what he wanted in life for himself and others.

For himself, Gideon had only one wish—to have his reputation restored so he would be permitted to resume command of his ship. Had he been guilty of taking the blessings of an honorable reputation and a fulfilling career for granted in the past? If so, then his present difficulties might yield a worthwhile outcome, after all—by reminding him to appreciate all he had achieved.

When the pudding was served, Gideon cast an expectant glance toward the dining room door, half hoping Miss Murray might appear to discuss some matter about the children. He could not stifle an unaccountable pang of disappointment when she did not.

Though he had not been pleased by the governess's sudden appearance on Saturday evening, he'd soon found himself enjoying her company. At first he'd been reluctant to grant her request to accompany her and the girls to church, but now he was grateful she'd persuaded him.

He'd discovered his young cousins were not quiet the alien beings he'd dreaded, but two small people, each with her own feelings and personality. He could not help but be drawn to the younger one, any more than he could resist a frolicsome kitten that rubbed its head against his hand, hungry for attention.

The elder girl was a good deal more reserved and appeared every bit as wary of him as he was of her. Gideon could hardly fault the child for that since it showed her to be similar to him in temperament.

"Can I get you anything more, Captain?" asked the footman as he removed Gideon's plate. "Another helping of pudding? More tea?"

Gideon shook his head. "I have had my fill, thank you. More than is good for me I daresay. If I keep on at this rate, my girth may soon rival the Prince Regent's."

The young footman strove to suppress a grin but failed. "You won't be in any danger of that for quite a while, sir. When you first arrived, Mrs. Wheaton said you needed filling out. I reckon she's made that her mission."

Though he knew such an exchange between master and servant was more familiar than it should be, Gideon could not bring himself to discourage it. He had opened the door, after all, with his quip about the Regent. Besides, he preferred a little cordial familiarity to the hostile silence with which he'd been treated upon his arrival at Knightley Park.

"When I return to sea, I shall have to send my ship's cook to Knightley Park so Mrs. Wheaton can train him properly." Gideon pushed away from the table. "I have no doubt my crew would thank me for it."

In search of something to occupy him until bedtime, he headed off to the library. He had recently finished the books he'd brought with him, and he was confident he would find some suitable replacement on the well stocked shelves.

Uncertain whether he would find the room lit, Gideon took a candle from the hall table as he passed by. But when he pushed open the library door, he glimpsed the soft glow of firelight from the hearth and the flicker of another candle. It danced wildly as the person holding it gave a violent start when he entered.

Not expecting to find the room occupied, Gideon started, too. A quiver of exhilaration accompanied his surprise when he recognized his young cousins' governess.

"Forgive me for disturbing you, Miss Murray." He explained his quest for fresh reading material.

Clearly the young woman did not share his welcome of their unexpected encounter. Her eyes widened in fright and one hand flew to her chest, as if to still her racing heart.

When she answered, her voice emerged high-pitched and breathless. "It is I who should beg your pardon, Captain, for making free with your library."

She offered a halting explanation of how his late cousin had permitted her the use of it.

"Then, by all means, you must continue," Gideon assured her. It troubled him that she had feared he would be unwilling to extend her the same courtesy as Cousin Daniel had. "Though I enjoy the pleasures of a good book more than your late master, I have never had the knack of reading more than one at a time, let alone all of the hundreds collected by my family over the years. Having so many books for one person to read strikes me as a singularly inefficient arrangement. I would appreciate your assistance in making better use of this library."

Miss Murray did not appear to grasp his attempt at levity.

"That is very kind of you, sir." She bobbed a hasty curtsy. "But I still should not have presumed without asking your permission. If you will excuse me, I shall return at another time when my presence will not disturb you."

Her eyes darted as if seeking the quickest route to the exit that would give him the widest possible berth. Did she really find him so alarming still?

"You are not disturbing me in the least, Miss Murray," Gideon insisted, though he knew it was not altogether true. Her presence *did* affect him, though not in an unpleasant way. "Besides, if one of us must withdraw, it should be me. You were here first, after all, and I believe you have far more claims upon your time than I. If you were to go away now, I doubt you would easily find another opportunity to return."

"Not very easily perhaps, but—"

"I will hear no *buts,* Miss Murray. I should feel like the worst kind of tyrant if you left this library empty-handed on my account. Surely you would not want that?"

"Of course not, Captain."

"Good. Then we are agreed you must stay long enough to choose a book at the very least."

"If you insist, sir." Miss Murray reached toward the nearest shelf and pulled out the first book she touched, without even looking at the title. It might have been in

Latin, for all she knew, or a sixteenth century treatise on agriculture.

It was clear she wanted to make her escape as quickly as possible. A few days ago Gideon would have wanted the same thing. But having dined with Miss Murray and escorted her and the children to church, he'd discovered he preferred her company to his accustomed solitude.

Was there any way he might detain her there and keep her talking?

Perhaps...

"Before you go, Miss Murray, I hope you will not mind informing me how your pupils are getting on. Is Dolly still as determined to resist going to church? She seemed in fine spirits on Sunday and quite attentive to the service for a child her age."

His words had the most amazing effect on Miss Murray. All trace of diffidence fell away, and a winsome smile lit up her features. Clearly he had discovered the key to engaging her interest.

That accomplishment brought him an unexpected glimmer of satisfaction.

Chapter Five

Captain Radcliffe's inquiries about the girls banished any thought of leaving the library from Marian's mind. However uncomfortable she might feel in the captain's presence after the way she had imposed upon him, she could not neglect such a golden opportunity to further her plans. She fancied she could feel the warm hand of Providence resting on her shoulder, approving her efforts and helping to move them forward.

"The girls are quite well, thank you, Captain," she assured him, encouraged by his sudden concern for their welfare.

When he'd first entered the library to find her there, Marian had feared her presumption might cost her beloved pupils dearly. All she'd wanted was to apologize and make her escape as quickly as possible so the captain might forget she'd ever been there. To her surprise he seemed anxious for her to stay and not at all offended that she had made use of the library without his permission. Such generosity only made her more ashamed for sneaking around and assuming he would refuse her if she had asked.

"As for Dolly," Marian continued, "she has not uttered a single word of complaint about church, though she has asked a great many questions about ships and the sea. I believe you sparked her interest in those subjects. I hope to make use of that enthusiasm to engage her more fully in her studies."

The captain's brow furrowed. "And how do you propose to do that, pray?"

Did he truly want to know? It sounded as if he did.

"Today, for instance," she explained, "I had Dolly read a little verse about the sea, then choose a particular line to copy to practice her penmanship. Later we examined the atlas, and I pointed out some of the waters in which you might have sailed."

"I believe I understand your method." Was it a trick of the candlelight, or did a twinkle appear in the captain's gray eyes? "For sketching you would have her draw a ship. In music you would have her play or sing a sea shanty…one of the less bawdy variety, I hope."

His unexpected jest surprised a gush of laughter out of Marian and brought an answering quip to her lips. "Is there such a thing?"

The instant the words were out, she clapped her hand over her mouth, but it was too late. How could she have said such a thing, least of all to a man of the sea? Her years at school and later serving as a humble governess had trained Marian to guard against giving offense. Yet something in the captain's manner seemed to invite her to speak her mind.

His rumbling chuckle assured her he did not resent

her thoughtless jest. "I have never heard one. Still, I approve of your manner of teaching. I wish my old tutor had used something like it."

The captain's sincere interest in her profession gratified Marian. "Thank you, sir. Far too many people regard the education of girls as nothing more than furnishing them with a few superficial accomplishments necessary to snare a suitable husband."

That was one positive thing she could say about the Pendergast School. Its pupils had received a rigorous education, training them to make their own way in the world. It had been continually impressed upon them that their lack of fortune made it highly doubtful they could ever hope to marry.

"What about you, Miss Murray?" The captain set his candle on a low table beside one of the chairs upholstered with dark leather. "How do you view the education of girls—my young cousins in particular?"

No one had ever bothered to ask her any such thing, especially in a way that suggested respect for her opinion. For that reason, the captain's question flustered her, though in a strangely pleasant way.

"I—I suppose it means cultivating the development of my pupils in all areas—not only their intellect, but artistic sense and character—to the best of which they are capable. No doubt that sounds like a lofty ambition for a simple country governess."

The captain shook his head. "It sounds like a fine aim to me, Miss Murray. My young cousins are fortunate indeed to be taught and cared for by someone so devoted to them. Your task cannot have been easy considering the losses they've suffered."

Marian raised a silent prayer of gratitude for this unexpected encounter with Captain Radcliffe. Talking to
him about Cissy and Dolly was a perfect means to stir
his sympathy for the girls without forcing him to spend
time with them—something he was clearly reluctant to
do.

"It has been difficult to witness them suffer such sad
losses at so young an age. I have tried my best to fill
some small part of the void left by the passing of their
parents. I want them to feel secure and loved."

"It is obvious how much you care for them."

"Thank you, Captain. They are very easy children
to love. There is little I would not do for them." Her
greatest fear for the girls and for herself was that they
might be removed from her care. Though Marian was
satisfied she loved Cissy and Dolly Radcliffe more than
anyone, she had no legal right to decide their future or
make certain they stayed with her.

Tempted as she was to confide her worries in the
captain, Marian sensed it was far too soon to raise the
matter. If he suspected her hope that he might become
the girls' guardian, she feared he would retreat into his
earlier solitude. She needed him to learn to care for his
young cousins as she did. Then he, too, might be willing to take any action necessary to protect them.

"Very commendable," he replied, though Marian
sensed a slight chill of formality in his manner. Had
her talk of love made him uncomfortable?

Perhaps so, for he hastened to change the subject.
Gesturing toward the tall shelves crowded with books,
he observed, "You must be far more familiar with this

collection than I, Miss Murray. Are there any books you would recommend?"

Though part of her wished they might continue discussing the girls, Marian could not resist the chance to talk about books with someone above the age of ten or who did not live many miles away and must communicate exclusively by letter.

She swept an appreciative glance around the library, grateful to Captain Radcliffe that she would not have to give it up, as she'd feared. "I have derived many hours of entertainment and instruction from your family's books, sir. But I would hesitate to recommend any one in particular without first discovering what subjects interest you. Are you partial to poetry, biography…gothic novels?"

What had made her offer such an absurd suggestion? Could it be the hope of coaxing that twinkle back into the captain's eyes? Indeed it must have been, Marian realized when her effort succeeded, and her heart gave a sweet little flutter of triumph.

"I must confess, Miss Murray, I am not well acquainted with gothic novels. Though the two I have read proved exceedingly amusing."

She could not help but laugh. "Poor Mrs. Radcliffe read little else, rest her dear soul, and constantly urged them upon me. I must confess I found their dark melodrama and sensational subject matter all rather silly. I prefer heroic adventures or stories with intentional comedy."

The captain nodded. "Life can be quite dark and sensational enough at times without carrying those over into our reading."

Marian wondered if he could be thinking of his own situation—unjustly accused of dark deeds that would not be out of place in the pages of a gothic novel.

"What *do* you enjoy reading, Captain? What is your favorite of all the books you've read?" She did not tease him with facetious suggestions this time for she was sincerely interested in hearing his answer. His reading tastes might reveal aspects of this very private man that she might not discover any other way.

But why was she suddenly so eager to be well acquainted with Gideon Radcliffe? For the girls' sake, of course, Marian insisted to herself. The better she came to understand the captain, the better she would know how to appeal to him on Cissy and Dolly's behalf.

Captain Radcliffe stared toward the shelves with a look of intense concentration. "I like history. Gibbon's *The History of the Decline and Fall of the Roman Empire* is a work I admire. When I was younger, though, I had a thirst for adventure stories. *Robinson Crusoe* was a favorite of mine for many years. Have you read it, Miss Murray?"

Marian shook her head, almost ashamed to admit such a lapse. "I have heard of it, of course, but never actually read it. That is an oversight I must rectify at once. I know I have seen a copy in this library."

She turned toward the nearest shelf, scanning the titles. "Here it is. To think I could have passed over it so many times."

Pulling down the book, she replaced the other volume she had taken earlier. For the first time she glanced at its title. "I have no doubt I will find Robinson Crusoe's adventures more stimulating than *The*

History and Art of Chalcography and Engraving in Copper."

"They could hardly be less." Captain Radcliffe tried to suppress a grin. "So tell me, Miss Murray, if you were stranded on a deserted island, like Robinson Crusoe, what is the one book you would want to have with you?"

An answer to his question sprang immediately into Marian's mind, though she hesitated to reveal it. "There are many books I would like to take with me in such a case, but only one I could not do without—my Bible."

The captain rolled his eyes. "I should have guessed. A very pious choice, indeed. I hope you will pardon me if I do not take your recommendation as eagerly as you took mine."

"I did not *recommend* you read the Bible, sir. You asked what one book I would want to have with me if I was castaway on a deserted island. I did not mean to give you a pious answer, only a true one. If I were to endure such a trial, I would need the consolation I could only find in that particular book."

"Forgive me, Miss Murray." The captain looked as if he might approach her, then changed his mind. "I did not mean to question either the sincerity or suitability of your choice."

Although she believed him, Marian felt compelled to defend her decision in a way he might understand. "Even if those writings did not hold such power for me, I still believe it would be a worthwhile book to possess if I had no others. It contains a whole library in a single compact volume. It has a great history of the Hebrew people and adventure stories of Daniel, Jonah and other such heroes. It has biography, law, romance as well as some of the most beautiful poetry ever written."

As she spoke, Captain Radcliffe nodded in earnest agreement. Then a quicksilver twinkle lit his eyes once more. "But, alas, no gothic fiction. Could you survive without that?"

"Very easily, thank you." She did not resent his good-natured teasing for it showed they could disagree without creating hard feelings. "You must admit, though, the story of Salome demanding the severed head of John the Baptist in return for her dance verges on the gothic."

"You have me there, Miss Murray. I see I may have to read the Bible again more carefully, if only so I can hold my own with you in conversation."

They continued to discuss their other favorite books until the pedestal clock beside the door chimed the hour of ten. Marian gave a start and fumbled the book she was holding. Where had the time gone? She'd only meant to stay here long enough to return one book and take another. But talking with the captain had made the evening fly by. Though she'd started out wanting only to talk about the girls, she had soon come to enjoy his company for its own sake.

But realizing how long they had been talking together also made her aware of how long they'd been alone in this room. What if one of the servants came into the library to check the fire or deliver a message to the master? Their conversation had been perfectly innocent. She trusted Captain Radcliffe would never do anything improper, even if he thought of her as anything more than a servant—which she was quite certain he did not.

Still, if they were discovered together, it might lead to gossip in the servants' hall.

The captain's recent troubles proved what a danger the *appearance* of impropriety could pose to a person's reputation. Marian could not afford the slightest blemish on her character. Her livelihood depended on it.

"If you will excuse me, Captain, I must get back to the nursery." Clasping the copy of *Robinson Crusoe* tightly to her chest, she made a hasty curtsy. "Cissy sometimes wakes with bad dreams. She would be very upset if I wasn't there to comfort her."

"Of course." Was it her imagination, or did the captain also seem surprised by the swift passage of time? "I am sorry to have kept you from your duties, though I must admit I have enjoyed this opportunity to talk to someone about books."

"As have I, Captain." Was that the only reason the evening had passed so quickly and pleasantly, because they'd been conversing about a subject she enjoyed but seldom had the opportunity to discuss?

Marian edged between the writing desk that stood against the far wall and a trio of leather upholstered arm chairs clustered in the center of the room.

Meanwhile, Captain Radcliffe moved toward one of the chairs as if he intended to sit and read awhile after she'd gone. "Do not forget, Miss Murray, you have my express permission to continue making use of this library as often as you wish. And do let me know what you think of Mr. Defoe's book. Good night."

"Good night, Captain. And thank you." Marian

fled from the library as if to escape some unnameable danger. And yet, she could not deny her reluctance to part from Gideon Radcliffe.

All the way back to the nursery she cradled the book in her arms as if it were the most precious object she'd ever held.

The next evening Gideon rushed through his dinner, exchanging a few pleasantries with the young footman who served him. Afterward, he sent his compliments to the kitchen, for the chine of beef had tasted even better than usual.

The moment he finished his last bite of pudding, he rose and headed for the library. On his way, he paused for a moment to adjust his neck linen in front of a pier glass in the hallway.

The cloth was pristine white and perfectly tied, yet Gideon still scowled at his reflection. He had never noticed before that his face was so long and angular or how his sailor's tan accentuated the fine crinkled lines that fanned out from the corners of his eyes. He looked every day of his seven-and-thirty years, something that had never mattered to him before.

Nor did it now. Gideon gave his reflection a final dismissive glance, then continued on to the library. When his hand closed over the knob, he hesitated an instant, making a deliberate effort to smooth the frown from his features.

He entered the room to find a small fire glowing in the hearth, just as it had the night before. The flickering light of his candle danced over the dark, polished wood of the shelves and the rows of richly colored book spines, many with their titles embossed in gold letters. The chairs looked as inviting as ever. The portrait of his great-grandmother looked down on him with a brooding gaze that reminded him of the way Marian Murray regarded her young pupils.

Yet somehow the library felt much colder and emptier than it had the previous night. Gideon strove to ignore a vicious little stab of disappointment at finding it empty.

That was ridiculous. Until recently, he'd been quite content with his own company. Indeed, he often preferred it.

But not this evening.

His unexpected and surprisingly enjoyable encounter with Miss Murray must have spoiled him.

Slowly Gideon paced the length of the library, his gaze drifting over the book titles, hoping one might catch his interest. Yet even as he read them, the words ran through his mind in a meaningless litany while his thoughts returned to the previous evening and his conversation with Marian Murray.

He almost fancied he could hear her voice, clear and melodious with that gently rolling Scottish cadence.

It was not only the way Miss Murray spoke that appealed to him, but what she had to say. Their opinions might differ widely, particularly when it came to spiritual matters, but he could not question her sincerity or her judgment. Indeed, he respected both. The differences between them added a certain zest to their discussion that made his conversation with anyone else seem stale.

Last evening, in Miss Murray's company, time had

flown by more agreeably than he'd ever experienced before. Tonight, as he paced the library, hoping she might appear again, every minute crawled as if some physical force were hindering the movement of the clock's hands. When those hands finally struggled to half-past eight, Gideon reluctantly acknowledged that he would not likely see Miss Murray that evening.

What had made him imagine he might? A sigh gusted out of him as he sank onto the nearest of the armchairs. Miss Murray had no reason to visit the library so soon again. Last evening she had procured a book that might take her many hours to finish in what little free time she had for pleasure reading. It was doubtful she would return to the library for a week at least.

To his bewilderment, Gideon found himself counting the days until Sunday when he could be certain of spending time in her company again.

"Will Captain Radcliffe be coming to church with us again this week?" asked Cissy as Marian fixed her hair the following Sunday morning. The child sounded as if she were bracing herself for something unpleasant.

"I'm not certain." Marian tried to ignore the odd little spasm that gripped her stomach when Cissy spoke the captain's name. "I suppose I ought to have asked him."

She had been strongly tempted to seek him out the previous evening for that very reason, but she'd feared she might find him at dinner again and he might feel obliged to invite her to join him. Not that she would have found it unpleasant—quite the contrary. But a repetition of such behavior might provoke comment among the servants. She did not want to risk exposing the captain to more undeserved gossip within his own household.

Now she almost wished she had consulted him, so she would know whether she and the girls could expect to see him this morning. The uncertainty made her rather anxious.

"I hope he will come." Dolly looked up from the atlas she had been examining with unaccustomed concentration. "It's much nicer driving to church in the carriage than walking. Besides, I have lots more questions I want to ask him."

"If the captain does accompany us," Marian said, brushing a lock of Cissy's lustrous dark hair around her finger to make a final ringlet, "please try not to pester him with too much chatter."

"Why not? He didn't seem to mind last week. He told me all sorts of interesting things."

So he had, Marian was obliged to admit. Just by listening to them, she had learned a few new facts. Captain Radcliffe had been remarkably patient in answering the child's endless questions about ships and the sea. In fact, he had appeared to welcome them to fill the awkward silence that might have pervaded the carriage otherwise.

"Get on your cloaks and bonnets, girls. If the captain is coming with us, we don't want to keep him waiting." And if he was not, she feared they might be late for church.

As Cissy rose from her chair in front of the dressing table, Marian stooped to glance at herself in the looking glass. She'd given in to an unaccountable whim to wear her hair differently this morning, parting it to one side rather than straight down the middle. For such a minor change, it altered her appearance considerably, softening the severe simplicity she had affected until now.

She noted other changes, as well, that the difference in parting her hair could not account for. Her lips looked fuller and her nose less prominent than usual. Her complexion had a youthful brightness that made her look less than eight-and-twenty, and her brown eyes sparkled. Marian scarcely recognized herself.

"You look very pretty today, Miss Marian." Cissy reappeared beside her, properly cloaked and bonneted.

Marian gave a guilty start. What was she doing, staring at herself in the mirror like some vain debutante when she and the girls were already running late? At school, her teachers had always impressed upon the girls the sins of pride and vanity. Humility, good character and diligence had been held up as virtues far more important than outward appearance.

Now she chided herself for forgetting those lessons. "That is kind of you to say, my dear. But remember, pretty is as pretty does. I should not have dawdled while you and your sister were busying yourselves to get ready."

Throwing her cloak over her shoulders, she snatched up her bonnet and began to tie it in place as she shepherded the girls out of the nursery. Her stomach seemed to churn harder with every step she took. Marian told herself it was only because she might have made the girls late.

Despite her earlier warnings to the contrary, Dolly hurried on ahead with a spirited skip in her step.

"What have I told you," Marian called after the child, "about bounding down the stairs two-at-a-time?"

But it was her heart that gave a bound when she heard Dolly cry, "Good morning, Captain! I've been learning all about ships and the sea. What is your ship called? How many masts does it have? Where is the farthest place you've ever sailed?"

Marian opened her mouth to remind the child not to plague the captain with questions. But just then she caught sight of him as he glanced up at her with a smile. It was unlike any expression she'd seen on his face yet. Not a wry grin at some jest. Not a cautious arch of one corner of his mouth. But an unreserved beaming smile that proclaimed his sincere pleasure at seeing them again.

The sight of it made Marian's voice catch in her throat.

Fortunately, Captain Radcliffe did not seem to notice as he turned his attention to Dolly.

"HMS *Integrity,*" he rattled off the answers to her questions. "Three masts. And the farthest I ever sailed from England was to a place called New Zealand—a pair of islands on the other side of the world."

Before Dolly could think of more questions with which to pepper him, Cissy addressed the captain for the first time. "Have you sailed all the way around the world?"

He nodded gravely. "I have, though that was quite a few years ago, when I was not very much older than you are."

"How old are you now?" Dolly demanded. "May we call you cousin...what is your name again?"

"Dolly!" Marian gasped. "Mind your manners!"

But the captain gave an indulgent chuckle that would have astonished her if she had not previously discovered his droll sense of humor. "You are welcome to call me Cousin Gideon if you wish. As for my age, I must confess it is seven-and-thirty. Perfectly ancient, don't you agree?"

The child nodded gravely. "That is old."

"Dorothy Ann Radcliffe!"

"Don't fret, Miss Murray. When I was her age I would have said the same thing." Captain Radcliffe opened the door for them.

To Marian's surprise, Cissy spoke up. "I don't think seven-and-thirty is so very old."

Clearly she was trying to spare the captain's feelings. Marian gave the child's hand a squeeze as they made their way out of the house to the waiting carriage. "I would say it is quite the prime of life for a man— an age when his character is set in a way it is likely to continue."

Though she addressed her remark to the girls, it was intended for the captain. While he gave the appearance of not being offended by Dolly's brutal honesty, Marian sensed that perhaps their opinion did matter to him.

Chapter Six

Did Miss Murray consider him as ancient as her young pupils so obviously did? When Gideon made his self-deprecating quip to Dolly, he stole a glance at the child's governess, fearing her countenance would betray agreement.

To his relief it did not. The only reaction Miss Murray's expression communicated was concern for his feelings. Not pity, though, fortunately. His pride could not have abided that.

He appreciated the older girl's effort to relieve any sting her sister's remark might have inflicted. Until now, he'd suspected Cissy Radcliffe might resent him for taking over as master of Knightley Park. He was touched by this sign that her feelings toward him might be thawing.

Once the girls and Miss Murray had passed through the open doorway, Gideon strode out and overtook them. With a pointed look, he dismissed the footman waiting by the carriage door so that he might help the ladies in himself.

When he overheard Miss Murray telling her pupils that she considered a man of his age to be in his prime, Gideon's chest expanded as he stood taller. At the same time, he felt vaguely disturbed by her suggestion that his character was irrevocably set.

He had little time to dwell on it, though, for no sooner had they gotten seated than Dolly demanded, "Tell us more about how you sailed around the world, Cousin Gideon. How long did it take? What places did you visit?"

"Please," Cissy added.

Although Miss Murray said nothing, the fact that she refrained from telling Dolly to stop asking questions made Gideon suspect she might also want to hear about his experiences. That made it impossible for him to refuse, even if he'd wanted to.

"Let's see." He plundered his memory for incidents that might entertain them without taking too long to tell on their short drive to church. "We set sail in 1789. The captain was an acquaintance of my uncle who had been among the crew on one of Captain Cook's famous expeditions. I was a twelve-year-old cabin boy, eager to become a midshipman."

As he told of the expedition to the west coast of North America to obtain furs for sale in China, two things surprised Gideon. The first was that young girls seemed to relish tales of adventure every bit as much as boys. The second was how flattering he found it to have a group of females hang on his every word.

Despite his best effort to keep his story brief and relate only the most interesting parts, he had just begun to describe how his ship had been captured by the Spanish when they reached the church.

"Bother!" Dolly muttered. "I wish we could keep on driving and listening to your stories."

Gideon cast a furtive glance toward Miss Murray. She had asked him to accompany her and the girls so he could be a good influence. He did not want his presence to have the opposite effect.

"Now, now," he replied. "There are plenty of fine adventure stories from the Bible, you know. I have had some interesting experiences during my career at sea, but nothing equal to being swallowed by a whale or slaying a giant with only a sling and a stone."

He climbed out of the carriage, then helped the girls and Miss Murray alight. His hand lingered on the governess's longer than he intended, but she did not seem to mind. Her eyes met his for a moment with a glow of gratitude that warmed him in spite of the November frost.

"The captain is right, girls. I should read you more of those stories. Besides being thrilling adventures, they teach important lessons about trust, faith and courage."

"It's not the same." Dolly shook her head. "I shall never meet David or that man in the whale. I can't ask them about what happened like I can with Cousin Gideon and *his* adventures."

Reluctantly, Gideon let go of Miss Murray's hand and took the child's instead. "I shall make you a bargain, then. If you can sit still in church and attend to the vicar, on the way home I'll continue my story."

"What if you're not finished by the time we get home?" Dolly was clearly a shrewd negotiator for her age. "Will you come and have tea with us in the nursery and tell us the rest?"

Gideon pretended to mull over his answer, though in truth there was no question in his mind.

"I believe I could be persuaded," he said at last. "That is if Miss Murray does not object."

"Not at all, Captain. We would be very glad to have your company." The notion sincerely pleased her. Gideon felt certain of it. She had an air of satisfaction that verged on smugness, odd as that seemed.

"Then we have a bargain," Dolly declared in a loud whisper as they moved through the church vestibule into the sanctuary.

A curious sensation spread through Gideon's chest as he looked down at the child and felt her small hand enveloped in his. There was a heaviness about it that did not burden him like too much ballast, but rather promised to anchor him when the seas of life grew rough.

But what if Dolly could not keep her part of their bargain? That tiny worry nagged at Gideon far more than it should have. She was a naturally boisterous child, after all, who reminded him of her father at that age. If she squirmed or chattered or otherwise misbehaved during the service, he would have to enforce the consequences and save the rest of his stories for another day.

Yet he feared missing out on tea in the nursery might be more of a hardship for him than for the girls.

To his relief, Dolly proved as good as her word, conducting herself with perfect restraint for every minute of the service, though it ran longer than usual. Such docility did not come easily for the child, Gideon sensed as he watched her clench her small fingers together and squeeze her eyes tightly shut during the prayers. He respected her strength of will and determination to honor their agreement. It flattered him to realize she considered his company and stories such a worthwhile inducement to put forth that kind of effort.

While they sat in the pew, his young cousin nestled up close beside him, warming his arm and his heart. During the liturgy, he held his prayer book down where she could easily see it, pointing to each word with his forefinger to help her follow along. The proportion of those words Dolly was able to read increased his respect for the skill and diligence of her governess.

As the service progressed, Gideon found himself intensely conscious of Miss Murray's presence so nearby. Twice he glanced down at Dolly, only to look up and find her governess watching them with a tender glow in the brown velvet depths of her eyes. And when she sang the hymns, the mellow sweetness of her voice lent those familiar lyrics fresh significance.

Though perhaps there was something more to it, as well. He had only come to church to oblige Miss Murray and set a good example for the children. But now that he was here, the prayers, scripture readings and sermon all engaged him in a different way than they had for many years. Somehow their message felt far more personal—as if someone was calling to him in a soft but insistent whisper.

But did he dare to heed it?

After the vicar had pronounced the benediction, Dolly looked up at Gideon with a triumphant grin. "I did it!"

He could not resist smiling back at her. That smile lingered on his lips when he looked up at Miss Murray. "It appears you may be saddled with a guest for tea. I hope it will not be too great an inconvenience."

"None at all, Captain." She leaned toward him, lowering her voice so the children would not hear. "Fond as I am of my pupils, I sometimes hanker for someone older to talk with."

"I certainly qualify." Gideon could not keep a shard of bitterness out of his quip. It wasn't that Miss Murray had any particular liking for *him.* She was so desperate for a little adult conversation that anyone would do.

He told himself he had no right to resent her motives. No doubt this bewildering fancy he'd conceived for her was only the natural attraction he might feel toward *any* woman with whom he spent time, after his long years away at sea.

Be that as it may, he made certain to spin out his story on the drive back to Knightley Park. By the time they reached the house, he had only gotten to the point where the Spaniards had finally released the ships, which then set sail for the Hawaiian Islands.

"Remember your promise," said Dolly as he helped her out of the carriage. "You must come to the nursery and tell us the rest over tea."

He nodded. "I would not think of going back on my word after you kept your part of our bargain so faithfully."

A few minutes later they entered the bright, cozy set of rooms with its bank of bowed windows overlooking the lake.

"Welcome to our nursery." Dolly ushered Gideon in with a flourish.

"Fancy that," he murmured, more to himself than to his young cousins and their governess. "This place is still exactly as I remember it. Even the old stool in the corner where Danny was made to sit when he grew too boisterous."

"You've been here before?" Dolly demanded.

"Danny?" cried Cissy. "Do you mean our papa?"

"Yes to both." Gideon made a slow circuit of the room as a host of memories came spilling out of some long locked compartment in his mind. "My family used to visit here sometimes in the summer and always at Christmastime. Your father and I were near in age and both the only children."

Only *surviving* children, but he did not want to bring that up with two young girls who had suffered more than their share of bereavement.

"Danny and I always enjoyed the holidays together," he continued. "Sometimes he and I would pretend we were brothers."

"What was Papa like as a boy?" Cissy asked in an almost pleading tone. "What did the two of you do together?"

Concerned that such reminiscences might only upset the girls, Gideon looked to their governess for guidance. She replied with a slight lift of her brows and shoulders, followed by a subtle nod.

"Let me think." He sank onto the window seat, and the two children flew to nestle on either side of him. "It has been many years, but I recall he had hair the color of yours, Cousin Celia, and a dimple in his chin like your sister. He was a year younger than me—not as tall but sturdier. He loved to be out-of-doors riding or throwing sticks for the dogs."

Gideon could picture his cousin so clearly he fancied he had only to look out the nursery windows to glimpse their boyhood selves larking about. "At Christmastime, we loved to skate on the lake and help gather boughs to deck the house. There was one special holly bush that always had the greenest leaves and the fattest, reddest berries. Afterward, we would hang about the kitchen and beg hot cider and nuggets of gingerbread from the cook."

Those memories filled his heart with wistful pleasure.

"What else?" Dolly prompted him eagerly.

But Cissy grew quiet, her head bowed. A tiny wet spot appeared on the lap of her dress, made by a fallen tear.

Suddenly Gideon felt badly out of his depth and overwhelmed by the situation into which he'd blundered. It was as if he'd waded into inviting waters only to find himself caught in a powerful current with no idea how to swim. Perhaps his first instinct upon coming to Knightley Park had been right after all. Cousin Daniel's young daughters did need things he was totally unequipped to provide.

Then Miss Murray spoke, and her words seemed to extend him a lifeline. "The captain can tell you more about all that later, girls. We invited him for tea, remember. Now we need to get ready."

Dolly leapt up at once, but Cissy hung back, swiping her forearm across her eyes. Gideon pretended not to notice, as he would have wanted if the situation had been reversed.

As he watched the girls do as their governess bid them, he recalled more of those happy Christmases when their father had so generously welcomed him to this nursery. He and his cousin had never met again after he'd been sent away to sea, something he regretted deeply.

Now another Christmas was coming—the first one Cousin Daniel's young daughters would spend without their father and the last they would likely celebrate at Knightley Park.

Somehow that regretful thought gave birth to a much happier idea—one that brought Gideon a sweet thrill of anticipation he had not experienced in years.

He only hoped Miss Murray would approve.

Her plan to encourage Captain Radcliffe to care for his young cousins had been going so well. But as Marian headed down to the library two evenings later, she feared it might have begun to flounder.

She'd been vastly encouraged when the captain had appeared to escort them to church again without having to be reminded. Clearly when he agreed to assume a responsibility, he could be relied upon to fulfill it to the best of his ability. Knowing what she did of him, it came as no great surprise he possessed that admirable quality. His skill at storytelling, however, had come as a pleasant revelation. Hearing about his adventures on the high seas had made Cissy begin to warm to him. But listening to the accounts of his childhood visits with her late father must have been a bittersweet experience at best.

Marian had sensed Captain Radcliffe's ambivalence to relate those stories when the girls pleaded to hear them. Then, after Cissy had tried to hide her tears, the captain had grown quiet and seemed to withdraw. Marian hoped he had not been so disturbed by Cissy's reaction that he might resist her future efforts to bring him and the girls together.

At the threshold of the library, Marian paused to smooth her skirts. This dress was one she seldom wore, its rich burgundy-red a bright contrast to her usual somber browns and grays. Was she foolish to have worn it this evening? The captain might not even be in the library. And, if he was, why should he take any notice of her appearance?

Still, Marian could not keep her pulse from beating a little faster when she nudged open the library door and entered the room. Neither could she suppress an unaccountable pang of disappointment when she saw it was unoccupied.

Chiding herself for being so foolish, she strode to one of the shelves and replaced the book she'd brought. She found herself reluctant to part with it after such an enthralling read. She'd hoped to find Captain Radcliffe here so she could thank him for recommending *Robinson Crusoe* and tell him how much she'd enjoyed it. Having missed that opportunity must be the source of her disappointment. Now she wished she'd thought to mention it to him on Sunday and tell him how much his personal stories put her in mind of the book.

Carefully she scanned the shelves looking for something new to read. Twice she pulled down books and read the first page only to put them back when neither piqued her interest. Whatever she chose, she feared it would suffer in comparison to *Robinson Crusoe.*

At last the clock chimed nine. Marian told herself to choose a book and go. If one of the girls had been here in her place, she would have accused them of dawdling.

Forcing herself to take action, she pulled a copy of *The Vicar of Wakefield* off the shelf and headed for the door. Just as she reached for the knob, it turned and the door swung inward to reveal Captain Radcliffe. The sudden meeting made them both start, but the sight of him brought Marian a bewildering rush of happiness along with an almost painful self-consciousness at being so close to him with no one else around.

Marian retreated a few steps to give the captain room to enter. "Good evening, sir. I just came to return the book I borrowed and select another."

Caution warned her she should not linger alone with the captain; but now that he was here, she did not relish the prospect of leaving.

Fortunately, he gave her an excellent excuse to stay for at least a few more minutes. "I hope you enjoyed the adventures of Robinson Crusoe."

"Very much. I must admit, I pictured Mr. Crusoe looking and sounding very much like you, especially after you told the girls and me about your adventures sailing around the world."

"Did you, indeed? Well, well." The captain seemed more embarrassed than flattered.

"Ever since I first read that book, I felt a kinship with the character," he confessed.

Could that be because he'd felt so isolated and lonely, even with many people around? Marian sensed he might harbor such feelings. For his sake, as much as the children's, she longed to breach the invisible barrier around him and bring them together...if only he would let her. "Speaking of books, do I take it you have been revisiting the one I mentioned, Captain?"

He gave a rather shame-faced nod. "I suppose I gave myself away with that little lecture to the children on Sunday. Indeed I have been delving into the Bible again and finding more within its pages to engage me than I ever expected. I have gained a deep appreciation for the wisdom of your choice."

"I am pleased to hear it." Marian was more than pleased to think she might have helped Captain Radcliffe see that God was not as distant and disinterested as he had long supposed. "I respect your willingness to keep an open mind."

If only he could do the same where Cissy and Dolly were concerned. Though in their case she felt it was more important for him to keep an open *heart*.

"If there is nothing more, sir, I should be getting back."

"Actually, there is something, Miss Murray, if you would oblige me for a few minutes more. I have a proposal to make."

Proposal?

The captain must have noticed her stunned expression, for he hastened to rephrase his request. "That is...a proposition...I mean...there is a matter I wish to discuss with you...about the children."

"Of course, Captain." Marian welcomed any excuse

to stay, though she still tingled from the rush of astonishment his use of the word *proposal* had provoked.

How foolish! As if a gentleman of property like him would ever think twice of someone like her...even if he wanted a wife, which Captain Radcliffe clearly did not.

She didn't want a husband either, Marian insisted to herself. Over the years, she had lost everyone she'd ever cared about. She did not want to leave herself vulnerable to that kind of hurt again. Bad enough she had allowed Cissy and Dolly deeper into her heart than she'd ever meant to. The fear of losing them reminded her how dangerous it could be to let herself care too much.

Then her befuddlement cleared and she wondered what he meant to say about the girls. Would the captain remind her of their original agreement to keep the children away from him in exchange for permitting them to stay on at Knightley Park until after Christmas? Was he going to point out that Christmastime was fast approaching, and the New Year hot on its heels? Did he want to discuss plans for tracking down the girls' aunt or what might be done with them if Lady Villiers could not be located?

That would certainly explain his sudden pensiveness in the nursery on Sunday. And his present anxious frown.

Those fears flooded Marian's mind in the instant it took for Captain Radcliffe to regain his composure and continue. "My conversation with the children about past Christmas celebrations got me thinking..."

As it had her. In previous years, Cissy and Dolly's father had made a great occasion of the season—hosting a dinner for all his tenants, the house crammed with

candles and greenery and special outings and gifts for
his young daughters. If Captain Radcliffe could not
be persuaded to seek guardianship of the girls, then
this would be their last Christmas at Knightley Park.
Marian longed to make it a memorable one for them.
But she had neither the resources nor the authority to
re-create the kind of celebration they were accustomed
to.

She feared this Christmas might only be memorable
for what it lacked…beginning with a father.

"…since this will be the children's first Christmas
without their father…" The captain's words echoed her
anxious thoughts.

Marian's lower lip began to tremble. She wanted
to beg Captain Radcliffe to reconsider whatever he
was about to suggest, but she feared her voice might
break or a tear might fall. After seeing how he had reacted to Cissy's furtive tears, she did not want to make
things worse for the girls by blubbering in front of their
cousin.

"I can see you are inclined to disapprove, Miss
Murray, but pray hear me out. I would like to do something special for the children this year to provide a
distraction from any mournful thoughts that might otherwise trouble them."

What was he saying? Marian wondered if she could
trust her ears, or was she only hearing what she so desperately wanted the captain to say?

"I thought perhaps it might amuse them to re-create
Christmastime as I remember it at Knightley Park."
He spoke in a rather defensive tone, as if he expected
her to interrupt at any moment with a long list of ob-

jections. "Feasting, decorating, music and gift giving. But I have never organized any such festivities before. I would not know where to begin."

Bless his kind heart! Captain Radcliffe was proposing precisely the opposite of what she'd expected. He wanted the same things for Cissy and Dolly as she did.

The curdled brew of sorrow and dread inside Marian suddenly distilled into a bubbly elixir of joyful excitement, which she found even harder to contain than her tears. Those still hovered, making her eyes tingle. Only now they were tears of happiness.

"What I am trying to say, Miss Murray, is that I will need your help if I am to realize these plans. I know it may mean extra work for you and perhaps you do not approve of any activities that might excite the girls or disrupt the orderly running of the nursery. But I would be heartily grateful if you would be so kind as to assist me."

The captain rushed through this last part as if he feared she would refuse if he stopped for breath— when instead she was fairly bursting with eagerness. By the time he paused to let her answer, her feelings had grown too volatile to contain.

"Of course I will!" Letting the book in her hands drop to the floor, she flew toward him and threw her arms around his neck as she had not done with anyone since her childhood. "I shall be delighted to help you in any way I can. Thank you, Captain! Thank you!"

It felt so natural to embrace him, soaking in his resolute strength, inhaling his brisk, briny scent. Yet Marian realized almost immediately that it was wrong.

Even with a family member or close friend, such an

unrestrained gesture would be questionable. But with the master of the house in which she was employed, a man with whom she was barely acquainted, it was an act of the most grievous impropriety.

One that might cost her everything she cared about.

Chapter Seven

When Miss Murray threw herself at him with such joyous abandon, Gideon had no idea what to do.

He was not accustomed to physical contact, least of all a hearty embrace from a very attractive woman. Before he could make any conscious decision, his body reacted on instinct. His muscles tensed and he drew back.

The instant he did, part of him wished he hadn't. The soft warmth of her touch promised to restore something he'd been missing for a very long time. The scent of her hair put him in mind of a freshly washed handkerchief just taken off a clothesline on a summer's day.

Of course, it would not have been proper to wrap his arms around her and hold her close, as part of him longed to. He respected Miss Murray far too much to do anything that might frighten her or compromise her reputation. But could he not have held still and let her cling to him for as long as she would?

There was no use speculating now for the damage was done. The moment he tensed, Miss Murray jumped back like a scalded cat, refusing to meet his gaze, stammering apologies.

"Forgive me, Captain! I didn't mean…I never should have…" With every word the northern lilt of her accent grew stronger. "I was just so happy to hear what you wanted…."

She looked so distraught and mortified by her behavior that Gideon forgot all about his own feelings on the matter, anxious only to protect hers. "Please, Miss Murray, I understand. And I assure you I am not offended. You took me by…surprise, that's all."

She scarcely seemed to hear him over her own condemnation. "I don't know what came over me. I've never done anything like this before."

Could her reaction to what she'd done involve more than regret for the impropriety? Gideon wondered if she found such close contact with him repellent. Or perhaps she realized what could have happened if he'd been a less honorable man.

Stooping to the floor, she groped for the book she'd dropped. "If you will excuse me, Captain, I must be going."

Miss Murray made a rush for the door, clearly expecting he would move out of her way. This time Gideon held his ground. If he let her go before they had resolved this awkward incident, he feared his Christmas plans might fall by the wayside.

"Please stay a few minutes more. I beg you not to reproach yourself for…your actions. I assure you, I do not."

When she realized he intended to stay put, Miss Murray staggered back as if she had struck an invisible wall. "You are very understanding, sir. I promise you, nothing like that will ever happen again."

Her reassurance brought Gideon a stab of disappointment, but he did not dare let his true feelings show. "I hope this one small…lapse in self-control will not prevent us from working together to make this a merry Christmas for my young cousins."

His appeal on behalf of the children seemed to penetrate her barrier of self-recrimination. Inhaling a deep breath and squaring her shoulders, Miss Murray met his gaze. "If that is what you wish, Captain, I can assure you it will not."

"Very good." A powerful wave of relief threatened to swamp Gideon, but he took pains to conceal it from Miss Murray. "Since we have barely a fortnight to lay our plans, I believe we should arrange to meet again and discuss what needs to be done."

She gave a solemn nod. "I agree, sir. When would you like us to meet next?"

Miss Murray was more than solemn. It seemed as if she had reverted to the stern-faced governess he'd encountered when he'd first returned to Knightley Park. This woman would never think of teasing him about gothic novels. Nor would she permit herself to become so overjoyed that she would throw her arms around him. Gideon considered that a pity.

He had been inclined to suggest they sit down and start making plans immediately. Now he wasn't so sure that would be a good idea. Perhaps they both needed time to let the memory of that impulsive embrace fade a little.

"Tomorrow evening at this time?" he suggested.

Then, lest Miss Murray suspect he was anxious to spend time alone with her, he added, "I would prefer to keep all this as a surprise for the children, until the time gets closer…if you don't mind."

"Not at all." She clasped the book in front of her chest like a shield. "If Dolly found out what you're planning too soon, she would get so excited I'd be up until midnight getting her to sleep. Then we would never be able to meet. So back here tomorrow night, then. At eight o'clock?"

Her gaze flitted from him to the library door and back again.

He deduced what she wanted and stepped aside to let her pass.

"I look forward to it, Miss Murray." As he spoke those words, Gideon realized he meant them far more than the usual hollow pleasantry.

The next day Marian tried to keep as busy as possible so she would not fall to brooding about the thoughtless indiscretion she'd committed. Of course, that meant keeping the girls busy, too, which did not sit well with Dolly.

"Why are you making us work so hard, Miss Marian? Is it punishment for being naughty? What did we do?"

"I haven't been naughty," Cissy protested before Marian could reply. "It's not fair if I'm being punished for something Dolly did. You should just make her sit in the corner."

Dolly stuck her tongue out at her sister. "I'd rather sit

in the corner than do all this work. It would be a good rest."

"You haven't been naughty." Marian came between the children before they tried to take out their frustration on each other. "Though making faces at your sister is highly impolite and I expect you to apologize. Your lessons weren't intended as punishment. I didn't realize how hard I was making you work."

She must stop this foolish preoccupation with Captain Radcliffe. It was having an adverse affect on her dealings with the girls, and she could not permit that. Cissy and Dolly mattered more to her than anything. "I'll tell you what. Since you've managed to do a whole day's work this morning, you can spend the afternoon enjoying yourselves. We'll go out for a walk in the garden, then later we can go down to the music room and practice on the pianoforte. What do you say to that?"

"Practice?" Dolly wrinkled her nose. "That sounds like more work."

"What if I cut your practice shorter, then I play some music for you to sing and dance to? Would that be better?"

Both girls nodded eagerly.

"Let's get ready then." Marian beckoned them up from their work and supervised their dressing for outdoors.

With the help of the nursery maid, she made sure the girls put on thick wool stockings, sturdy half boots, cloaks, bonnets and gloves, for the day was clear and cold enough that the lake had frozen over.

"Can we go skating?" pleaded Dolly after they'd gotten outside.

Marian shook her head. "I'm certain the ice won't be thick enough yet. If it stays as cold as this for another fortnight, it should be safe."

Perhaps that was something she should mention to the captain at their meeting in the evening. The late Mr. Radcliffe had enjoyed every sort of outdoor activity, and skating was one in which he'd been able include his young daughters. Marian had preferred to watch from the shore, not trusting her balance on those slender metal blades.

Looking ahead to the evening, a sense of acute embarrassment overwhelmed her again. But it could not entirely stifle the sparkle of anticipation at spending time with Captain Radcliffe.

In the course of their brief acquaintance she had come to appreciate a number of fine qualities he possessed. He was hardworking, dependable and well-read. Though rather solitary and self-reliant, he could tell an entertaining story and keep up a most engaging conversation when he tried. He had a streak of ironic wit, often at his own expense, that was all the more amusing for being so unexpected.

But none of those things drew her to him as much as his kindness and willingness to forgive. After the way she'd behaved last night, the captain would have been well within his rights to demand her removal from his house. At the very least, he could have changed his mind about his Christmas plans for the girls. But he'd done neither of those things, choosing instead to excuse her outrageous conduct and seeking to ease her shame over it.

She almost wished he would do something to lessen her liking for him before it grew to threaten her happiness.

After an invigorating walk, she and the girls returned to the house for steaming cups of chocolate and currant buns warm from the oven. When Martha set down the tray she had fetched from the kitchen, Marian spied a letter propped up against the chocolate pot. She snatched it up, recognizing the handwriting at once.

"Who sent it," asked Cissy, "one of your friends from school?"

Marian nodded as she broke the seal. "I have no other correspondents, as you know."

That reminded her she must get busy writing her own Christmas letters to her friends. She was certain they would all want to know how her master's unexpected passing had affected her and her young pupils.

"Which one is it from?" Dolly said, helping herself to a bun. "Miss Beaton in the Cotswolds? Miss Fletcher in Kent? Or is it the one in Lancashire? I forget her name."

The girls had long been curious about the friends she had not seen for years, but with whom she faithfully exchanged letters. She had used that interest to foster their knowledge of geography.

"Miss Ellerby," Marian reminded Dolly. "Yes, the letter is from her."

Anxious to glance over it, she quickly filled their chocolate cups. While they all ate and drank, she skimmed Grace's letter. After her meeting with the captain this evening, she would read it over more carefully and perhaps begin her reply.

"But she is no longer in Lancashire," Marian murmured as she read. "She is looking for a new position elsewhere."

"Why?" asked Dolly, between bites of her bun. "Did she do something she oughtn't and get dismissed?"

"Of course not." Marian answered rather too emphatically, glancing up from the letter. "She is seeking a better position, that's all."

That wasn't altogether correct, but she could not possibly confide the true reason to her innocent young charges. Although Grace had been discreet in her letter, Marian gathered her friend had been the object of unwanted attentions from her master's brother. Poor Grace had been afflicted with a degree of beauty that might have been a great asset to her if she'd been born into a wealthier family. Instead, her looks had provoked charges of vanity at school, when nothing could have been further from the truth. Since they had completed their education and gone out into the world, this was the third time her friend been obliged to seek a new position because of difficulties with gentlemen in the household.

Would Captain Radcliffe have shirked her embrace if she'd had Grace Ellerby's golden hair and exquisite features? Of course he would have, Marian's reason insisted. The captain was too honorable a gentleman to take advantage of such a blunder no matter what her appearance. Reading about Grace's difficulties made Marian all the more grateful for his restraint.

"You aren't going to find a better position and leave

us, are you, Miss Marian?" Cissy inquired in an anxious tone.

"Of course not!" Marian folded up Grace's letter and tucked it away to read more carefully in private. "What better position could I possibly find than here at Knightley Park with two such sweet, clever girls?"

The thought of being separated from them was like a sharp knife pressed between her ribs. But she must not worry the girls by letting on how near that danger loomed if she could not persuade Captain Radcliffe to take responsibility for them.

"Wrap your hands around your cups." Marian picked up hers to demonstrate and to divert them. "That will warm your fingers so they won't be too stiff to play."

She kept up an animated chatter until they'd finished eating, then the three of them trooped down to the music room. There the girls faithfully practiced their scales and went over the new pieces they were learning. Finally, Marian showed them a little duet with a very easy part for Dolly. The girls managed to stumble through it without many mistakes.

"There," Dolly huffed, as if she'd just finished a very strenuous chore. "Now will you play for us, Miss Marian?"

"I don't know that it's such a great reward." She bent between the girls and wrapped an arm around each of them. "But if that's what you want..."

"It is." Cissy rose from her chair, offering it to Marian. "Play something we can dance to, but not too fast."

She held out her hand to Dolly. "Come, you be the lady and I'll be the gentleman. I'll show you what to do. First you must curtsy and I will bow. No, wait until the music starts."

Taking that as her cue, Marian began to play, all the while watching the girls out of the corner of her eye. She stifled her laughter as Cissy tried to instruct her sister in the steps while Dolly proceeded to do just as she pleased.

After the girls tired of dancing, they came and stood on either side of her while she played several favorite tunes for them to sing.

"Now will you sing for us, Miss Marian?" Dolly leaned against her, resting her head on Marian's shoulder.

How could she deny the child anything when she asked in such a way?

Marian's fingers began to move almost without conscious thought and familiar words rose to her lips. *"The water is wide, I cannot get o'er and neither have I wings to fly. Bring me a boat that will carry two and I will sail my love to you."*

It astonished her that her fingers still recalled the notes to this old song, one of the first she'd ever learned. What had made her think of it now after so many years? Marian shrank from admitting why she might have chosen to sing a love song involving ships.

"A ship there is and she sails the sea. She's loaded deep as deep can be. But not so deep as the love I'm in. And I know not how I sink or swim." As she continued on with the next verse and the next, Marian could not keep from imagining the events of the ballad played out by her and Captain Radcliffe.

"Must I be bound and he go free?" The words of the

final verse sent a shiver through her. *"Must I love one that cannot love me? Why must I play such a childish part, and love a man who will break my heart?"*

No sooner had the final notes died away than a burst of energetic applause rang out behind her. Marian gave a violent start and spun around to find Captain Radcliffe standing in the doorway clapping his hands.

"Well done, indeed, Miss Murray. You have a fine voice and a most expressive manner of conveying the meaning of the piece."

His praise set her aflutter. But it alarmed her to wonder what he might make of her singing such a song the day after she had thrown her arms around him.

"Forgive me, Captain!" She leapt up and performed an awkward curtsy. "I was only obliging the girls with a song after they concentrated so well on their music lesson. I had no idea you were at home. I did not mean to disturb you."

Dolly must have taken note of her agitation for the child dashed toward Captain Radcliffe and seized his hand. "Please don't be cross at Miss Marian, Cousin Gideon! We asked her to sing for us."

A quiver ran through Marian at the sound of their first names spoken together like that.

As the child drew him into the room, Captain Radcliffe shook his head. "What makes you think I am angry? On the contrary, I wonder what feat I might perform to earn more of Miss Marian's singing as a reward."

Did he realize he'd just spoken her Christian name? It was a natural enough mistake, since it began with the same letter as her surname. No doubt he'd simply repeated what the girls called her. Still, it took Marian by surprise what a jolt of pleasure such a small error could bring her.

"I assure you, Captain, you have done it already and more with all your kindness to me and the girls." That gave her an idea for something they could do at Christmastime. She had no intention of mentioning it to him when they discussed his holiday plans that evening.

Instead, it would be a secret and a surprise for him.

Gideon could not recall a time when he'd enjoyed himself so thoroughly as in the weeks leading up to Christmas. Each morning he woke eager to experience what the day would bring. He looked ahead to the approaching holiday season with a level of anticipation that was almost childlike. He relished all the planning and the delightful secrets.

In the past he had made plans and kept secrets of an entirely different nature. Readying his crew for battle, supplying British troops on the Continent and maintaining the blockade of French imports and exports had all been vital duties, but hardly a source of pleasure. The secrets he'd kept had been a matter of life and death rather than a source of future happiness for others.

"What else needs to be prepared for our Boxing Day festivities, Miss Murray?" Gideon glanced up from the writing desk in the library, where he sat making lists of errands to run and supplies to purchase.

"I believe we've taken care of all the details for the dinner itself, sir," she replied. "Do you wish to give out hampers to the tenants, as your cousin used to?"

Gideon raised an eyebrow. "Hampers?"

She nodded. "Hampers of fruit, sugar, tea and the like. Those little comforts people cannot produce for themselves and are most likely to do without when times are hard."

The way she spoke, Gideon sensed she had known such need in her own life. Though he longed to learn more about her past, he knew it was not his place to inquire.

"An admirable tradition." He dipped his pen into the inkwell and began adding to his list. "One we must maintain. Anything else?"

Miss Murray thought for a moment. "If you're set on keeping things the same as other years, you might want to engage a few musicians to play for dancing after the dinner."

"And where would I find these musicians?"

"I can give you some names, sir."

He glanced up at her again with a grateful smile. "I don't know how I would manage all this without your assistance."

Gideon could not deny that one of the pleasures of this time was the certainty of enjoying Miss Murray's company almost every day. At first he'd told himself he would have relished any woman's society after all his years at sea. Now he was not so certain.

Marian Murray possessed a fortunate combination of the qualities he most admired. She was clever, well-read and accomplished. Ever since the day he'd overheard her singing to the girls, her clear, sweet voice had woven its way into his dreams. She was sensible and sincere, unlike some women he'd had the misfortune to encounter in various ports of call. Even that embrace, which he could not forget, had been a spontaneous mistake, not a calculated flirtation. She was open-minded and open-hearted, the first person who had been willing to believe in his innocence and trust in his honor.

But what he liked best about Miss Murray was her open affection for his cousin's orphaned daughters and her warm, nurturing spirit. From what he had observed, she was more like a mother to the girls than a governess. If he were ever to want a wife, Miss Murray would answer all his requirements and more.

His words of praise seemed to fluster her. Or was it the fact that he was staring at her like a calf-eyed schoolboy?

"I'm happy to help." She ducked her head, and her lips rippled in a self-conscious smile. "It was so kind of you to think of this."

He had no intention of taking a wife, Gideon reminded himself sternly. His heart belonged to the sea, and his first duty was to the Royal Navy. That solitary life suited him. He had been for too many years away from the company of women and children. His one recent attempt at a closer relationship had ended in failure of the worst kind. He could not bear to fail anyone else like that.

"Kindness? Tosh!" He forced his gaze away from her face and back to the safety of his list. "It is pure self-interest, I assure you. These festivities will give me an opportunity to celebrate Christmas in a way I have not had the pleasure in years."

"How did you mark the season on your ship?" Miss Murray asked.

Much as he would have liked to look up at her again,

Gideon gave a shrug and continued writing. "With very little fanfare, I'm afraid. I increased rations and tried to make certain there was tolerable meat for our cook to prepare. I had plugs of tobacco and other such minor comforts distributed, when we could get them."

"It sounds like Christmas might have been nothing at all for your men if it hadn't been for you," Miss Murray suggested. "You must have been something of a father to them."

"I wouldn't go that far," Gideon muttered, though her words struck a chord. He had once considered himself a father figure to his men—a sort of Old Testament patriarch who could be depended upon. One who rewarded the good and punished the bad. "If my crew had respected me like a father, I doubt I would have found myself in my present difficulties."

With his two engaging young cousins, he saw the opportunity to experience a different kind of family relationship, however temporary.

"If you don't mind my asking, Captain, how did you come to be in your troubles? I know you could never have done what you're accused of. But I cannot understand how anyone could have accused you of such a thing in the first place. How did that poor boy come to die?"

Gideon winced, for her questions revived memories he had worked hard to suppress.

"Have you ever talked about it with anyone?" Miss Murray's voice fell to a beseeching murmur he found impossible to resist.

With a weary shake of his head Gideon laid aside his pen.

"It would do you good," she persisted. "I wouldn't repeat a word to anyone."

He knew he could trust her to keep his confidence. He had been looking forward to giving his testimony at the inquiry. But how much better would it be to unburden himself to someone he knew would sympathize and believe his side of the story? "Perhaps I was getting too soft, wanting to be a father figure to the younger members of my crew. Harry…that is, Mister Watson… reminded me of myself at that age. He'd been sent to sea as a boy after losing his family. He was a quiet lad, but diligent and dependable. I didn't mean to favor him, but perhaps I did. I reckon that was what got him killed."

When he paused to collect his thoughts and master his emotions, Gideon expected Miss Murray to jump in, firing off questions as Dolly would. But she did not. Instead, her expectant, understanding stillness invited him to continue when he was ready.

"The other midshipmen all knew one another. They came from families with more influence. They tried to curry favor with me, but when they realized their efforts were having the opposite effect, they turned their attention to my second-in-command, an ambitious young fellow itching for a ship of his own."

He should have seen the direction in which events were drifting and corrected his course, but he'd been too trusting of his men. It had never occurred to him that others might place self-interest above honor and duty.

"When Mister Watson would not countenance some of the mischief they got up to, the others started bullying him. I sensed something was wrong but when I asked, he always denied any trouble."

"Of course he would." Miss Murray's pitying whisper reminded Gideon of her presence. "He wouldn't want to worry you. He probably thought if he said anything it would only make matters worse."

"Then he was right." How did she understand the situation so well?

Gideon had been staring down at his list of Christmas preparations, not really seeing it. Now he cast a glance at Miss Murray and saw her emotions etched plainly on her irregular but appealing features. Her outrage stirred something deep within him.

"One day I overheard them threatening what they would do if he complained to me of their mistreatment."

"What did you do?" The words burst out of her as if she could not contain them.

If he had still been holding the pen, it would have snapped when his hands clenched. "I informed them in no uncertain terms that if Mister Watson so much as stubbed his toe again, I would hold them responsible no matter how strenuously he denied it. And I would punish them with the utmost severity the Royal Navy would permit."

He'd been trying to protect the lad, but he had failed. "I thought they wouldn't dare lay a hand on him after that. But one night I returned to my cabin and found… his body. I went after those despicable bullies in a rage, vowing to make them pay for what they'd done. But my second-in-command gave them an alibi and persuaded the doctor to have me restrained. The more vigorously I protested, the more I sounded like a raving madman who had murdered one of his crew and gone after others."

Again Miss Murray could not restrain herself. "Surely anyone who knew your character…"

"My sterling record was all that saved me from immediate prosecution the moment we arrived back in port. But those allied against me have powerful friends, while I have made more than one enemy in the Admiralty with my intolerance for bungling and politics."

"What about the rest of your crew? Surely others must have known what was going on and could speak in your defense."

Gideon heaved a disillusioned sigh. "Perhaps, but I imagine they are frightened for their own safety if they testify against that wicked cabal, led by the villain who is now their commanding officer. They have seen what such men are capable of."

"I don't understand. Why did your second-in-command protect those miserable bullies? Just because they made up to him?"

"It had nothing to do with *them*. I told you he was ambitious. During the war there were more rapid promotions. Now that peace has come, it could take years for him to earn his first command. The opportunity to remove a superior officer who stood in the way of his advancement was one he could not resist."

"I'll tell you one thing…" Miss Murray's voice rang with righteous indignation. "If I'd been a member of your crew, I would have stood by you and told the truth about what happened, no matter what the consequences. If there's one thing I can't abide in this world, it's bullies. Fair makes my blood boil!"

Her fierce declaration of loyalty brought the shadow of a smile to Gideon's lips.

"I suppose you think that's no way for a woman to talk," she snapped. Clearly her blood was still up. "Or do you doubt I'd do what I said?"

"Not for a moment, my dear." Gideon leaned back in his chair, bathed in an unexpected release of tension and frustration. "I overheard you giving those two footmen a vigorous dressing down, remember? I only smiled now because I relished the thought of you making mince of those bullies aboard my ship. I know you would stand up for anyone you believe in, and I am flattered to count myself among that company."

If only he had as able an advocate as her to present his case at the inquiry, he would feel much less doubtful of its outcome.

Chapter Eight

If the Royal Navy could not appreciate what a fine officer they had in Gideon Radcliffe, then the service did not deserve him!

In the wake of his confession about all that had happened aboard HMS *Integrity,* Marian could not help reassessing her hopes and plans for the future of those she cared for at Knightley Park. That now included not only her dear young pupils but also the captain.

When she'd first come to realize what a good, honorable man he was, she had hoped to enlist him as an *absentee* guardian for the girls. Now she thought it might be better for everyone if he put the Navy behind him and stayed here in Nottinghamshire.

From all she'd seen of his interaction with the girls, she believed he could be an ideal surrogate father to them. She hadn't realized how much they needed a man in their lives until he'd begun spending time with them. Dolly responded so well to his kind firmness and his attention. Even Cissy, who had viewed Gideon as an interloper at first, was beginning to warm up to him.

Much as the girls needed him, Marian sensed he might need them even more. When he'd spoken of his ship and the way he'd treated his crew, she could tell the man secretly yearned for a family. Surely that deep need would be better filled by two dear girls who could reciprocate his feelings for them, rather than a pack of bullies, traitors and cowards who weren't worthy of his regard.

As she and the girls headed out with Gideon to gather Christmas boughs, Marian told herself she should put aside all her planning and worries for the future and savor the joys of the season.

They made quite a numerous party, setting out from the house on Christmas Eve morning—along with the groundskeeper, a footman and a stable boy. The latter led a sturdy brown pony, which pulled a two-wheeled cart.

"This will be great fun!" Dolly skipped along at Gideon's side, clinging to his hand as they headed toward a nearby coppice to harvest all the greenery they would need to deck the halls and rooms of the house. "Other years we always had to wait back in the nursery until the boughs were brought. I'd rather go out and fetch them."

"At least the nursery was warm," Cissy grumbled under her breath.

Marian flashed the child a warning look and hoped Gideon had not overheard. She knew Cissy was only reacting to Dolly's implied criticism of how things had been done in their father's time. Still, she did not want the captain thinking the girls were as ungrateful as his former crew for everything he tried to do for them.

Dolly must not have heard her sister or she would surely have had something to say about it. Instead she asked, "Can I have a hatchet to cut some boughs myself?"

The very idea of Dolly wielding an ax brought a half stifled gasp to Marian's lips. Gideon would not agree, would he? Lately he'd become more and more indulgent of the little scamp.

"I believe it would be better to leave the actual cutting to those who know what they're doing." Gideon made it sound as if he'd actually considered the child's outrageous request. "Besides, there will be plenty of work for the rest of us, choosing what we want cut and loading it into the cart."

Dolly didn't seem too disappointed. "Maybe next year."

Marian lofted a heartfelt prayer toward the overcast heavens that they would all be together next year, gathering Christmas greenery. Even then, she doubted she or Gideon would be inclined to trust Dolly with a hatchet.

"Tell me, Cousin Celia," Gideon called over to the older girl. "How are you accustomed to decorating the house for Christmas?"

Marian caught his eye and gave a discreet nod of approval. He seemed to understand that the quickest way to Cissy's heart was to honor the traditions of the past.

Just as Marian expected, the first words out of the child's mouth referred to her late father. "Papa always liked to have evergreen boughs over the windows, with holly and ivy on the sills and over the mantelpieces."

"That sounds very festive," Gideon replied as the

cart stopped before a patch of woodland. "I remember the place being decked that way in our grandparents' time. Did he still like to have the pictures hung with bay?"

"Yes, that's right." Cissy began to sound more enthusiastic.

"Don't forget the kissing bough," Dolly chimed in. "And mistletoe for over the doorways."

"No, indeed," Gideon replied. "We mustn't forget those."

Marian thought he sounded rather uneasy. Was he afraid of being accosted in doorways by a certain forward governess? She would have to make sure she gave him no such reason to want to leave Knightley Park and return to his ship.

Ah, the kissing bough. How could he have forgotten it?

As they collected boughs and other greenery for the Christmas decorating, Gideon thought back to his first and only experience with that perilous object. On his final Christmas at Knightley Park, a young lady from the neighborhood had managed to catch him beneath the kissing bough and demand the customary favor, much to his mortification.

He would have to beware of it and all the mistletoe-hung doorways throughout Knightley Park this Christmas season. Not that it would be a great hardship to kiss Marian Murray if they happened to be caught under the mistletoe—quite the contrary. The difficult part might be stopping.

Unlike her unexpected embrace in the library, a

public mistletoe kiss would not pose a threat to her reputation. Still, Gideon was reluctant to risk the pleasure of it. In the unlikely event that Miss Murray did entertain any particular fancy for him, he did not want to encourage her. He thought too highly of her to toy with her affections. He did not want to risk having her feelings injured if the inquiry found in his favor and he was returned to command.

But what if that did not happen? For the first time, Gideon permitted himself to entertain the possibility with something less than dread.

For who could be low in spirits on such a day, in such good company? True, the sun was hidden behind a thick bank of gray cloud, and the ground was a damp mixture of dull greens and browns. But his young cousins scampered about in bright wool cloaks, their cheeks nipped pink and their faces alight with eager smiles. When Gideon placed an armload of fresh-cut boughs in the cart, his nose tingled with the sharp tang of evergreen.

A vigorous tug on the hem of his coat made him look down at Dolly, who immediately darted away calling, "You can't catch me, Cousin Gideon!"

She reminded him so much of her father that his years and cares seemed to fall away until he felt almost like the boy of those long-ago Christmases.

"Oh, can't I?" He lunged toward the child, but she dodged around the cart with a gleeful shriek.

"Too slow! Too slow!" She taunted him.

"We'll see who's slow." He ran after the little minx, but she picked up her skirts and tore off, leading him a merry chase.

"Be careful, Dolly," her governess warned. "The ground is muddy, and the laundress won't thank you if she has to scrub a lot of dirt out of your skirts."

Cissy laughed. "You made a rhyme, Miss Marian. Scrub the dirt from Dolly's skirt!" Perhaps wanting a share in her little sister's fun, she skipped away. "Can't catch me!"

Much running and dodging ensued to the accompaniment of more taunts, squeals and wild laughter. By the time Gideon and Miss Murray cornered the two little runners, they were all red-faced and winded. For the first time in many years, Gideon's sides ached from laughing. And he had forgotten all about the inquiry.

"Thank goodness…the others have not…shirked the job," he panted. "Or we might have…a sadly bare house…for the holidays."

"I thought we needed to get warmed up." Dolly chortled. "And it worked, didn't it?"

"I cannot deny that." He reached over and tipped down the brim of her bonnet. "But now that we are warm, hadn't we better lend a hand with the work?"

"What can I do?" The child held out her empty hands. "You wouldn't let me have a hatchet."

A hatchet, indeed—the little monkey!

Gideon tossed her a sack from the cart. "Let's go see if we can find some holly."

They located a fine bush not too far away and collected plenty of sprigs for decorating—the leaves a bright, waxy green, the clusters of berries plump and crimson.

By noon they had managed to fill the cart with

everything they needed. They headed back to the house triumphant.

"My legs are tired," Dolly complained.

"No wonder," Marian Murray said, shaking her head. "After all that running around, which was your idea, don't forget."

"I know." Dolly heaved a sigh and trudged on.

"Here." Gideon picked the child up and hoisted her onto the pony's broad back. "Is that better?"

Dolly bobbed her head. "Much better, thank you, Cousin Gideon."

"It's not fair," Cissy muttered. "She gets to ride while I have to walk."

"We can't have that, can we?" replied Gideon. "If you would like to ride, I reckon this fellow can carry one more."

Cissy gave a solemn nod. She stiffened when Gideon swung her up beside her sister, but soon relaxed and seemed to enjoy the short ride home.

Once they had arrived back and removed their wraps, Gideon ushered "the ladies" into the parlor, where the Yule log crackled and glowed in the hearth, giving off fragrant, earthy warmth. Pulling chairs close around the fire, they extended cold fingers and feet to thaw. One of the maids appeared with a tray of cake and mugs of hot, spicy-sweet cider to complete their warming from the inside.

While they ate and drank, Dolly proceeded to interrogate Gideon. "Tell us all the places you've spent Christmas on your ship."

He took a long sip of cider and thought back over the years. "Out in the Channel for many of the last several.

Before that, once in Mexico, which I told you about. Twice each in Malta and Jamaica. Once in Naples. Once in Nova Scotia."

"Where's that?" asked Cissy.

"Across the Atlantic, north of the American states. There is enough evergreen there in a single acre to deck a hundred-thousand halls, and a vast deal of snow."

"I wish we had some snow." Dolly took a large bite of cake. "It makes all outdoors look like it's covered in a white blanket."

Gideon glanced toward the window. "You may get your wish before the day is out."

"What makes you say that?" Cissy nibbled daintily at her cake.

"The way the clouds are massed in the northwest and the smell of the air." Gideon explained how the welfare of his ship and crew often depended on his ability to foretell the approaching weather.

Miss Murray remained quiet, yet Gideon still found himself conscious of her nearness. While he addressed his conversation to the girls, he watched out of the corner of his eye to see how she reacted. Did she lean forward to catch every word? Did her clever dark eyes sparkle with interest? Did some little quip of his coax a fleeting smile to her lips?

When all the cake and cider had been consumed, Gideon rubbed his hands together. "Now we had better get to work and deck these halls, don't you think?"

Dolly jumped from her chair. "The kissing bough first!"

The footmen fetched in boughs and bags of other greenery. Then they set up an occasional table and brought wire and trimmings for the construction. Acting on the girls' directions, Gideon bent and wrapped lengths of thick wire into several large hoops. Then he joined and fastened the hoops into the skeleton of a globe.

The procedure required additional hands to hold the hoops in place while Gideon lashed them together with finer wire. Miss Murray quietly lent her assistance. The supple strength of her long-fingered hands made her perfect for the job. As he worked, Gideon could not prevent his hands from brushing against hers. Every time it happened, his heart seemed to beat a little faster.

"Not too dismal for a first effort." He looked the thing over with a critical eye when he'd finished.

"It's fine." Miss Murray hastened to reassure him. "The frame doesn't need to be pretty. No one will see it when all the boughs and trimmings get attached. As long as it's strong and holds together, that is what matters."

She was right, Gideon acknowledged as he fastened fir and cedar boughs to the bare wire frame in overlapping rows. Gradually the kissing bough took shape. Then the girls and Miss Murray took over, adorning the plain evergreen globe with red velvet ribbons and oranges he'd purchased from the market in nearby Newark. The tart aroma of the fruit mingled with the spicy fragrance of cloves. Cissy and Dolly had studded the oranges with those in fanciful patterns.

The finishing touch was the choicest sprig of mistletoe with a rich cluster of pearly white berries. Fastened into place and trimmed with a scarlet bow, it hung down from the bottom of the kissing bough. Then the chandelier in the middle of the high parlor ceiling was lowered and the kissing bough attached to it, as had been the tradition at Knightley Park for so many years past.

When the chandelier was raised back into place and their creation hung above them in all its Yuletide glory, Dolly broke into a cheer. "You see, Cousin Gideon, it looks wonderful!"

Standing back with his arms crossed, Gideon gave a nod of satisfaction. "We can all be proud of our handiwork. I must admit, I would have had no idea how to begin without all your advice and assistance."

Though he addressed his words to all three of them, it was to Miss Murray in particular he intended to speak. He and she made a very capable partnership.

"It is a beauty." She gazed up at the kissing bough with a glow of admiration in her dark eyes.

While Marian Murray's attention was fixed elsewhere, Gideon stole the chance to admire *her* beauty. He hadn't been much impressed with her looks when they first met. But as he'd become better acquainted with her, that had changed. Now he glimpsed intelligence and humor in her eyes, courage in the tilt of her chin and tenderness and generosity in her full lips. None of her features, on its own, measured up to an accepted standard of feminine beauty. Yet, taken together, and illuminated by her indomitable spirit, they became something far more rare.

As he watched her stare up at the kissing bough, he sensed the shadow of some darker emotion beneath her initial wonder. Was she perhaps as anxious as he not to be caught beneath the mistletoe?

* * *

How had that festive symbol of Christmas come to be associated with such an amorous activity? Marian surveyed their handiwork, suspended from the chandelier in the parlor. Was it the invention of some long ago gentleman who'd wanted the opportunity to kiss a number of ladies without committing himself to only one? Or perhaps a single lady who wished to enjoy a kiss or two without ruining her reputation?

Marian could not deny she'd felt more than a trifle stirred by Gideon's nearness as they worked together to construct the kissing bough. The frequent, glancing contact of their arms and hands had made her wonder what it might be like to share a proper embrace with him.

At the same time, she knew she did not dare try to discover. Perhaps if she had not thrown herself at him that evening in the library, she could risk being caught under the mistletoe with him. But after taking such a shocking liberty, any further behavior in that vein would make it appear she was actively pursuing the master of the house. She could not afford to have him suspect any such thing, for fear it would frighten him off before he'd come to care enough about the girls.

That part of her plan was progressing too well for her to jeopardize. Watching him chase Dolly around during their morning outing, as if he were a carefree boy again, had brought her a sweet, secret pang of satisfaction. It was clear the girls' well-being and happiness had begun to matter to him. Why else would he have taken such pains to give them a merry Christmas?

If anything more were needed to dispose Marian in his favor that would have been it.

"I'm certain it is the finest kissing bough in the neighborhood." She caught Cissy by the hand and gave an affectionate squeeze. "But we mustn't rest on our laurels. Or perhaps I should say, *rest on our evergreens.* There is plenty more decorating to do. The mantelpiece and windowsills are still bare and the other rooms haven't even been touched."

Realizing it might sound as if she were assuming the role of mistress of the house, she added, "Don't you agree, Captain?"

He gave a decisive nod. "Indeed. This may be our masterpiece but we do not want it to be our only decoration." He turned to Dolly. "What should we tackle next?"

"The mantelpiece." The child grabbed a fir bough from the pile they had discarded and handed it to him. "One set this way and one the other with some holly and oranges. We spent all yesterday sticking cloves in them. Don't they smell good?"

"Delectable." Gideon arranged the greenery as Dolly had bidden him. "This should look very festive indeed."

"What shall we do?" Marian asked Cissy.

The older girl glanced around the room. "Put candles in the windows with ivy and yew around them."

In far less time than it had taken to construct the kissing bough, the whole parlor was colorfully adorned for the holidays. Then they moved on to another room and then another. On the main staircase, they twined boughs through the banisters and secured them with red ribbons. Still more boughs and holly adorned the sideboard in the dining room as well as running up the middle of the long table.

When Marian glimpsed Gideon lifting Dolly up to add another orange to the mantelpiece decoration, she smiled to herself.

Later when he was trimming one of the family portraits with bay leaves, he beckoned Cissy over. "Do you know who the people in this painting are?"

"No. Who?"

"That is my grandmother." He indicated a handsome young woman who sat holding an infant. "Her name was Celia, too. The baby in her arms is my father and this little boy beside her is your grandfather."

"Who is the little girl?" asked Dolly, peering hard at the painting.

"That is their sister. Her name was Dorothy."

"Like me."

"Like you." Gideon cast her a fond look. "Now since we have all worked so hard and the dining room looks suitably festive, I hope you ladies will do me the honor of joining me for dinner."

Marian was not certain what to make of his sudden invitation. It had not been part of the Christmas plans he'd discussed with her.

But when the girls appealed to her, "Can we, please, Miss Marian?" she could not deny them. The more time they spent in the captain's company, the better, after all.

"Very well. Since it is Christmas, I suppose it will not hurt to alter our usual nursery routine."

"Excellent." The captain made it sound as if she had granted him a great favor. "It would be most unfortunate if I was obliged to dine alone on Christmas Eve."

Marian could not disagree with that.

"The invitation includes you, of course, Miss Murray," he added.

She opened her mouth to protest that it was not her place when a particular look from the captain changed her mind. It seemed to suggest he was not yet so accustomed to the girls' company that he would be comfortable dining with them on his own.

"Thank you, Captain." She curtsied to remind herself of her place in the household. Though she might care for the Radcliffe girls like a mother, she was only a hired employee. "If that is what you wish."

"It is," he replied, "and the girls', as well, I'm sure. Our celebrations would not be the same without Miss Marian, would they?"

There he went again, referring to her by her Christian name, as the girls did. Was it only a slip of the tongue or did he mean something more by it?

"Of course you must eat with us." Dolly's brow furrowed as if she was trying to puzzle out why there should be any question. "You always do."

"Then that is settled." The captain seemed well satisfied with the arrangements. "Let us retire to dress for dinner and meet back here in half an hour."

After a parting bow, he strode away before Marian could inform him that it took longer to change and groom two little girls than for him to don a fresh coat and linen.

"Come along, girls." Marian seized them each by the hand. "We'll have to hurry."

Hurry they did, racing up the stairs to the nursery where they scrubbed evergreen sap off their hands, then changed into their Sunday dresses with colorful plaid sashes and kid slippers. While Marian helped Cissy dress, Martha combed Dolly's hair and retied her ribbons. Then they switched.

The three of them made it back to the dining room with a full minute to spare, though Marian regretted having no time to do more than quickly smooth down her hair. She told herself it did not matter. She would only be there to supervise the girls and see that they minded their manners.

Yet she could not help wishing she'd been able to make a better appearance for the occasion when the captain joined them. He was freshly combed and shaved, wearing crisp snowy linen and a smart blue coat that emphasized his fine bearing. It was all she could do to stifle a sigh of admiration.

Until that moment, she had not realized how much his rugged looks had come to appeal to her. Every other man she'd ever met now suffered by comparison. The angular features and firm mouth that had appeared so severe at their first meeting now struck her as noble and courageous. Had she once thought his gray eyes cold? Now she could see the intelligence, honesty and kindness in them, as well as the occasional glimpse of wistful longing.

If he noticed her appearance for good or ill, Gideon Radcliffe gave no indication.

"I hope all our work today has given you ladies a good appetite." He held out the chair at one end of the table and beckoned Marian to be seated in what was traditionally the place reserved for the mother of the family.

Then he held chairs halfway down each side for
Cissy and Dolly. "I believe the cook has prepared a
fine meal for us tonight."

So she had. The soup was followed by slices of
savory brawn. Then the game pie was served, its flaky
golden crust encasing great lashings of meat and gravy.
Though Marian felt too full to eat another bite, she
could not refuse the airy lemon sponge cake and fine
fruit that were served for dessert.

While they ate, Dolly interrogated the captain further about his ship and his travels while Cissy quizzed
her cousin about their forebearers and times past at
Knightley Park. Captain Radcliffe answered all their
questions patiently and in an entertaining way. He also
used the opportunity to draw the girls out, asking about
their favorite colors, foods and activities.

From her place at the end of the table, Marian quietly tucked into her dinner while she listened to the
others converse. Now and then, she leaned over to catch
a glimpse of the captain around the pyramid of fine
fruit that served as an elegant centerpiece. Whenever
he glanced up to catch her watching him, she ducked
back out of sight like a bashful schoolgirl.

Though the steady stream of courses brought by the
footmen seemed as if it might never end, eventually
their delightful meal drew to a close and their whole
pleasant day with it. Marian could have stayed and listened to Gideon Radcliffe for many more hours, but it
was already past the girls' bedtime. Duty won out over
inclination.

"If you will excuse us, Captain." She rose from her
chair when he paused to take a drink. "I believe the

girls ought to get to bed soon, or they will be in danger of nodding off in church tomorrow."

The captain got to his feet. "We cannot have that, can we? Thank you, ladies, for a most enjoyable evening."

Cissy slipped out of her seat and went to join Marian, but Dolly's bottom remained firmly on her chair. "But I'm not tired!"

Her claim might have been more persuasive if she had not broken into a wide yawn.

"Come along now," Marian insisted. She knew it would be a grave mistake to put up with any nonsense so early in the Christmas season. "If you behave well, the captain may be more likely to include you in other holiday festivities."

"Will you?" the child appealed to her cousin.

"Without a doubt," he replied in a solemn tone, though Marian glimpsed a subtle twitch at one corner of his mouth.

Dolly yawned again. "All right, then."

She scrambled out of her chair and started toward her sister and governess when something outside caught her attention. She raced past them toward the window. "Look, it's snowing!"

"So it is." Marian and Cissy followed her to peer out the window that overlooked the garden.

Outside, in the frosty darkness of midwinter, large lacy flakes of shimmering white drifted lazily down from the sky. Whenever a breath of wind stirred, it set them dancing and swirling.

Behind her, Marian heard the captain's footsteps approach as he joined their huddle around the window. "I told you it would snow."

"Yes, you did." Dolly continued to stare outside. "Now everyone make a wish on the first snowflakes of the winter."

Cissy shook her head. "It's the evening star you're supposed to wish on, not snowflakes."

Dolly tilted her chin defiantly. "I think people should be able to wish on whatever they like. I'm going to wish on the first snowflakes."

Marian had no faith in Dolly's snowflake fancy. But a prayer directed heavenward on Christmas Eve— surely that would have a greater likelihood of being answered.

Intensely aware of Gideon hovering so close beside her, she repeated her often raised prayer that he might become Cissy and Dolly's guardian. But this time she neglected to ask that he be returned to his ship.

Chapter Nine

Wishing on a snowflake?

After Miss Murray took the children off to bed, Gideon lingered at the window watching the snow drift down. He shook his head and smiled to himself over Dolly's childish fancy.

Of all the things to attach one's hopes to—a tiny wisp of ice crystals that would melt away in an instant if it landed on his bare hand. At least a star, however impossibly distant, was constant and lasting.

Somehow that thought reminded him of what Miss Murray had said when they'd first talked about the power of prayer. She'd suggested that God could be infinitely small as well as infinitely great. The force that had created those massive, brilliant heavenly bodies and flung them across the universe had also wrought the transient delicacy of a single flake of snow. Who could say in which of those labors the Creator took greater satisfaction?

To humor his young cousin, Gideon made a wish, though he had no more expectation of it yielding what he desired than a prayer. What had he wished for? The thing he wanted most in the world, of course. Justice for him and for poor young Watson. A return of his life to what it had been—once again in command of the *Integrity,* serving his country and watching over his crew.

Yet when he pictured himself returning to his ship and putting this interlude at Knightley Park behind him, Gideon found it difficult to put his whole heart into that wish.

He slept well that night. Was it the belly full of hearty country fare that brought him such a peaceful rest? Or was it a daft sense of hope spawned by the wish he'd made? Gideon assured himself it must be the former. Not that it made any difference. He woke on Christmas morning with a sense that he was where he belonged on that particular day. Hard as he tried during his years at sea, he had never quite managed to quench his boyhood longing for Knightley Park at Christmastime.

On his way to breakfast a while later, he caught a whiff of spices and spied one of the maids bearing a tray to the nursery. He could not keep from following that alluring aroma.

"Pardon me," he said when Miss Murray answered his knock. The sight of her fresh-faced loveliness at this early hour felt like its own kind of Christmas present. "I thought I smelled frumenty."

"That's right, Captain." She looked surprised to see him, but not displeased. "Frumenty for Christmas breakfast in the nursery is a tradition at Knightley Park, I gather. Was it when you used to come here as a child?"

Gideon nodded and inhaled a deep breath of the rich, sweet aroma. "I have not tasted frumenty since then."

Miss Murray seemed to guess his thoughts, though it could not have been difficult. "Would you care to join us for breakfast?"

"I would not want to deprive you or the girls of your share."

Before Miss Murray could reply, Dolly appeared at the door and practically dragged him into the nursery. "Don't fret about that. Cook always sends up more than we can eat."

He did not resist as the child drew him in and offered him a seat at the table.

"Why, thank you." He sank onto the chair after the girls and Miss Murray had taken their places.

Gideon felt rather overgrown and awkward sitting at the nursery table with three diminutive females, but he forgot all about that as soon as he consumed his first spoonful of frumenty. It was just as he remembered, the wholesome goodness of wheat boiled in milk, spiced with cinnamon and nutmeg, sweetened with sugar and dried fruit. One taste brought back all the happiness of his childhood Christmases.

"Did you see how much it snowed last night?" asked Dolly between heaping spoonfuls of frumenty. "I'm afraid the carriage might get stuck on the way to church."

Gideon exchanged a significant look with Miss Murray. Was Dolly afraid or hopeful the snow might prevent them from attending the service?

"In that case, perhaps we should travel by sleigh,"

Gideon suggested. "We wouldn't want to miss church on Christmas Day, after all."

"A sleigh ride!" Dolly clapped her hands, and even her more reticent sister looked pleased at the prospect.

Once he had eaten as much breakfast as he could hold, Gideon excused himself and headed off to bid the stable men to harness the sleigh instead of the carriage.

A while later, with the girls wedged between him and their governess, they prepared for the drive to church with hot bricks at their feet and thick robes over their legs. As the sleigh skimmed over the snow-covered road, the girls squealed and giggled, and the cold air nipped their faces. Though Gideon had not had much practice handling horses, the team seemed familiar with the way and got them to church swiftly and safely.

That morning, as he sang the familiar carols and listened to readings of the Christmas story, Gideon could not help thinking what a special gift a child was. A God who could bestow such a blessing must care deeply for the people He had created, in spite of their weaknesses. A God who bestowed such a blessing might well heed and answer prayers.

Celebrating Christmas at Knightley Park with his young cousins had clearly brought the captain many happy memories.

During the Christmas service, Marian stole frequent glances at him, pleased to note how much more relaxed and at peace he appeared. Could it be that he was getting more out of his attendance at church than simply setting a good example for the girls? For his sake, she hoped so. Anyone who had been so unappreciated and badly betrayed surely needed the consolation of God's love.

After the service, she noticed him slip a large contribution into the poor box when he thought no one was watching. His actions did not surprise her. He had proven himself a charitable man who cared about those in need of his help. Yet his reserved nature clearly made him shrink from being publicly acknowledged for his generosity.

Though she admired such behavior, in contrast to some of the self-righteous but mean-spirited patrons of the Pendergast School, she wondered if the captain's reticence would make it difficult for him to present an effective defense at the inquiry. Marian reminded herself that she wanted him to stay on at Knightley Park with the girls. Yet it offended her sense of justice to think of his reputation being permanently tarnished.

As they left the church, a number of parishioners offered Captain Radcliffe the compliments of the season, including one or two who had been rather cool to him when he'd first begun attending services. It heartened Marian to realize that their neighbors appeared willing to make up their own minds about the man in spite of whatever gossip might spread from London. Even if the inquiry did not find in the captain's favor, she assured her conscience the decision would not affect local opinion of him.

When they reached the sleigh, Squire Bellamy was waiting to greet the captain. Marian liked the squire, a jovial sportsman who had been a particular friend of Cissy and Dolly's late father.

He and the captain exchanged seasonal good wishes, then the squire asked, "I wonder if you might do me the honor of attending a ball I am hosting on New Year's Eve for some of the neighbors? It would be a welcome opportunity for you to become better acquainted with the local families."

Captain Radcliffe seemed taken aback by the invitation. "I...er...that is very kind of you but—"

"No *buts.*" The squire waved away any objections with one beefy hand. "My wife is determined you shall attend. She says it will put her numbers at table out if you do not. Surely you would not wish to be the cause of ill-feeling between a man and his wife on Christmas Day."

Mrs. Bellamy had a reputation in the parish as an irrepressible matchmaker. No doubt she had a lady all picked out for the captain. As Marian got the girls settled into the sleigh, she strove to quell a stab of irritation. She had no right in the world to feel possessive of Captain Radcliffe, after all.

"Since you put it that way," the captain replied, "I most certainly would not wish to cause dissention in your house. Tell your wife I appreciate the invitation and mean to accept."

"Capital!" The squire beamed. "We shall look forward to seeing you on the thirty-first, then."

"New Year's Eve?" Dolly whispered. "But that was when we were going to—"

"Hush." Marian twitched the sleigh robes over their legs. "There will be plenty of other opportunities."

"Opportunities for what?" The captain suddenly turned back toward them.

"Opportunities…to celebrate the season with you." She recovered awkwardly. "The girls must not monopolize your company. I'm sure you would enjoy spending time with other adults."

"Not particularly." He climbed in beside Dolly and picked up the reins. "My dancing skills are almost as lamentable as my polite conversation."

"What's wrong with your conversation?" demanded Dolly. "You have heaps more interesting things to talk about than most grown-up people."

"Except Miss Marian," Cissy chimed in loyally.

Under the sleigh robe, Marian reached for the child's hand and gave it a squeeze.

Meanwhile the captain responded to Dolly's compliment with a wry chuckle as he jogged the reins, and the sleigh started back toward Knightley Park. "I'm afraid most ladies of mature years are not excessively interested in all the details of life at sea."

"I don't know why not." Dolly changed tack. "If you need to learn how to dance, Cissy can show you. She's teaching me."

"Don't be silly," her sister protested. "I don't know that much about it. I only had a few lessons with the dancing master."

"That is more instruction than I can boast." A hint of desperation tightened the captain's voice. "I would be grateful, Cousin Celia, for whatever help you can provide."

"Very well." The child looked secretly pleased with the idea, and Marian welcomed the opportunity for Cissy and the captain to become closer. At times she seemed to warm to him, then something would make her grow cool again.

"Can we play out in the snow, Miss Marian?" asked Dolly as the sleigh neared Knightley Park.

"I suppose..." It would do the girls good to have an outlet for some of their energy. "But you will have to change clothes and back before Christmas dinner."

They agreed readily and scampered off toward the nursery the moment they reached the house. Marian followed, as did the captain. She assumed he must be on his way to his rooms to change clothes or rest before dinner.

"Pardon my curiosity, Miss Murray, but are you quite well?" he asked. "You seem rather subdued on such a festive occasion. Are you missing your family in Scotland?"

His question caught her off guard. It was kind of him to notice her demeanor and care about her well-being. "I am not ill, Captain, nor am I pining for distant family. My parents and brother are all long dead and this day stirs no particular memories of them. Where I come from, we made more celebration of the New Year than Christmas."

"I should have known. I have served with a number of Scottish officers over the years. As for your family, forgive me for reminding you of your loss."

"You could not have known, sir."

They walked a few steps in silence before he spoke again. "May I ask what age you were?"

It had been so long since anyone cared to inquire about her background. Neither Mr. nor Mrs. Radcliffe had ever asked about her family. Though Marian was reluctant to disclose too many details about herself, she could not forget all that the captain had told her about his past. How could she refuse to return a confidence?

"I was nine when my father died. My mother passed away when I was much younger."

"Nine," he repeated, his voice suffused with a world of sympathy. "Who took care of you after that?"

She was even less inclined to talk about her years at school than about the loss of her family. Fortunately, they had reached the spot where they must part ways, he going off to his quarters and her to the nursery.

"If you will excuse me, Captain, I must go see to the girls."

"Is it such a long story?" A look of puzzlement and tender concern made his features more attractive than ever.

Marian shook her head. "I had no family but a widowed aunt who was hard-pressed to care for her own fatherless brood. So it was decided I should be sent to a charity school in England for orphaned daughters of the clergy."

Hard as she tried, she could not keep her face impassive when she spoke of that wretched institution—any more than if she'd bitten into a lemon.

The captain was too perceptive a man not to notice. "Were you ill-treated there?"

He fairly radiated fierce indignation at the mere possibility. Such sentiment proved impossible for Marian to resist. "Very ill indeed."

Bitter memories rose to torment her. If she stayed there, she feared she might lose control of her emotions.

She could not afford to let that happen again. Spinning away from Gideon Radcliffe, she fled down the passage to the nursery.

No wonder the poor lady had not been able to fully embrace the joyous spirit of Christmas.

As the patter of Miss Murray's footsteps retreated into the distance, Gideon stood frozen in the grip of pity and anger far too powerful for his comfort. He had experienced something similar when Harry Watson confessed to the bullying he'd endured. But those feelings had been tempered by the belief that he had the power to remedy the situation. He'd turned out to be wrong, but he hadn't known that then. In this case, he knew very well there was no assistance he could render Marian Murray.

Whatever she'd suffered as a child at that charity school was over and done. But he sensed it had left wounds that might never fully heal, like the old injury to his hand that made it ache in certain types of weather. The scars on her spirit must trouble her more at Christmas, when the pervading happiness of the season created such a severe contrast to her childhood memories.

A potent conviction welled up in Gideon as he recalled the anguish in her eyes. He must do everything in his power to make *this* Christmas one on which she could look back fondly in future years. He must also encourage Miss Murray to confide in him about her experiences. After all, he felt much more at peace since he'd told her the truth of what had happened aboard the *Integrity*. The least he could do was offer a sympathetic shoulder on which to unburden her troubles. Knowing what she did of his past, surely she would realize he was better capable of understanding than most people.

He changed into his warmest clothes and ventured outside to join Miss Murray and the girls in the snow-covered garden. Sensing his unexpected appearance flustered her, he refrained from asking any more questions about her experiences at the charity school. Instead, he put aside his accustomed reserve and larked about with the children until he glimpsed a tentative smile on her lips.

Later, as they headed back inside to dress for Christmas dinner, he made a point of saying, "I hope it is understood that you must accompany the girls whenever they dine with me. While I have come to enjoy their company more than I ever expected, I am all too aware of my lack of experience with children. I am certain we will all be more comfortable together if you are with us."

"Thank you, Captain." She acknowledged his invitation with a curtsy. "Of course I shall supervise the girls at all times if that is what you wish."

"It is." He did not care to be reminded that Miss Murray would only join in the festivities as part of her terms of employment.

Remembering the mission he had set himself, to give Miss Murray as happy a holiday as her pupils, Gideon went out of his way to include her in table conversation while they ate Christmas dinner. To begin with, he banished the tall centerpiece of fruit to the sideboard so it would not obstruct his view of her as it had the day before.

After their play outside in the fresh, cold air, all four of them had hearty appetites to do justice to the succulent stuffed turkey and all the other holiday delicacies.

As the mince tarts were being served, Gideon addressed Cissy. "I wonder if I might begin my dancing instruction after dinner? New Year's Eve is less than a week away and there is the dinner for our tenants tomorrow. I believe I may be expected to perform a turn or two afterward. I would prefer to embarrass myself as little as possible."

The child replied with a grave nod. "Of course. We can go into the music room. Miss Marian, will you play for us?"

"I shall be happy to do whatever I can to assist your efforts. I reckon the captain will be a very apt pupil in spite of his claims to the contrary."

Her tone of friendly banter appealed to Gideon.

He could not resist replying in kind. "You think I exaggerate my ignorance, do you?"

"I believe you exaggerate all your shortcomings and minimize your accomplishments." This time he could not tell whether the lady was teasing or perfectly sincere…or perhaps a little of both. "In any case, I shall be happy to play for your dancing lesson."

Once they had eaten all they could hold, the four of them retired to the music room where Miss Murray seated herself at the pianoforte. Gideon would much rather have listened to her sing again than stumble his way through a dancing lesson, but he supposed it was necessary if he hoped to avoid humiliating himself too badly in the coming days.

Cissy took her role as instructress quite seriously.

"Come stand here, please. Dolly, you stand there. Now, Miss Marian, please play that same piece as the other day."

As the music commenced at a steady, stately pace, Cissy began issuing directions. "First you must bow and curtsy to one another. Now turn to face me and join hands. Take two steps forward, then two steps back. Now face each other. Each take a step toward me, then close—that means bring your other foot over. Now bow and curtsy again...."

He and Dolly tried their best to do as they were bidden, but the dance quickly degenerated into a flat-footed muddle.

"It's no use." Cissy shook her head in disgust. "In the first place, Dolly is far too small...or you are far too tall to be proper dance partners. Besides that, the music room isn't big enough for dancing, you know."

Gideon shrugged. "Thank you for trying."

"Don't give up so soon." Dolly pressed her forefinger to her temple in thought. "We could go into the great parlor. It has plenty of space. And Miss Marian could take my place as Cousin Gideon's partner. She's much taller than me."

The child's suggestion that he dance with her pretty governess tempted Gideon far too keenly for his peace of mind. However, he feared Miss Murray might shrink from the prospect of being so near him and often taking his hand as dancing might demand.

Her response confirmed that. "But who will provide the music? There is no instrument in the great parlor and even if there were..."

But Cissy seemed quite taken with her sister's idea.

"We don't really need music, just a rhythm for you to keep time. Dolly and I can clap our hands for that."

"If Miss Murray would rather not…" Gideon tried to sound as reluctant as his proposed partner, but he could not manage it. Though he did not care for idea of dancing in general, he could not deny a wish to dance once with her.

Cissy frowned. "Do you want to learn or don't you?"

For some reason, the child's response seemed to overcome Miss Murray's reluctance. "Of course he does. And I am willing to try if he is."

She cast Gideon a look of appeal that he could not resist. "I suppose it couldn't hurt…except perhaps your toes."

Her lips blossomed in a luminous smile that felt like a rich reward for his cooperation.

"Good." Dolly took Gideon by the hand. "Let's get started then."

They moved to the larger room and pushed some pieces of furniture against the walls to create a spacious area for dancing. Then Gideon and Miss Murray took their places and Cissy resumed her instruction.

Gideon found it far easier to follow the steps and figures with a partner nearer his own height. Miss Murray claimed to have no prior experience dancing, yet she seemed to possess an instinct for graceful movement. Gideon had only to mirror her actions to feel a growing sense of confidence.

"Try that bit again," Cissy ordered, "and pretend there are other couples on either side of you. One, two, three."

As she clapped out the rhythm and Dolly joined in,

Gideon fancied he could hear the melody their governess had been playing earlier.

"Very good." Cissy nodded approvingly when they had gone through the step without any mistakes. "Now one more time from the beginning. Then I think we had better stop for tonight."

She glanced toward Dolly, who was endeavoring to stifle a yawn. "It is past our bedtime again."

Miss Murray peered toward the mantel clock and gave a start. "So it is. I have been concentrating so hard I did not notice the time passing."

Gideon had not realized how late it was getting either. Could that be because he'd been so occupied with the dancing lesson? Or might it have been his enjoyment of Miss Murray's close company that made time fly? Recalling the swiftly passing evenings he'd spent with her in the library, he was inclined to credit the latter.

"Once more, then." Cissy began to clap out the time again.

Off they went, performing the steps of the dance with greater ease than Gideon had believed possible. It occurred to him that they made excellent partners. Each seemed able to anticipate the other's movements and adjust their own accordingly, with the happy result that he did not once tread on the lady's toes.

"There," he declared when they had exchanged their closing bows. "With a patient teacher and a naturally skilled partner, it appears I am capable of improvement after all."

"Once again, you do not give yourself enough credit,

Captain." Their mild exertions had brought a becoming flush of color to Miss Murray's face.

Something made her dark eyes glow. Could it have been his praise?

Then Dolly broke out in an infectious chuckle. "Look, you've ended up right under the kissing bough!"

A quick glance aloft assured Gideon it was true. He'd been so agreeably occupied he had not given the kissing bough a single thought.

"Come now, you must kiss." Cissy sounded impatient with their hesitation. "Or all our hard work making it will have been for nothing."

Swallowing the lump that suddenly formed in his throat, Gideon gave an apologetic shrug. "We wouldn't want that, would we, Miss Marian?"

For all his show of reluctance, he felt a great bubble of elation swell within his chest. With a sense of trepidation he had never felt in the heat of battle, he searched the lady's eyes for any sign of aversion. To his vast relief, he found none.

"I suppose not." She caught her full lower lip between her teeth but could not quite bite back a self-conscious grin. "It is a long-standing tradition, after all."

Clearly she had received Christmas kisses under the mistletoe before this and knew they were simple holiday pleasantries of no particular significance. Gideon wished he could view it that way.

"Go on then," Dolly urged.

The child's prompting made him realize any longer postponement could prove more embarrassing than to simply go ahead.

Inhaling a deep breath, he bent toward Miss Murray and aimed his lips to meet hers. It was a more delicate procedure than he had reckoned and one with which he was not especially familiar. Yet, as with their dance, he seemed able to anticipate her, tilting his head slightly so their noses did not collide.

There! His lips pressed against hers with what he hoped was the proper amount of pressure. The smooth warmth of hers was the single most delightful sensation he had ever encountered. It brought him a feeling of connection…belonging…homecoming. The only thing he could imagine better would be if she wrapped her arms around his neck and pulled him close, as she'd tried to do that evening in the library.

Just as he had feared the first time his young cousins mentioned the kissing bough, Gideon discovered how difficult it was to take leave of Marian Murray's soft, sweet lips.

Chapter Ten

She was actually receiving her first kiss from a man—and such a man!

When Gideon Radcliffe's lips sought her in a tender, restrained connection, Marian's breath stuck in her throat and her knees threatened to give way.

The harsh, sensible voice of reason chided her not to be such a sentimental fool. This was not a proper kiss, bestowed out of affection for her. It was only a token gesture to satisfy Christmas tradition and two insistent little girls.

Yet it felt the way she'd imagined a proper kiss might, those few times she had permitted her thoughts to stray in that improbable direction. His lips pressed against hers, warm and gentle, kindling fancies of a chivalrous knight pledging his chosen lady his loyalty, his protection…and his heart.

But that was preposterous.

Captain Radcliffe had commanded great ships in defense of King and Country. Now he was also the master of a fine estate and a gentleman of fortune. What could he want with a plain, orphaned governess of no particular distinction, who had scarcely a penny to her name? He had treated her with courtesy because of his kind nature…and perhaps out of loneliness. She must not mistake his feelings for anything more.

If she hung on to his kiss an instant longer, she risked humiliating herself with a yearning sigh or worse yet, swooning to the floor. Mustering every scrap of restraint she had cultivated during those miserable years at school, Marian pulled away from the captain.

"There, are you satisfied, girls?" She strove to curb her ragged breath, lest it betray feelings she had no business entertaining.

"Oh, yes." Dolly sounded rather smug about something. "That was a fine, long kiss. Not the quick peck I saw Wilbert give Bessie in the dining room doorway. Of course that sprig of mistletoe is much smaller than the bough. Perhaps that's why."

Had she permitted their kiss to go on for too long? Marian fled from under the kissing bough, fussing around the girls like a ruffled mother hen with a pair of chicks. "I'm glad you approve. Now you must get to bed or you'll be out of sorts tomorrow."

She refused to let her gaze stray toward the captain for fear of detecting signs that her behavior had shocked him. "Say good-night, then we'll be off."

"Good night, Captain." Cissy dropped him a curtsy. "Perhaps I can give you another dancing lesson before New Year's Eve."

Dolly followed her sister's example. "Good night, Cousin Gideon."

"Good night," he replied in a subdued tone that made Marian certain he must be displeased with her.

She never should have agreed to take part in the dancing lesson, especially in the face of Captain Radcliffe's obvious reluctance. But Cissy had been so set on it, and Marian was committed to encouraging any possible connection between the girls and their cousin. Their entire future might depend upon it. Bitter memories of school that the captain's earlier questions had revived made her more determined than ever to spare her dear pupils a similar fate. A place even half as bad would crush Cissy's sensitive nature, while Dolly's high spirits and strong will would be harshly repressed at every turn.

And yet her concern for the girls did not account for how sincerely she had enjoyed the opportunity to be near Gideon Radcliffe, with his hand often holding hers. All the years she'd sat quietly in the corner at assemblies or glimpsed a ball from the top of the stairs had stood her in good stead as she'd executed the steps she had often seen performed by others. Just as she had suspected, the captain was far more agile than he claimed. Marian found a sweet sense of satisfaction working with him to accomplish something worthwhile, be it making Christmas plans or learning the steps of a dance.

Then that ridiculous kissing bough had spoiled everything.

Although she cherished the opportunity to receive a kiss from a man like Gideon Radcliffe, she wished it had not brought her so close to losing control of her secret feelings.

As she ushered the girls off to bed, a sweet sound drifted toward them from the entry hall.

"Carol singers!" Dolly dug in her heels and refused to budge another inch toward the staircase. "Can we go listen to them? Please, Miss Marian!"

"Please!" Cissy echoed. "Just for a little while. Then we'll go straight to bed."

"It is Christmas," Dolly reminded her, as if she could forget after that tender, terrifying kiss under the bough.

Marian could only resist their combined coaxing for so long. "Oh, very well, but only for a little while. When I say you must come away, do you promise you will, without any arguing?"

The girls nodded vigorously. Then Dolly sped to the doorway of the great parlor and called in, "Carol singers, Cousin Gideon! Can you hear them? Miss Marian says we may go listen. Will you come, too?"

A quiver went through Marian as she tried to decide whether she wanted the captain to join them. Her sense of duty urged her to seize every opportunity to bring the girls together with him. But could she bear to be near Gideon Radcliffe again until the memory of their kiss had dimmed a little? It might not take long for him to forget, but she doubted the same could be said for her.

Whether she wanted his company or not, it appeared they would have it. Just as she and Cissy caught up with Dolly, he emerged from the great parlor and took the child's hand. "Carolers is it? Of course we must listen to them. I believe it is an offense against the spirit of Christmas to do otherwise."

A soft sigh of relief escaped Marian's lips as the four

of them headed to the entry hall. Whatever the captain's reaction to their kiss, he sounded as if he had put it out of his mind already. She should have known better than to suppose it would matter to him one way or another.

When they reached the front door, Captain Radcliffe pulled it open, and they filed out under the portico. Marian wrapped her arms around the girls and pulled them close to keep them from getting too cold. The night was clear and crisp, the winter moon a slender sickle in the black, star strewn sky.

A little ways away, a group of men and boys clustered, well-muffled against the cold. In the flickering light cast by several lanterns they bore, their breaths frosted the air as they sang. *"Whilst shepherds watched their flocks by night all seated on the ground, the angel of the Lord came down and Glory shone around."*

Marian could picture local shepherds guarding flocks in the surrounding fields of Knightley Park, when angels robed in glittering starlight appeared with glorious news.

When the final notes of the carol died away, Captain Radcliffe led Marian and the girls in a round of applause.

"Come sing some more for us inside." He beckoned the group.

As Marian drew the girls back into the entry hall, the captain called to her over his shoulder, "Kindly summon any of the servants who might wish to hear, Miss Murray. And ask Mr. Culpepper to fetch mulled cider and pies for everyone."

She acknowledged his order with a nod. "Right away, sir."

Though he had phrased it as a request, she wondered if he meant to remind her, or himself, of her position in his household.

Kissing Miss Murray under the mistletoe had been a mistake. Gideon knew it the instant she'd pulled away from him so abruptly. Now, as she headed off to the servants' hall, he sensed a chill in her manner as cool as the winter night outside.

Why had his self-control chosen the worst possible moment to desert him? He had faced many a moment of crisis in his career, including some in which life and death had hung in the balance. Yet he had always managed to keep a cool head and act as reason and honor demanded. Unfortunately, he had no experience in how to curtail a kiss with an attractive woman—one he liked too much for his own good...and hers.

The last thing he wanted was for her to think he would use his position to impose himself upon her. By the nature of their work, men of sea had a reputation for seeking female companionship where they could find it, without regard for morality. He could not bear to have Marian Murray think he would stoop to such behavior.

Until that moment, he'd been celebrating his best Christmas in years, and he congratulated himself that Cousin Daniel's young daughters seemed to enjoy the day, too. Having threatened his very agreeable friendship with their governess, Gideon decided he must make an even greater effort to ensure the children a happy Christmas.

Once all the carol singers had filed in, he asked the

girls, "Is there a particular favorite you would like to hear?"

Dolly only shrugged, but Cissy answered readily. "Could they sing 'The Holly and the Ivy'? Miss Marian has been teaching me to play it on the pianoforte."

Gideon turned toward the leader of the group. "Do you know that one?"

"Indeed we do, sir. Come, lads. For the little lady. *The holly and the ivy when they are both full grown, of all the trees that are in the woods, the holly bears the crown.*"

The others joined in, singing lustily on the chorus. *"Oh the rising of the sun and the running of the deer, the playing of the merry organ, sweet singing in the choir."*

By the time they had sung through all the verses, the servants had begun to slip into the entry hall to swell the audience. This continued while the carolers sang two more pieces. The group had just finished "The Boar's Head Carol" when Miss Murray, the cook and the scullery maid appeared bearing trays of cups. Mr. Culpepper followed with a large crock borne upon a wheeled serving table. An enormous covered platter rested on its lower tier. The mellow, spicy aroma of mulled cider seeped into the room along with a hearty, savory smell. Several of the younger singers broke into broad grins at the prospect of refreshment.

"Singing is thirsty work," said Gideon. "Since you have done such a fine job of entertaining us, I hope you will accept our hospitality."

The carolers did not hesitate to accept. Soon the maids, assisted by Miss Murray, set about serving hot

cider and small pork pies. As they all ate and drank together, the servants from Knightley Park mingled with
the carol singers, some of whom appeared to be friends
or relations. A satisfying sense of community stirred
in Gideon, which he had never expected to feel for any
folk other than the crew of his ship.

After they had partaken of refreshment, the carolers
sang a few more pieces. The whole company joined in
on a spirited rendition of "Joy to the World." Finally,
the performers wished them all a Merry Christmas in
song before going on their way. Gideon thanked them
and made certain they were well-rewarded for their efforts.

He turned back into the entry hall to find Miss
Murray trying to coax Dolly up from a low stool where
she had fallen asleep, resting against Cissy's shoulder.
"I should have known this would happen. Come now,
Dolly, you can't spend the whole night here."

Gideon approached them, still rather uneasy in Miss
Murray's presence. "May I be of assistance?"

She started at the sound of his voice but quickly re-
gained her composure. "Perhaps you might have more
success trying to wake her than I've had, sir. Imagine
falling sound asleep in the midst of all that hubbub. It's
my fault, of course. I should never have let the girls stay
up for the whole thing."

Perhaps if he hadn't sent her away to fetch the servants, she might have been able to keep her mind on
her duties.

"I have a better idea." He bent down and hoisted
Dolly up until her small golden head lolled against his
shoulder and her body hung limp in his arms.

He had never thought it could feel so natural and pleasant to clasp a sleeping child to his chest. Yet, at the same time, it provoked a mild ache in his heart, rather like hunger pangs in his stomach.

Forcing himself to ignore it, Gideon strode off toward the staircase with Cissy and her governess trailing behind him. When they reached the nursery, Miss Murray scurried ahead to open the door for him.

"Thank you for your help, Captain. Dolly's bed is this way." She led him through the dimly lit nursery, then turned down the child's bedcovers.

With a gentleness of which he'd never suspected himself capable, Gideon eased his small burden down. In spite of his best effort not to wake her, Dolly stirred and blinked her eyes.

"Where are the carol singers?" she asked in a drowsy, puzzled voice. "Please let us listen to one more, Miss Marian."

Her governess perched on the edge of the bed, removing Dolly's slippers and stockings. "The carol singers have gone. You fell asleep listening to them. If the Captain hadn't carried you up to bed, you might have had to sleep in that drafty entrance hall. Now what do you say to him?"

Dolly yawned. "Thank you, Cousin Gideon."

He was certain she'd be back to sleep in no time. She might not even recall this brief half-waking. "You're quite welcome, my dear. Good night and Merry Christmas."

He turned to leave when the child's reply stopped him in his tracks. "When Papa came to the nursery he would always kiss us good-night. Will you, Cousin Gideon?"

The request rather unnerved him. One kiss this evening had already gone badly. Still, that empty ache in his heart urged him to reply. "I...suppose I could, if you wish?"

He looked from Dolly to Cissy. The older girl shook her head. "Not tonight, thank you."

"Well, I do!" Dolly sounded wider awake than she had a moment before.

Approaching gingerly, as if putting his head in a lion's mouth, Gideon brushed a feather light kiss on her plump cheek. But when he tried to draw back, the child threw her sturdy arms around his neck and planted a hearty smack on his cheek, much to his disquiet and secret pleasure.

At least he could offer Dolly some of the affection he dared not show her pretty governess.

On New Year's Eve, in her small, spartan chamber adjoining the nursery, Marian rolled over in her bed and sought to find her way into the elusive state of sleep. But all the paths she tried only circled back on themselves. The Land of Dreams seemed to have closed its borders to her.

She must get some rest soon or she would be perfectly useless tomorrow. Keeping up with two young girls, one a high-spirited bundle of energy, could present a challenge under the best of conditions. Besides, she was not certain what sort of festivities Captain Radcliffe had planned for tomorrow. Since Christmas Day, there had been all manner of special activities and outings, beginning with a feast for Knightley Park's tenants on Boxing Day. Dolly had enjoyed mixing with the tenants' children while Cissy had been pleased to help dispense the hampers, in keeping with family tradition.

This evening had been unusually quiet with the captain going off to Squire Bellamy's ball. But that had *nothing* to do with her present sleeplessness, Marian told herself.

She wondered how he was managing on the dance floor. They'd had two more lessons in the past week, neither of which had been as successful as the first. Could that be because she and the captain were constantly aware of the kissing bough and taking more care to avoid it than to perform the proper steps?

She also wondered with which lady the Squire's matchmaking wife hoped to pair him. Part of her questioned whether it might benefit the girls if Gideon Radcliffe took a wife. Marriage would give him a reason to stay at Knightley Park, even if the inquiry decided in his favor. And if it came down to a legal battle between him and Lady Villiers for guardianship of the girls, surely it would look better before a court if he were a married man.

In spite of all that, when she considered the possible matches Mrs. Bellamy might have in mind for the captain, none met with her approval. The Squire's widowed sister was as incurably silly as a green girl half her age. Miss Hitchens was notorious in the parish for her temper and sharp tongue. Miss Piper spent money like water. Unfortunately, all three were quite handsome and much more suitable wives for Captain Radcliffe than...

Marian rolled over and pounded her pillow to relieve her feelings. It did not help nearly as much as she'd hoped. She needed some diversion to occupy and calm her thoughts. Reading would be the perfect activity, if only she had a book on hand. But she had returned *Evelina* to the library three days before Christmas, then neglected to borrow another book to replace it.

After another hour taunted by thoughts of which she wanted no part, Marian rose and fumbled her candle alight. Shivering, she pulled on her dressing gown, shawl and slippers. Then she crept out of the nursery and headed down to the library. A glance at the pedestal clock surprised her with the information that it was not much past eleven. She could have sworn she'd been lying awake for hours.

It did not take her long to select a book, for she only wanted something capable of holding her attention without being too stimulating. Once she found a promising volume, she hurried back toward the nursery as quickly as she'd come. Yet she was not quick enough.

Marian had only gone a few steps when she heard the main door open and shut, and Captain Radcliffe came striding in. "Miss Murray, what on earth are you doing up at this hour? Is one of the girls unwell?"

Her unease at being seen by the captain in her nightclothes was tempered by the evidence of his concern for Cissy and Dolly.

"Don't fret, sir. They are both quite well and sleeping soundly. I only wish I could say the same for myself." She held up the book. "I hoped having something to read might help me sleep."

"A good idea." The captain seemed to be making an

effort to ignore her state of dress. "I have read myself to sleep on a number of occasions. Warm milk is another useful remedy. Perhaps you should investigate whether there is any to be had in the kitchen."

"Thank you for the suggestion, sir. I may try that another time. I wouldn't want to disturb anyone tonight."

"Of course you wouldn't." He spoke in a low murmur, as if musing to himself. "May I ask if there is some particular difficulty that keeps you from sleeping? No problems with the children, I hope?"

"None at all, Captain." The last thing Marian wanted was for him to guess what sort of thoughts had kept her awake. She had a guilty feeling he would unless she offered him some other reason. "I must admit I have been rather worried about a friend of mine. We met at school and have kept in contact ever since. This is the first Christmas I have not received a letter from her."

Everything she'd said was true—Marian could not bring herself to tell him a falsehood. She *did* wonder what could have happened to prevent Rebecca from writing. A stab of guilt pierced her for having lain awake thinking about something other than her dear friend.

"You met at *that* school?" Gideon Radcliffe's tone grew harsh. "The place you told me about? Was your friend also the orphaned daughter of a clergyman?"

She should not stand there conversing with the master of the house at this hour, in her nightclothes, Marian's sense of propriety warned. But after imagining him dancing, dining and talking with a bevy of marriageable ladies, it felt so pleasant to have him all to herself for a few stolen moments.

"We all were. The only thing that made my years at the Pendergast School remotely bearable was the support and affection of the friends I made there. Several of us became especially close—almost like sisters. Though we have not seen each other since we left that institution, we have tried to remain in contact, scattered about as we are."

He nodded gravely. His palpable concern enveloped Marian like a thick wool blanket on a cold winter night. "Is there any way I can assist you? Where was your friend when you last heard from her? Perhaps I could dispatch someone to make inquiries on your behalf?"

Send someone over a hundred miles to the Cotswolds, paying for food, inns and stabling for no other purpose than to set her mind at ease? His generosity touched her. Yet his caring gesture made her feel even more ashamed for making him believe her concern for Rebecca had prevented her from sleeping.

"You are too kind, Captain. I would not want to put you to so much trouble on my account. It may be that my friend's letter is only delayed by bad roads. If I have not received word from her by Twelfth Night, I will write to one of our other friends to inquire whether they have had news of her."

"I would consider the effort well worthwhile if it set your mind at rest."

His assurance made Marian's pulse quicken. But it was only a measure of his thoughtfulness...wasn't it?

"Speaking of rest, I should retire for the night and let you do the same for the hour is late. It will soon be eighteen-hundred and fifteen." In spite of that, part of her searched for an excuse to linger. "I am surprised to see you home so soon from the Bellamys'. I thought you would stay at least until they rang in the New Year. Did you not enjoy yourself at the ball?"

He gave an indifferent shrug. "Squire Bellamy neglected to inform me that tonight's entertainment would be a *hunt ball* and that I would be the principle prey."

"I beg your pardon, Captain?"

He rolled his eyes. "I was the only bachelor in a company that included several marriageable ladies. Not merely marriageable, but rather desperately intent on securing a husband. It is not a pleasant experience to be stalked that way."

So he had not taken a fancy to any of the ladies Mrs. Bellamy threw in his path? Marian struggled to keep from smiling.

But with her self-control concentrated on that task, she had none left over to govern her tongue. "Perhaps you ought to consider taking a wife, now that you have a good income and a settled abode."

"*Et tu,* Miss Murray?" His upper lip curled. "Do you reckon it is my social obligation to wed, simply to furnish some spinster with a home and generous pin money?"

"Of course not!" She turned defensive, stung by his question and what it implied. "Surely you don't suppose every woman who shows an interest in you is only after the comfortable life you can afford to give her?"

"What else?" he demanded. "That was clearly the object of those ladies at the ball tonight."

Marian struggled to frame a reply that would not betray the kind of feelings he did not seem inclined to trust.

"Who would want a husband like me otherwise?" he continued. "I am hardly the answer to a maiden's prayer."

He'd been the answer to her prayer…as a responsible, caring guardian for her young pupils. As for the other, Marian had never bothered to pray for a husband. It had seemed so futile. "Not every woman is looking for Romeo or Sir Galahad. You have a great many qualities a sensible woman would look for in a husband."

She meant that as high praise, but the captain flinched at her words. "A sensible woman—you mean the kind with bluestockings, a plain countenance and rapidly advancing years, who knows enough to settle for what she can get by way of a husband?"

Now it was her turn to flinch from his brutally accurate assessment of her. His lip had curled into a full sneer. It proclaimed his distaste for such a woman and his certainty that she would only want to wed him for mercenary reasons.

Marian's throat tightened until she wondered how she could draw any air down into her lungs, much less force words up. What a perfect fool she'd been to worry herself sleepless about potential rivals for Gideon Radcliffe's affections when it was clear he would never think of her in that way.

"All that aside," he continued in a gruff tone. "Even if I were capable of making a lady attached to me, I am not cut out for marriage. I had better stick with my mistress."

"Mistress?" The word burst from Marian's lips like a stopper from a jug of fermented cider.

"It does sound ridiculously unlikely, doesn't it?"

Not to her. In fact, it explained a great deal. And yet it puzzled her, too. He was such a fine, honorable man. That was why she'd never been afraid to be alone with him, apart from her concern for appearances and propriety. She'd never entertained a moment's worry that he might take advantage of her. Even if she'd been as beautiful as her friend Grace Ellerby, Marian believed she would still be safe in Gideon Radcliffe's company.

"I didn't mean I was surprised you could attract a... mistress, if you wanted one. Only you seem too respectable a man to—"

"I am the one who should explain, Miss Murray. I meant, of course, that the sea is my mistress—a demanding one but not all that discriminating."

Marian scavenged up a wan smile at his self-deprecating jest. But all the while her heart was sinking. Even if she were more attractive and eligible, even if she could persuade the captain that she cared for *him,* not his fortune and position, the sea was a rival with whom no woman could hope to compete. She must take care to remember that.

As she strove to master her voice so she could make her excuses and escape to the nursery, several clocks in the house began to chime the hour of midnight. From off in the distance came the muted sounds of church bells ringing.

"There we are," said Captain Radcliffe after the noise had died away. "The New Year has arrived. I wonder what it will bring us?"

His use of the word *us* made Marian's heart give a broken-winged flutter, even though she knew he only meant it in a general way to include everyone at Knightley Park. Perhaps the whole of Great Britain.

"I hope it will be a quiet one with no great events to make it memorable in the future. After so many years of war, I pray for one of peace. As for you, Captain, I wish a year of health, happiness and justice."

"Why, thank you, Miss Murray." He extended his hand almost gingerly, tensed to pull away if she tried to surprise him with a kiss or embrace. "A happy New Year to you. I hope God will answer all your prayers."

She took his hand and shook it, savoring the contact between them while trying to maintain all possible restraint. "I thought you didn't believe in prayer."

"I'm not certain I do. But since coming to Knightley Park, I am less certain that I don't." Like that kiss under the mistletoe, their handshake went on longer than it should have. "Perhaps I should have said I hope all your wishes for this New Year come to pass."

"Thank you, Captain." Slowly, reluctantly, she disengaged her hand from his.

Would he still extend her such a hope if he knew what secret wishes she kept locked in her heart?

Chapter Eleven

Would God answer his prayers for the New Year? It might help if he was certain what he wanted to ask for. Those thoughts lurked in the back of Gideon's mind the next day and the next, along with an unsettling realization he'd come to on New Year's Eve.

Attending the Bellamys' ball had been one sour note in an otherwise happy, harmonious Christmas season. When he'd been besieged by those ladies at dinner, he'd felt like a stag set upon by a pack of she-hounds! The whole ordeal had made him see he was quite mistaken about his liking for Marian Murray.

Until then, he had tried to dismiss his feelings as the natural reaction of a man enjoying the company of *any* woman after many years at sea. Now he could not deny there was more to it than that. If anything, his lack of experience had prevented him from recognizing just how rare and fine a woman she was. A few hours spent with those friends of Mrs. Bellamy's had made him properly value Miss Murray's good sense, compassion and loyalty.

Like the Christmas season itself, his acquaintance with her had transformed what could easily have been a period of barren darkness into something festive... perhaps even blessed.

But that did not change their situation, he sternly reminded himself as he stared out the great bay windows of the Chinese drawing room toward the frozen lake. Like Christmas, this surprisingly agreeable interlude must soon come to an end one way or another. The girls' aunt would return from her travels to whisk them and their governess away. Gideon hoped with all his heart that he would be acquitted of any wrongdoing by the Admiralty and returned to active duty before then. He could not bear to contemplate staying on at Knightley Park without them.

As if drawn by his thoughts, the swift patter of footsteps approached, and Dolly raced in, warmly dressed in her scarlet pelisse and matching bonnet. "Where are you taking us, Cousin Gideon? Miss Marian won't tell me."

"That's because I swore her to secrecy." The moment the child appeared, his lips relaxed into a broad smile and a sense of well-being engulfed him. "I am happy to hear she has kept her word."

Miss Murray appeared then with Cissy. "I'm not certain you ought to take that wee scamp anywhere, Captain, after the way she ran ahead and wouldn't come back when I called her."

Gideon tucked his arms behind his back and strove to force his countenance into the stern stare that used to come so easily to him. It no longer did—at least not when Cissy and Dolly were around. He could scarcely believe how much he had come to care for them in such a short time. It was as if his young cousins had woken and befriended the lonely boy he'd once been.

"I am disappointed to hear of you running in the house and failing to heed Miss Marian. Do you remember what I told you about that?"

Dolly gave a chastened nod. "You said I'm not a filly and the house is not a racecourse. You won't leave me at home, will you, Cousin Gideon? I'm sorry I ran, but I was so excited to find out where we're going."

He could understand that. Perhaps her behavior was partly his fault for keeping the children in suspense. "I reckon we can still take her this time, don't you, Miss Murray? But if she makes a habit of this sort of conduct, I fear she will miss out on future excursions."

"I suppose," Marian Murray said, pretending to be persuaded against her will, "provided she stays on her best behavior while we're away from home."

"What's an *excursion?*"

"It's another way of saying an *outing*," Gideon explained. "Going somewhere a bit different and doing something rather special."

"Going where?" Cissy piped up. "Doing what?"

"Well, since Twelfth Night is approaching—" Gideon watched the girls' faces for their reaction to his announcement "—I thought you might like to go shopping for gifts…in Newark."

"In town?" Dolly bounced up and down on her toes, clapping. "Oh, yes! We haven't been there in ever so long."

"After we've made our purchases," he continued. "I

wondered if you might care to see a pantomime at the theater."

"I would." A subdued sparkle in Cissy's wide blue eyes betrayed her excitement.

"What's a pantomime?" demanded Dolly.

"Something you will enjoy, I believe," Gideon replied. "I can tell you more about it on our drive into town. But we must be on our way soon if we want to get our shopping done and have something to eat before the curtain rises."

The weather had turned milder, so their drive to Newark was a pleasant one. Dolly chattered away, scarcely able to contain her excitement. Even Cissy seemed more talkative than usual. Now perfectly at ease in their company, Gideon sometimes joined in the conversation and other times simply basked in the enjoyment of it. Miss Murray said little but watched him and the children with a brooding air that lent her features a glow beyond mere beauty.

Now and then their gazes met, and they exchanged brief smiles of shared affection for the girls. That's all it was, Gideon insisted to himself. That was all it could ever be.

By and by they reached Newark, a prosperous, bustling town that straddled the Great North Road where it crossed the River Trent. They drove into the market stead, a large open square surrounded by shops, inns and public houses. The magnificent spire of the parish church loomed behind the southeastern side of the square, dwarfing all the buildings in its shadow.

"I suggest we go separate ways to make our purchases," said Gideon as their carriage drew to a stop in front of an inn called The Kingston Arms. "Each of us can take one of the girls. That way the presents may be a surprise when they are opened on Twelfth Night."

"That's a very good idea." Dolly latched onto the sleeve of his coat.

"I'm glad you think so." He fought back a grin. "Though it was Miss Murray's approval I was seeking."

"I agree with Dolly." She took Cissy by the hand. "It is a good idea."

When they alighted from the carriage, he drew Miss Murray aside and slipped her a sum of money. He pitched his voice low and leaned in close so the girls would not hear. "Help the child pick out a gift for her sister. And if you should see anything the girls need or might enjoy, I would be grateful if you make the purchase on my behalf. If the sum I have given you is not sufficient, kindly take note of the item and the shop so I can return for it later."

"I shall be happy to help, Captain." She slipped the money into her reticule. "Where and when should we meet up again?"

He nodded toward the inn. "I shall order us dinner and a private parlor where we can eat. Let us meet back here in two hours, if that will give you enough time?"

"I believe it should." As she and Cissy headed toward a nearby shop, Miss Murray called back. "We will see you in two hours, then."

With Dolly dancing along at his side, Gideon entered The Kingston Arms and made arrangements for their dinner. Then he and the child began walking around the cobblestoned square in the opposite direction from Cissy and their governess.

A year ago, if anyone had told him he would take pleasure in shopping with a high-spirited little girl, he would have dismissed such claims as the ramblings of a lunatic. Yet here he was, going from shop to shop, seeing everything with fresh, wondering eyes, evaluating every possible purchase in terms of the enjoyment it might bring his young cousins.

Then his gaze lit upon an item he felt certain their governess could use. Never in his life had he wanted so badly to give someone a particular gift. If only that harsh taskmaster, propriety, did not make it impossible.

Suddenly he became aware of a persistent tugging on his coat sleeve. How long had Dolly been trying to get his attention? "Forgive me, my dear. What do you want?"

"I was thinking," Dolly pressed her forefinger to her temple. "We should buy a present for Miss Marian."

The child's idea was like the answer to a prayer, only better, for he had not even formed his wordless longing into a petition. Instead, it felt as if someone knew him well enough to anticipate his need and supply it.

"That is a fine idea!" He wrapped his arm around Dolly's shoulders and pulled her close. "What's more, I believe I know just what she might like."

"I'm glad the Captain suggested we go our separate ways to do our shopping," said Marian as she and Cissy skirted the perimeter of the cobbled market square, peering into shop windows. "It isn't often you and I have a chance to be by ourselves."

Perhaps, in future, she could persuade the captain to take Dolly now and then so she could spend more time with Cissy. It couldn't be easy for the child, always having to share attention with her boisterous little sister.

"Yes." Cissy tugged her toward the confectioner's shop, which had a mouthwatering display of Twelfth Night cakes in the window. "If Dolly came with us, she would try to peek all the time at what I was buying for her."

Marian chuckled. "And I don't suppose you would ever think of doing that?"

"Of course not." Cissy seemed mildly offended. "That would spoil the surprise."

"So it would," Marian agreed. "See that cake decorated with all the marzipan fruit? The tiny grapes and cherries look so real."

"I like that one best." Cissy pointed to a cake with seven swans swimming around the edge. "Mrs. Wheaton's Twelfth Night Cake may not look as fancy as these, but I'm sure it will taste every bit as good."

"I have no doubt of that." Marian nodded toward the milliner's shop next door. "These cakes are lovely to look at, but this isn't getting Dolly's Christmas present bought."

"What do you think I should get her?" asked Cissy as they entered the milliner's and began to look over the colorful array of bonnets and hats on display. "I'm not certain she'd want any sort of clothes."

"I suppose not." Marian gazed with longing at a blue hat trimmed with lace and white silk flowers. She had never owned anything so pretty in her life and probably never would. But she should not be ungrateful. Her present circumstances were a vast improvement over her wretched years at school.

With Cissy's hand firmly in hers, they emerged back onto the market square. "If you don't want to give her clothing, that narrows down our search. We needn't bother looking in any of the drapers' shops."

They passed by two of those.

"Or the shoemakers."

"What about that place?" Cissy pointed toward a shop that sold china, glassware and cutlery.

"It looks worth a try." Marian doubted Dolly would care for a piece of decorative china, either. But she might find something for Cissy from her cousin. "It was very kind of the captain to bring us shopping in Newark, wasn't it?"

"Yes." Cissy did not elaborate.

"Do you like him better now than when he first came to Knightley Park?"

The child nodded, though not with the degree of enthusiasm Marian had hoped for. "He isn't very much like Papa, but he is rather nice in his way. You seem to like him a great deal more than you used to."

Were her feelings for Gideon Radcliffe so transparent? Marian tried not to let on how much Cissy's remark flustered her.

Fortunately, they had reached the china shop which provided plenty of distractions. It turned out the place also sold toys. Away from the fragile china and glassware were several shelves containing jacks, marbles, toy soldiers and the like.

"I should be able to find something here for Dolly." Cissy looked carefully over the items for sale.

Marian did too, taking note of one or two that Captain Radcliffe might wish to purchase for the girls.

Though she wanted to carry out his commission, she felt uncomfortable spending his money without consulting him.

She hoped the girls would like the beaded coin purses she had made for them. How she wished she could afford to give them special shop-bought presents. But her salary was not large and she needed to save every penny to support herself when she got too old to work.

After careful deliberation, Cissy made her choices. Marian counted out from her reticule the sum they would cost so the child could pay for her purchases.

As they headed back out to the market square, Cissy clutched her parcel as if she feared someone might try to take it from her. Without any warning she asked, "When is Aunt Lavinia coming? Has there been any word from her? I hoped she would be here to spend Christmas with us."

Marian hoped Lady Villiers would stay away from Knightley Park for at least ten years. "Your father's solicitor has tried to contact her but no one is quite certain where she might be...Paris...Vienna...Naples."

Cissy's questions dismayed her even more than the too-perceptive remark about her feelings for the captain. She had been trying so hard to make him care for his young cousins. Now it seemed she should have done more to foster Cissy's liking for him.

"The bookseller's." Marian headed toward a handsome stone building that occupied the south corner of the square. "Let's see what they have, shall we? I could happily browse there for hours."

The shop was quite crowded with prosperous-looking

people in search of gifts for friends and family. Marian inhaled the mellow pungency of ink, paper and leather as avidly as the children might sniff sweet smells coming from a bakery.

No sooner had they arrived than a friend of Cissy's came to greet her. "Merry Christmas! Have you had a pleasant holiday? We've come to town to see the pantomime."

"So have we," Cissy announced proudly. "And to shop for Christmas presents."

The girls wandered off, chatting together, while Marian perused the shelves that reached all the way to the high ceiling.

"May I help you find a particular title, ma'am?" A young shop assistant approached her. "*Mansfield Park,* perhaps? It is the newest work by the authoress of *Sense and Sensibility* and *Pride and Prejudice.* All the ladies are clamoring for it."

Marian would have liked very much to purchase all three books by that lady. Her friend Rebecca had read the first two and praised them highly in her letters. Ah, well, she had the Radcliffes' whole library at her disposal. Those books might not be the newest, but there were many good ones among the collection. "Thank you, but I am not looking to make a purchase for myself."

"For a gift. Of course." The young man held up a book he was holding. "I highly recommend this for a father, brother or husband. *Waverley,* a historical novel set in Scotland."

That sounded good, too, though Marian feared it might make her homesick to read about the land she had been forced to leave so long ago. Even if she could afford to buy the novel, she had no male relative to whom she could give it. She would have liked to give a copy to Gideon Radcliffe, but that was impossible for so many reasons.

"I'm sure it's excellent," she replied, "but I am looking for gifts for two young girls."

The assistant beckoned her over to the counter. "We have a fine selection of books for children, printed on Dutch paper with tinted engravings, as well as some new items that have proven very popular."

As he brought out several of these for her inspection, Marian kept casting glances over her shoulder to make certain Cissy's friend was keeping her well occupied.

She was just about to check again when she heard the captain's voice behind her. "I thought we might meet up here, since it is halfway around the square from where we started."

A sharp gasp burst from her lips as she spun around. "Captain, you startled me! Where is Dolly? I don't want her to see what I've been looking at."

He nodded toward Cissy and her friend, whom Dolly had joined. The three girls seemed to be discussing the pantomime and their Christmas celebrations. "She appears to be diverted for the moment. Do I take it you have found some suitable gifts?"

"I believe so." Only now did Marian notice his arms were filled with a number of parcels, one quite bulky. "Though perhaps you have already found what you would like to give them."

"These, you mean?" He rested his parcels on the edge of the counter, shielding the items she'd been looking over from Cissy and Dolly's view. "No, indeed. So tell me what we have here?"

He stood close beside her, their arms touching. Was that also to prevent the girls from spying?

Whatever the reason, Marian savored his nearness, happy to see him again after even such a brief absence. "I am certain the girls will find these things both amusing and instructive. What is even better, I doubt they are aware such playthings exist. That should make their surprise all the greater."

As the shop assistant showed them to him, Captain Radcliffe nodded. "Well done, Miss Murray. These will do very nicely."

"Which do you wish to purchase, sir?" asked the young man.

"Why, all of them, of course." The captain turned slightly toward Marian. "Could I trouble you to fetch the girls back to the inn so I can pay for these without fear of discovery?"

"Of course, sir." She hastened to do his bidding, though she would rather have lingered there at his side.

The girls reluctantly bid Cissy's friend goodbye and headed back to the inn with Marian. On the way, they traded accounts of what they had seen on their shopping excursions. When Dolly heard about the cakes in the confectioner's window, she insisted on stopping so she could see them for herself.

They were still lingering there when the captain caught up with them. Though he was laden with even more parcels, he whisked the girls into the shop and proceeded to buy a bag of barley sweets and toffees for them to eat during the pantomime.

Marian could not imagine they would have much appetite for those treats after the excellent dinner they tucked away back at The Kingston Arms—cold meats, salads, pies and delicious cheese.

"There." The Captain leaned back in his chair with a contented sigh. "That should give us the strength to walk to the theater. It is only a little way past the other side of the square. The carriage can wait here to drive us home."

Dolly jumped up at once. "Let's go, then. Nell told us we want to be there early to get good seats."

"Never fear," he assured the child. "I have sent Wilbert ahead to reserve us a box."

He had spared no effort or expense to make certain the girls enjoyed their excursion to Newark. Marian savored that thought like a sweet, creamy toffee that melted slowly in the mouth. Whether he realized it or not, Gideon Radcliffe had clearly become attached to his young cousins.

Later, as they watched the rollicking, riotous pantomime, Marian noted how his acquaintance with the children had done him so much good. Gone was the fiercely solitary man who had stalked into Knightley Park two months ago. In his place was one capable of laughter, thoughtful generosity and an ability to enjoy the small pleasures of life.

Newark's playhouse was not a large one, or so Marian guessed, having never attended the theater before. The compact box she shared with the Radcliffes had an excellent view of the stage, where the company performed *The Misadventures of Robin Hood,* a very popular production in Nottinghamshire. As Robin and his band of clownish outlaws cavorted about, playing tricks upon the foppish sheriff and his buffoon of a henchman, the crowded little theater throbbed with laughter.

Dolly fell about in fits of giggles whenever Robin stole up behind the sheriff and gave him a resounding smack on the bottom with his slapping stick.

Later, when the henchman stalked Robin and Maid Marian, Cissy got so caught up in the action she cried, "Look out behind you!"

The poor child hid her face in shame when she realized what she'd done, but the rest of the audience roared with mirth and the actors incorporated her warning into their performance.

Though Marian laughed as much as anyone at the exaggerated falls, blows, tumbling and comical songs, a tiny part of her remained detached, observing Captain Radcliffe and the girls, taking added pleasure in *their* enjoyment. The captain's plan to give Cissy and Dolly a merry Christmas had worked better than she could have hoped. It was quite clear that her prayers for him to care about the girls had been answered.

Now all that remained to crown her efforts was an opportunity to broach the subject of guardianship with Captain Radcliffe. Surely, when he learned what kind of woman Lady Villiers was, he would not wish to see his young cousins fall into her clutches any more than Marian did.

Glancing around at the other families who occupied surrounding boxes, she reckoned a chance observer might suppose she and the Radcliffes were also a close-knit, happy family. Spending so much time together over Christmas, they had come to feel like a family, too.

Knowing how unlikely it was that she would ever have a family of her own, Marian had never permitted herself to think too much about wanting one. But now that she had tasted the joy of family unity, she was not certain she could repress that longing.

After the curtain fell to thunderous applause and the performers took their final bows, Marian and the captain helped the girls bundle up for their return to Knightley Park.

"That was the funniest thing I ever saw," Dolly crowed. "My tummy hurts from laughing so hard."

"I wish we could see it all over again." Cissy pulled on her gloves. "Wasn't it lovely how Robin and Maid Marian were able to get married at last in spite of that awful sheriff?"

"Robin Hood had a *Maid* Marian," Dolly said, her eyes twinkling with mischief, "and we have a *Miss* Marian. I think after this, I will call you Maid Marian."

"Call me what you will." Marian playfully batted Dolly's nose. "But I will choose what name I answer to."

Over the child's head her gaze met the captain's, and they exchanged a comradely smile.

"May I have a barley sweet, now?" Cissy asked him.

"What do you say, Miss Marian?" He pulled the bag from his pocket.

"Go ahead." She plumped the bow of Dolly's bonnet. "Now that the pantomime is over, I won't be afraid of them choking when they laugh."

Having secured her approval, Captain Radcliffe fished out sweets for the girls. "And you, Miss Marian?"

"Yes, please." She held out her hand.

As he slipped her one of the hard-boiled sweets, she gave silent thanks for all the joys, great and small, that Gideon Radcliffe had brought into her life.

Once out on the street, they walked briskly toward The Kingston Arms and their waiting carriage. Marian wondered if the girls might fall asleep on the drive home, leaving her and the captain a chance to talk. If they did, it might be the right time to raise her doubts about Lady Villiers as a suitable guardian for the girls. But part of her shrank from spoiling this lovely outing by bringing up such an unpleasant subject.

They had nearly reached the inn when they met an elderly gentleman who doffed his hat and wished them a Happy New Year. Captain Radcliffe returned his cordial greeting.

"Have you seen the pantomime?" Dolly asked the man. "It's very funny, especially Robin Hood's slapping stick. I laughed and laughed!"

The old gentleman stopped in a pool of light cast by one of several street lamps scattered around the square. "Bless my soul, child, I have not seen a pantomime in years. But now that you mention it, I believe I shall go. I could do with a good laugh."

He beamed at the girls, then smiled up at Marian and the captain. "A very handsome family you have been blessed with, sir. I trust you appreciate your good fortune."

Marian sensed a sudden tension in the captain's posture, but he replied with only the slightest hesitation. "Thank you, sir. I do, indeed. Good evening to you."

As they hurried on, Cissy piped up in an accusing tone, "Why did you not tell that man we aren't your family?"

"Because you are…in a way."

Cissy was not satisfied with that excuse. "But you know he thought Miss Marian must be your wife and Dolly and me your daughters. You should have told him the truth."

"Perhaps," replied the captain. "But his praise was kindly meant. It would have been more awkward to explain. Besides, I cannot deny you are handsome."

"We *aren't* your family," Cissy repeated. "Not in the way he meant."

"I sometimes wish we were," announced Dolly, who had been unusually quiet during their exchange. "I sometimes wish Cousin Gideon was our papa and Miss Marian our mama."

Those words brought Cissy to an abrupt halt. She let go of Marian's hand as if it had suddenly caught fire. "Dolly Radcliffe, how could you wish such a wicked thing?"

"It isn't wicked!" Dolly cried.

"Please, Cissy." Marian had been afraid the late hour and all the treats and excitement might catch up with the children. "Your sister didn't mean—"

"Yes, she did!" Cissy backed away, glaring at all three of them. "And she had no business wishing any such thing. She should wish Mama and Papa had not died!"

With that, the child spun away and ran off across the square.

"Cissy!" Marian started after her only to feel Gideon's restraining hand on her arm.

"Stay with Dolly," he ordered in a tone of command the brooked no refusal. "Take her into the inn to keep warm until I fetch her sister back."

He spoke those words as he hurried past in pursuit of the fleeing child.

Marian wanted to protest. Cissy was much more likely to listen to her. But for that to happen, she would first have to catch the child. Gideon was better suited to that task for he had longer legs which were not hampered by skirts. Besides, it might not be prudent for a woman and young girl to be out at night on their own, even in a respectable town like Newark.

As she turned back toward Dolly, Marian raised a wordless prayer that Gideon would be able to catch Cissy quickly and somehow find the words to reach her heart.

Chapter Twelve

Dread clawed at Gideon as he raced across Newark's market square, trying to keep from losing sight of the fleeing child. If he did not catch up with her soon, he feared she might duck into one of the narrow lanes around the church and lose him.

What might become of her then? It was a cold night, and he doubted Cissy knew anyone in Newark with whom she might seek shelter. Even if she repented running away and wanted to return, would she be able to find her way back through unfamiliar streets in the winter darkness? The thought of her lost, alone and perishing with cold terrified Gideon as no peril to his own life ever had. Almost as acute as his fear for her safety was the alarming realization of how much his cousin's young daughters had come to mean to him.

Cissy had almost reached the other side of the square! How could such a slender little creature run so fast? She was like a frightened fawn fleeing for her life.

Out of his desperation, a plea rose in his thoughts. "Dear God, help me catch her before it's too late!"

A prayer? Part of him scoffed at the futility of it. Even if the Creator of the Universe did heed the pleas of insignificant human beings, why should God deign to answer his first prayer in nearly twenty-five years? If anyone was going to reach Cissy, it would have to be him alone, by his own efforts.

That thought spurred him to a final burst of speed.

Was the child slowing down a bit? Perhaps he might catch her yet.

Then in a confused instant, his foot landed on a patch of ice and flew out from under him. Gideon flailed his arms in a futile effort to regain his balance. A cry burst from his lips as he crashed down hard on the cold cobblestones.

Stunned and in pain, he struggled to drag himself back to his feet and continue the chase. A groan collided in his throat with a sob of despair, for he knew it was too late. Cissy would have disappeared from sight, and his chances of finding her would be far too slim.

But as he tried to pull himself up, ignoring a stab of pain in his ankle, Gideon heard footsteps. They could not be the child's, though, for the sound was coming closer rather than fading into the distance.

"Cousin Gideon?" That was Cissy's voice. Or had the fall addled his wits enough to make him hear things?

"Are you much hurt?" She gasped for breath. "I heard you fall. It's all my fault...if you are injured."

Hearing him cry out, she had stopped and come back? That mishap had accomplished his goal when his own best efforts might have failed. What strange irony. Or could it be the unlikely answer to a prayer?

"Don't fret yourself, child." Much as pride urged

him to get back on his feet as quickly as possible and pretend nothing was wrong, he sensed that might make Cissy run off again.

A soft whisper from deep in his heart suggested that perhaps an admission of weakness might serve him better that a show of strength. "You came back. That counts for a great deal more. Can I trouble you to help me up? I fear my leg may be injured and my balance is none too steady."

Cissy hesitated for a moment, then Gideon felt her hand on his. Leaning upon her, he struggled to his feet. "Could you assist me back across the square? I believe your Miss Marian will be worried about us, don't you?"

"Yes," came the forlorn answer. "Do you think she will be very angry with me for running off like that?"

"More relieved to get you back than angry, I should think." His arm slung over the child's shoulders, Gideon took one halting step forward, then another.

After a few more steps, he spoke again. He hoped— prayed—that what he was about to say would not make the child take flight again. "I understand why you were upset with me and with your sister."

"You do?" Cissy sounded skeptical yet mildly curious.

"Yes, indeed." Much as it went against his nature to speak of his past, Gideon sensed the child needed to hear about it. Besides, he now had some practice confiding in Marian Murray—enough to know that while the experience might be painful, it often brought a sense of relief. "I was around Dolly's age when my father died. My mother lingered after him for nearly two years, but she had never been strong...."

"Did you miss them very much?" Cissy asked in a plaintive murmur. "Did you pray they would come back again? Did you think if you were very, very good, they might?"

The anguish in her voice revived Gideon's deeply buried feelings of loss. Old wounds reopened, stinging and bleeding afresh. "During my mother's final weeks, I made all manner of bargains with God for good behavior if He would spare her life."

A long overdue realization gashed his heart. "When she died at last, I wondered if it was my fault for not behaving well enough."

Was that why he had blamed God—because it was easier than carrying that burden of irrational guilt?

Cissy sniffled. It might be just the cold air making her nose run, but Gideon did not think so.

"Now I understand," he continued, "that my mother's death was not my fault...nor was it God's."

He wasn't certain Cissy would be able to grasp that yet. It had taken him twenty-five years. Perhaps it would not have taken so long if he hadn't spent so much of that time trying to bury his memories and feelings about that part of his life.

In spite of their slow progress across the square, he and Cissy were drawing near The Kingston Arms. Since it was doubtful he would have another opportunity to talk privately with the child, there was one more thing he needed to say.

"I hope you know I have no desire to take your father's place in your life. Any kindness or affection you show me would not be disloyal to his memory. Indeed, from what I remember of him, I believe he would approve. Even in death, he would not want to cause you any guilt or sorrow. More than anything, I believe he would wish for you to be happy."

Beneath his arm, Gideon could feel the child's slender shoulders tremble and heave.

Oh, no. His effort to comfort her had only made her weep.

His first day back at Knightley Park, when he'd seen those two beautiful children, he had been beset by the conviction that he was not equipped to provide what they might need, though he'd only had a vague suspicion of what those needs might be. In the weeks since, he had gradually gained more confidence in dealing with the girls. False confidence apparently.

Now that he understood what they needed, the knowledge made him feel more inadequate than ever. That self-doubt urged him to hurry those last few steps to the inn and shift responsibility onto the capable shoulders of Marian Murray. But some other feeling he scarcely recognized pleaded with him to try at least. He was the child's flesh and blood after all, the closest living relative to the father she mourned so deeply.

Did he dare turn to the Lord for help again so soon, when he was not entirely convinced his first prayer had been answered? Perhaps he did not deserve the help he sought, but surely it could do no harm to ask. "Please, Lord, tell me what to say. Let me know what she needs to hear."

But no words leapt instinctively to mind. He could not summon any powerful phrases certain to reach her. Gideon tamped down a foolish sense of disappointment. How could he have been so daft as to expect an answer?

Or could his loss for words be part of the inspiration he sought? Was it a sign that no words could provide what a confused, guilty, grieving young girl needed now?

What *did* she need then? He was in no mood to puzzle out riddles from a Higher Power...or some forgotten corner of his own mind.

Then, without conscious effort on his part, the arm he had slung over Cissy's shoulders subtly increased its pressure, encouraging her to turn toward him. He expected her to resist, perhaps even take flight again. Instead, to his amazement, she surrendered to the gentle urging. As her weeping gained momentum, she slowly turned until her face rested against the breast of his coat.

There was only one thing to do at that point. In spite of how self-conscious it made him feel, Gideon raised his other arm to wrap the child in a comforting, protective embrace.

Perhaps he didn't know the right things to say, but at least he had a sense of what *not* to say. He would not try to shush her and tell her not to weep. It might make *him* feel better, but that was not the point.

"Go ahead," he murmured. "Cry as long as you like. I'm here."

Cissy accepted his invitation, letting her tears flow freely for several minutes, gulping in air to fuel her sobs. When she began to quiet at last, he rummaged in his pocket for a handkerchief and pressed it into her hand in silent sympathy.

The child wiped her eyes and blew her nose.

"We should get inside," she murmured. "It's cold out here and Miss Marian will be worried."

"An excellent suggestion." Gideon loosened his hold on her, only to discover how reluctant he was to let her go.

But that was nothing to his astonishment when instead of taking the opportunity to disengage from his embrace, Cissy pressed tight against him. "Thank you, Cousin Gideon. I still don't wish you were my papa, but I am glad you came to Knightley Park."

His throat tightened as he bent to drop a kiss on the crown of her bonnet. "Then we are in complete agreement, my dear."

"Cissy!" Marian swooped down on the child the moment she peeped into the waiting room at The Kingston Arms. "Thank God you are back!"

Noting Cissy's red, swollen eyes and nose, she asked, "Are you all right? You weren't hurt, were you?"

The child gnawed her lower lip as she shook her head. "Cousin Gideon was, though. He fell on some ice in the square and hurt his leg."

Cousin Gideon? This was the first time Marian had heard Cissy refer to him that way. An intense impulse of concern for him pushed that trifling thought out of her mind.

"Captain!" She was barely able to keep from throwing her arms around him. "Come in and sit down. Should I send for a physician?"

"Don't fret, Miss Marian," he bid her rather gruffly. "I'm certain nothing is broken. Only bumps and bruises. Fortunately, Cissy was kind enough to come to my assistance."

Seeing how he had one arm draped over Cissy's shoulders, Marian slid in under his other arm. She chided herself for welcoming this excuse to be close to him.

As she and Cissy helped the captain to a nearby bench, a loud yawn reminded everyone of Dolly, curled up half asleep at the far end of the bench. "Aren't you going to punish Cissy, Miss Marian? She shouted at me and ran away. It's her fault Cousin Gideon got hurt chasing after her."

"Not now, Dolly." Marian fixed her younger pupil with a firm stare. "We'll talk about all that later."

"We'd better." Dolly eyed her sister with a scowl. "You never wait 'til later to punish me when I've been naughty."

Marian was about to scold the child for her impudence, but the captain only chuckled. "Ah, Dolly, you are practically a pantomime all on your own."

The corners of her fierce little frown arched upward. "I wish I had a slapping stick. That would be great fun."

"Great *havoc* you mean." Marian gave an exaggerated shudder. "None of us would be safe."

After the captain had taken a few minutes to rest and get warm, he refused any suggestion of seeking medical attention but said they should head back home at once. To Marian's surprise, Cissy quietly insisted on sitting beside him in the carriage. It took some persuasion for Dolly to surrender her accustomed spot, but at last she gave in with rather ill grace and they were on their way.

"What on earth did you say to Cissy to bring about such a change in her?" Marian asked when the drone of the girls' breathing assured her they were both asleep.

"Not a great deal," Gideon replied. "I only told her a little about losing my parents when I was her age and how it affected me. Then I assured her I have no intention of trying to take her father's place in her life."

He didn't? Not ever, under any circumstances? His words made Marian rethink her intention to raise the subject of the girls' guardianship.

What had gone wrong? Until an hour ago, she'd been certain God was smiling upon her efforts. Could this be a test of her resolve?

"Strange that saying a thing like that should make her take such liking to you."

"Believe me, I am quite as surprised as you. Perhaps it helped her to know I understand her feelings because I have shared them."

Should she have told Dolly and Cissy about her experiences being orphaned at an early age? Marian wondered. She had held her tongue on the subject, fearing it might prompt prying questions about her experiences at the Pendergast School. She did not want to make them afraid of being sent to such a place. It was bad enough that she must live with that worry on their behalf.

A sudden thought drove every other from Marian's mind.

"Dear me. How could I have forgotten?" She groped for her reticule while trying not to disturb Dolly, who had fallen asleep with her head on Marian's lap. "That money you gave me, I only spent a wee bit of it on Cissy's gift to Dolly."

She fished out what was left—heavy gold guineas, silver shillings, halfpennies. "Here is the rest. I would have returned it to you sooner but with dinner and the pantomime and everything else, it slipped my mind until now."

She hoped he wouldn't suspect her of trying to keep his money.

"Oh, that?" Gideon sounded as if he had never given it a thought. Or was he only trying to be polite? "Do not trouble yourself over it, I beg you, Miss Murray. Please keep it, with my compliments."

"I couldn't do that, Captain." The very idea made her feel ill. "It is a great deal of money…at least to someone like me."

"Nonsense," he replied gruffly. "You deserve every farthing and more for the way you have looked after the girls since their father died. Consider it a Christmas box."

Though it pleased her to know he valued her efforts so highly, the notion of taking money from Gideon Radcliffe only emphasized the gulf between her position and his.

"Please, Captain, I cannot accept this." She held out the money to him, but she could not reach any farther without the risk of waking Dolly—something she was loath to do. "It would not be fair for me to take this when the other servants work so much harder than I do at far less congenial tasks."

"Servants?" Gideon Radcliffe sat stubbornly back in his seat, refusing to extend his hand and take the money she sought to return. "Surely you know I do not think of you as a servant!"

The fierce tone of his insistence rocked Marian back. How did he think of her then? She longed to know, but dared not ask for fear his answer might crush her foolish illusion that some degree of friendship existed between them.

"In that case," she edged a little closer and opened her palm. "Please do not insult me by insisting I keep this money."

"Fine." He snatched the coins out of her hand in a swift, almost violent movement. "If that is what you wish."

He'd told Marian Murray he did not think of her as a servant. Why had she refused to ask how he did think of her? In the final few days of Christmas leading up to Twelfth Night, Gideon could not decide whether he was sorry or grateful he'd been denied the opportunity to tell her.

Would he have been able to explain if she had asked? The privacy and darkness of the carriage box might have tempted him, but at what cost?

He admired the woman, liked her…even fancied her, heaven help him. But entertaining such feelings for her did not give him any right to reveal them or, worse yet, act upon them. He might not think of her as a servant, but she was employed in the house of which he was master. Any declaration would shatter the precious illusion of a family that he treasured more and more.

This time with Cissy and Dolly…and Marian…was only temporary. Gideon knew and accepted that. But for a short while he'd been able to experience the small domestic joys of family life. For that gift, he would be forever grateful.

What made it all the sweeter was knowing he had been able to do something for his young cousins. He'd given them the opportunity to remain in their home and grow accustomed to the changes that would soon take place in their lives. With Marian's help, he'd turned a Christmas that might have been shadowed with sad memories into a festive celebration of light and hope. On the most personal level, he had helped a grieving young girl understand that she was not alone.

Those accomplishments brought him a deeper sense of satisfaction than any of the battles in which he'd fought or voyages of exploration on which he'd sailed. Yet, as the last few days of the Christmas season passed, a hint of wistfulness colored the pleasure of his celebration.

On the day before Twelfth Night, they invited a number of children from the parish to a skating party. Round and round the youngsters glided on the frozen lake, laughing and calling to one another. Cissy and Dolly even persuaded Gideon to strap on skates for the first time in twenty-five years to help push a small sleigh full of younger children around the ice. Later, they gathered in the pavilion that stood on the little island in the middle of the lake. There, Marian and the kitchen staff dispensed cups of steaming cider and chocolate, baked potatoes, hot meat pies and buns, followed by gingerbread.

"I wish Christmas never had to end." Dolly took Gideon's hand as he and the girls stood in front of the house waving farewell to the last of their guests. "I'd like it to go on and on."

Her childish wish echoed his own recent thoughts so closely, it took Gideon aback.

"Now, now." He squeezed her hand, not looking forward to the day he would bid Dolly and her sister goodbye. "Don't let the thought of happy times coming to an end spoil your enjoyment of them. If every day were Christmas you'd soon grow tired of it. I reckon we enjoy special times all the more because they don't last forever."

"You sound just like Miss Marian," the child grumbled.

Once again, Gideon could not help but laugh at the things she came out with. They were a tiny pinch of yeast that leavened his day. "Why, thank you! That is one of the nicest compliments anyone has ever paid me."

"It wasn't meant to be a compliment," Dolly muttered, making him laugh again.

"Don't look so sour." He scooped her up and jiggled her until she began to chortle. "The best of Christmas is yet to come, remember? A fine dinner and presents and Twelfth Night cake. I have it on good authority that Mrs. Wheaton has quite outdone herself this year."

"Presents!" Dolly threw her arms around his neck, a gesture he had grown accustomed to and come to enjoy. "What did you get me?"

"He mustn't tell," piped up Cissy, who'd been standing quietly beside them. "It's meant to be a secret."

"So it is." Something in the look she cast him made Gideon set Dolly on her feet and pick up her sister.

"And speaking of secrets, I've noticed a bit of whispering going on and conversations that mysteriously stop when I enter the room. You wouldn't be planning some sort of trick to spring on me by any chance?"

"Not a trick," Dolly insisted.

"Hush!" Cissy bid her sister. "You mustn't tell."

"Now I am intrigued," said Gideon. "Come, don't keep me in suspense. Surely you can tell me something."

Cissy grinned and her eyes sparkled. "Wait and see."

The next morning Knightley Park was abuzz with preparations. Succulent aromas of roasting meat, fresh baked bread and cooking spices wafted up from the kitchen. Eager for every opportunity to spend time with the girls, Gideon joined them for their last breakfast of frumenty.

While they were eating and talking over plans for the day, Mr. Culpepper appeared with the post. "A letter for you, Captain Radcliffe, and one for Miss Murray."

Gideon's stomach sank at the sight of the Admiralty seal on his letter. Stuffing it in his pocket to read later, he hoped the ever curious Dolly would not quiz him about it. Fortunately for him, Marian's post diverted attention from his entirely.

"Oh, thank goodness." She pressed it to her heart with a look of relief.

"Who is your letter from, Miss Marian?" demanded Dolly.

Gideon found himself quite as eager as Dolly to learn the answer to her question. Everything about

Marian Murray had become of particular interest to him.

Perhaps she sensed his curiosity, for when she replied, she looked toward him. "It is a Christmas letter from my friend Rebecca Beaton. I was beginning to worry some trouble might have befallen to prevent her from writing."

"What does she say?" asked Dolly. "Why did her letter come late?"

"I won't know that until I read it, will I?" Marian turned the thick packet of paper over and over in her hands. It was clear she was as curious as her young pupil to learn those things.

"Go on then," Dolly coaxed her. Bolting her last spoonful of frumenty, the child leaned back in her chair, waiting to be informed.

"Don't be rude," Cissy chided her. "Letters are private, you know."

For all that, she eyed her governess's letter with ill-disguised interest.

"True." Marian stared at the letter longingly. "Besides, it would not be polite to read it at breakfast in front of everyone."

Would she have hesitated if he were not there, Gideon wondered. He did not want to stand between her and whatever news the letter might contain.

"Pray do not suppose I would object to you looking over your friend's message," he assured her. "At least enough to rest your mind that she is not in any difficulty."

"Thank you, Captain. That is most considerate of you." The gratitude in her voice made him feel a trifle guilty, for his suggestion had not been entirely free of self-interest.

Without further ado, she broke the seal on the letter with eager, jerky movements, as if she had been itching to do that from the moment it arrived. Pulling it open, she hurriedly scanned the page.

"Oh, my." Her eyes widened in wonder. From her tone it appeared the letter did not bear any bad news.

"Well, what does it say?" Dolly prompted Marian, ignoring a sharp look from her sister. "Why did Miss Rebecca take so long to write you?"

"She has been very busy." Marian continued to read the letter with a look of dreamy abstraction that Gideon found far too appealing. "Rebecca is engaged to be married. To a viscount, no less. Lord Benedict."

"What's a viscount?" asked Dolly.

"Lord Benedict?" Gideon repeated. "During the war, he once sailed aboard the *Integrity* to Portugal to see for himself how British troops were being supplied. He struck me as a fine man."

Clever, hardworking and passionately committed to his mission, but not necessarily cut out for marriage. Now that the war was over, perhaps Lord Benedict had decided to allow himself the luxury of a family life. Gideon wished him well. If Marian's friend was anything like her, then his lordship was a fortunate man to have secured her affection.

Chapter Thirteen

Rebecca was going to be married. Her friend's wonderful news hovered in Marian's thoughts as she got the girls ready for their Twelfth Night celebrations.

It appeared their teachers' stern admonitions were wrong after all—and how very wrong. Marian could not help gloating a little over that. She wondered what they would think if they knew one of their former pupils was betrothed to a peer of the realm.

She should not let any foolish ideas get into *her* head on that account. Marian fancied she could hear the voice of their strictest teacher reproaching her. Rebecca Beaton might have been the orphaned daughter of a clergyman, like all the other girls at the Pendergast School. But on her late mother's side, she had noble blood and aristocratic connections. Some of their teachers had treated her a little better because of her background. Others had been even harder on her, claiming a virtuous desire to help her conquer her pride.

Perhaps Viscount Benedict valued Rebecca's good breeding in spite of her humble position as a governess.

Marian had no such advantages. She came from a respectable, educated Scottish family, but nothing compared to the Radcliffes in wealth or social standing.

Still, Gideon had said he did not think of her as a servant. And Rebecca Beaton had proved it was possible for a pupil from the Pendergast School to secure a fine husband.

Encouraged by those thoughts, in spite of her doubts, Marian took special care with her appearance for the festivities. When the time came, she ushered the girls down to the Chinese drawing room, where Gideon was waiting to give them their presents.

Outside, tiny flakes of snow swirled in a cold breeze. Gideon beckoned them from the wide seat of the great bow window. A pile of packages rested on top of a small table beside him. Marian thought it was a nice informal spot for them to gather to give the girls their gifts. Anyone looking in the window at that moment might easily mistake them for an affectionate family group—like that kind old gentleman in Newark had thought.

"May I go first?" Marian asked in a rush the moment she and the girls were seated. Her gifts were certain to be the most modest. She would rather see the girls' pleasure mount after that humble beginning than face their disappointment if they opened her presents later.

"Certainly, if you wish," Gideon agreed. Perhaps he guessed her reason for the request.

"There you are, Cissy, and for you Dolly." She handed them each a small parcel, wrapped in colored paper and tied with pretty ribbons.

"Thank you, Miss Marian!" The girls opened their

gifts each in their accustomed manner. Cissy carefully untied the ribbon and pealed open the wrapping while Dolly ripped the paper off without ceremony.

"What is it?" She jiggled the small beaded bag in her hand.

"It's a coin purse, of course." Cissy gave the younger girl a pointed nudge with her elbow. "They're lovely, Miss Marian. The beadwork is beautiful. Isn't it, Dolly?"

"Oh, yes." Dolly took the unsubtle hint. "Very beautiful. They will come in handy if we go shopping in Newark again. And if we get any money to put in them."

"Since you mention it—" Gideon dug in his pocket and came out with several coins he divided between the girls "—I meant to give you these the other day, but since you had no purses, I was afraid they might get lost."

Dolly looked much more pleased with her purse now that it was no longer empty. She shook it to make the coins jingle.

After a few moments of that, she thrust a rather clumsily wrapped parcel into her sister's hands. "Now open mine."

Cissy returned the favor with a package upon which greater pains had been taken. She winced when Dolly proceeded to rip it open, then decided to do the same with the one she'd been given.

"A muff—how pretty!" She rubbed the handsome fur hand-warmer against her cheek. "How soft it feels. Thank you, Dolly."

Meanwhile Dolly gasped with delight when she

unwrapped the toy sailboat from her sister. "I hope the lake will thaw soon so I can sail it!"

When the girls opened their presents from Gideon a few moments later, they were equally pleased, though a little baffled at first.

"It's a dissected puzzle," Marian explained when Dolly's brow furrowed. "When you put each of the countries of Europe in their proper place, the edges will fit together to make the whole map. It will be a great help to you learning geography."

"Look at mine!" cried Cissy. "I thought it was a pretty book, but see it has a cut out figure of a girl with paper costumes to change how she is dressed through the story. Her name is Little Fanny. Isn't that clever? Thank you, Cousin Gideon!"

"Yes, thank you!" Dolly bounded up to give him a hearty kiss on the cheek.

The child's impulsive gesture seemed to please him. "I'm delighted you approve."

His obvious pleasure in the girls' happiness touched Marian. He might not intend to take their late father's place, but surely he would want what was best for Cissy and Dolly. He would never allow Lady Villiers to help herself to their inheritance or pack them off to school.

"While I was happy to make the actual purchases," he continued, "I would never have guessed what you might like without Miss Marian to advise me. I hope you will think of these gifts as coming from both of us."

Having said that, he leaned down and whispered something in Dolly's ear. She nudged her sister and pointed to the one remaining parcel on the table.

Scrambling up from the window seat, the girls retrieved the package and presented it to Marian. "Merry Christmas!"

"Cousin Gideon paid for it," Dolly confessed. "But he says it's from us."

"My goodness. This is quite a surprise." Like Cissy, Marian untied the string with great care and folded back the paper. "I cannot imagine what it might...oh, my!"

It was a writing box made of fine dark wood with a sloped lid, which folded open to reveal all the supplies she would need for letter writing—paper, ink, quills, a pen knife, sealing wax and a jar of pounce for drying the ink.

"Do you like it?" asked Cissy anxiously as a fine mist rose in Marian's eyes.

"Like it?" She swallowed the lump in her throat and sought to reassure the child with a wide smile. "I cannot imagine any gift I would like better. Thank you so much!"

She raised her gaze to meet Gideon's, eager for him to know how much she appreciated his thoughtfulness. Not only had he shown how well he knew her by choosing such an ideal gift, he'd also found a way to give it that would not violate propriety.

More than ever, she wished she could have afforded one of those new books for him. But she would have to be content with a different kind of offering—one she hoped would please him even half as much as his gift delighted her.

"We have something for you, too, Cousin Gideon." Cissy took the rolled paper tied with red ribbon that

Marian handed her. Turning toward the captain, she presented it to him with great ceremony.

"Really, this is not necessary." He seemed torn between self-consciousness and curiosity as he unrolled the little scroll. "What have we here? A program of festive music and recitations in my honor? What an excellent gift and a fine way to conclude the Christmas season!"

The silvery radiance of his eyes left no doubt of his sincere gratitude and desire to hear the girls perform.

After an excellent dinner, the four of them headed to the music room where the girls took turns playing simple renditions of Christmas melodies on the pianoforte. Their duet of "The First Noel" made the captain applaud so vigorously Marian feared he might hurt his hands.

Then it was her turn to take the keyboard and accompany the girls while they sang. Again Gideon proved a very appreciative audience. His attention did not flag for the recitations either—some little rhymes about Christmas the girls had practiced every day in the nursery. They concluded their concert by taking turns reading verses from St. Matthew's account of the wise men visiting Baby Jesus, followed by a spirited duet of "I Saw Three Ships."

"Bravo!" cried Gideon as the girls proudly made their curtsies. "That was a splendid evening's entertainment and without a doubt the best Christmas present I have ever received."

By now they had digested their dinner sufficiently to do justice to Mrs. Wheaton's Twelfth Night cake. Retiring to the dining room, they watched in amazement as it was brought out, swathed in snow-white icing and topped with a tiny sailing ship cleverly fashioned out of marzipan.

The girls clapped excitedly when they saw the marvelous confection. "It is fancier than any in the shop-window in Newark!"

Gideon sent for the cook to receive their praise and congratulations in person. Despite their frequent insistence that the cake looked too beautiful to cut, they could not resist the temptation indefinitely. When they finally began to eat, they were delighted to discover the cake tasted as good as it looked. They ate, drank and made merry until Marian reluctantly announced that it was long past the girls' bedtime.

Cissy and Dolly protested, but not as much as she feared they might.

As they gathered up their gifts from the drawing room, the captain picked up Marian's writing box. "Let me carry this for you. It is not heavy, but rather cumbersome."

Though Marian had no doubt she could have managed it on her own, she did not protest, but thanked him for his assistance. He probably wanted an excuse to be on hand in case Dolly requested another kiss good-night.

As they headed upstairs, Marian noticed dry evergreen needles on the floor from the decorative boughs. On closer inspection, the holly, mistletoe and ivy all looked badly wilted. It reminded her that while Twelfth Night was the culmination of the Christmas season, it was also the end of the festivities. Tomorrow, all the dried out, wilted greenery would be taken down, the kissing bough would be dismantled, and life at Knightley Park would return to its usual safe, dull routine.

"I meant to mention," Gideon's resonant voice interrupted her wistful musing. "While I was purchasing the girls' gifts at Ridges, that young clerk persuaded me to acquire a few new books for the library. One is a novel set in Scotland, which I am enjoying immensely and believe you will, too. The others are by an anonymous authoress whose work is said to be very popular."

Words of thanks rose to her lips, but Marian suppressed them firmly. Thanking the captain would imply that he had purchased those books for her benefit—another covert gift.

"An excellent idea," she said instead. "It is a fine collection, but it has not been added to in quite some time."

Searching for a way to change the subject, she recalled his presence at breakfast in the nursery. "I am anxious to use my new writing box to compose a message of congratulations to my friend on her betrothal. You received a letter in the morning post, as well, Captain. I hope the news it contained was equally good."

He hesitated a moment before replying. "It was. I am summoned to London to appear before the board of inquiry. At last I shall have the opportunity to present my case and defend my actions."

"That *is* good news," she replied in spite of her sinking spirits.

If the inquiry absolved him of any wrongdoing, would Gideon Radcliffe come back to Nottinghamshire, or would he return to his ship immediately?

The prospect of never seeing him again cast Marian

down lower than she had been for many years. She tried to tell herself it was on account of the girls. If he did not return to Knightley Park, there would be nothing to prevent their aunt from taking them.

Yet, deep down, she knew her feelings were more personal than that.

He was eager to get to London and face the inquiry. Gideon told himself so repeatedly during the following week as he prepared for his journey south. He had enjoyed his Christmas interlude playing happy family with the girls and their governess. But the time had come to stop pretending and remember his obligations.

As much as he longed to redeem his reputation for his own sake, he also had a duty to the crew of the *Integrity*. What a time they must have had of it, poor devils, serving under his ruthlessly ambitious second-in-command with his pet pack of bullies to intimidate any opposition. Though it troubled him that none of his crew had come forward in his defense, Gideon understood what was at stake for them. The worst that had befallen him was exile to a quiet corner of the country to enjoy a good rest, better food and the best possible company. His crewmen had far more to lose if they fell afoul of his enemies.

Now, as he prepared to leave Knightley Park, one of Gideon's most important tasks was deciding whether he dared leave Mr. Dutton in charge as steward during his absence. From what he could tell, the man appeared to have mended his ways. But could he be trusted to continue in that vein once his master left for London and perhaps even returned to sea?

Though Gideon was tempted to give him the benefit of the doubt, he recalled how dearly a decision like that had cost him before. And not him alone. His crew had paid a far higher price. In this case it was the tenants of Knightley Park who would suffer if the steward returned to his lax ways.

If only there was someone he could trust to oversee the overseer and report any problems directly to him. Gideon believed that was all it would take to keep Dutton from shirking his responsibilities in future. Unfortunately, the only person at Knightley Park he trusted that much would soon be leaving, too.

With that thought in mind, Gideon tried to keep busy to distract himself from the hollow ache that nagged at him. With the Christmas season over, the girls had returned to their usual nursery routine, meaning he saw much less of them...and their governess. Perhaps that was for the best, though. It would give him a chance to grow accustomed to their absence gradually before he must depart for London.

Yet he could not keep from straining his ears to catch the faintest cadence of their voices in the distance. On his way to breakfast in the mornings, he found all manner of ridiculous excuses to linger in the hallway, hoping a small human cannonball might come hurtling around the corner toward him. In the evenings he retired to the library, hoping those new books might lure Marian Murray to join him.

He had nearly given up hope when, on the fourth evening, the library door opened tentatively and she peeped in. "I hope I am not disturbing you, Captain."

"Not in the least," he assured her, though it was not altogether true.

During Christmas they had been so often together that his awareness of her had mellowed. But now that feeling had intensified again to the point where it was rather disturbing...in a pleasant way.

As she entered the room, Miss Murray seemed more self-conscious around him, too, without the girls present. Did she recall that meeting of their lips under the kissing bough and wonder whether she would be safe alone with him?

"I thought I might borrow one of those new books you acquired." She scanned the shelves. "If you don't mind."

"Not at all." Did she not realize he had purchased them for her benefit? "I have finished *Waverley* and just started *Pride and Prejudice*. The latter may be intended for ladies, but I am enjoying it very much."

He gestured toward the table beside him where the new books lay.

Miss Murray approached with an air of hesitation. She picked up one of the books and read a little from the first page, then laid it back down and tried another. In the end she chose the one titled *Sense and Sensibility*.

Once she'd made her selection, Gideon feared she would go away again. But she lingered, though her glance often flickered toward the door. "I must confess, Captain, I had more in mind than seeking a book when I came here. May I sit?"

"Please, do." Had their time together at Christmas made her realize she enjoyed his company?

When she sank onto the armchair opposite his, Gideon sat back down. "May I inquire as to your other reason?"

He wasn't entirely certain he wanted to know. Flattering as it would be to think that such an admirable young woman might have some slight fancy for him, their respective duties made it impossible for anything to come of it. He must return to the *Integrity,* and she must accompany her young pupils to their new home with their aunt. He knew better than to suppose she would ever desert them.

"It's about Cissy and Dolly, sir."

He should have guessed. Gideon strove to ignore a sting of disappointment. The girls were her top priority. He doubted there was anything in the world she would not do for them.

"They are well, I hope." That sting swelled to a stab of fear he could not ignore. For the past few days, he had missed the girls but never taken the trouble to inquire about them. "All the rich food, late hours and time out in the cold have not made them ill?"

A soft smile lit Marian Murray's features as she shook her head. It seemed to hold a warm glow of gratitude and a faint flicker of...triumph? "They are very well, Captain, though Dolly is having a little trouble settling back down to her lessons after all the excitement of Christmas. It is kind of you to inquire after them. I believe you have come to care for the girls."

He could not deny it. "I must admit, it is a great surprise how much they have come to mean to me in such a short time. They are so different from one another, yet each so dear in her way."

"That is exactly how I feel." Her warm brown eyes shone with a depth of love that Gideon might have envied if he did not share it. "Which is why I would like you to seek guardianship of Cissy and Dolly."

Her suggestion stunned him as badly as if she'd hurled the book at his head.

"Guardianship?" he stammered. "You must be joking!"

His reply ripped the smile from her lips and the glow from her eyes. "I would never joke about the girls' welfare. If you do not become their guardian, their future will be no laughing matter, I assure you. You would make an excellent guardian. It is obvious by the way you treated them at Christmas."

Now that the shock of Miss Murray's proposition was wearing off, Gideon could not deny a traitorous flicker of temptation, which alarmed him. "Nonsense! Playing father for a few days at Christmas hardly qualifies me to take permanent responsibility for the girls. I am simply not cut out for that sort of role."

"I reckon you could be if you wanted to. If you were willing to try." Gone was his congenial companion of the past few weeks. In her place sat the steely creature he'd had the misfortune to encounter when he first arrived at Knightley Park.

"It has nothing to do with wanting or trying." Gideon sprang from his chair and stalked around to stand behind it. This felt like a stronger position from which to repel her challenge. "I have responsibilities to my crew and my country. They are the most important things in the world to me. Besides, it is not as if the girls are without anyone to care for them. They will have you and their aunt. She is a much more suitable person to have charge of two young girls."

"You might not say that if you knew her." Miss Murray surged up from her chair, the better to confront him. "It has been months since the girls' father died, yet there has not been a word from Lady Villiers. Who knows when, or if, she will return?"

"She must have a man of affairs who can get in contact with her," replied Gideon. "I will look into it while I am in London. If you are concerned about the girls having to leave Knightley Park in the meantime, you may put your fears to rest. They are welcome to stay here until their aunt comes to collect them."

If he became the children's guardian, they would never have to leave until they were old enough to marry and have homes of their own. That would mean Marian Murray would stay, too, for many years. If by chance the inquiry went against him, guardianship of the girls would give him an alternative sense of purpose.

No! Duty and conscience protested. He must fight for his reputation and his command with every ounce of determination he possessed. Not just against the Admiralty and the powerful influence of those who had disgraced him, but against the siren song of home and family at Knightley Park.

Miss Murray drew a deep breath and squared her shoulders. It was clear she did not intend to make this easy for him. "It is kind of you not to turn the girls out, Captain, but there is far more to it. Lady Villiers is a woman of very different character from Cissy and Dolly's mother. She values her independence. She likes to travel and keep herself amused. The children need continuity and stability in their lives, especially after the upheaval they have suffered in the past few years. Please believe me when I say you would make a far better guardian for the girls than their aunt."

Marian Murray did not consider him capable of regaining his command. She could not propose such a scheme otherwise. After all he had confided in her, that felt like a betrayal.

"If you had such grave reservations about Lady Villiers, why am I only hearing them now?" he demanded in a tone as chill as the winter air that frosted the library windows.

His question rocked her back, putting her on the defensive. Her gaze shifted, guiltily. "Be-cause, I did not think it would do any good. I assumed there was no alternative to her ladyship. But when I saw how much you have come to care about the children, it gave me hope that you might be willing to intervene on their behalf."

An appalling suspicion took hold of Gideon. "You planned this from the very beginning, didn't you? Coaxing me to spend time with the girls, to become close to them so I could be persuaded to seek guardianship?"

Had their accidental meetings in the library also been in furtherance of her scheme? What about that impulsive embrace? Had she used her charms on a lonely man to lure him into spending time with her and her young pupils? Gideon cursed himself for a fool, being so quick to trust again after being betrayed. Worse yet, he had let the pretty Scottish governess far deeper into his heart and confidence than any of his officers aboard the *Integrity*.

The answer to his accusation was written plain on her pale features. "I...I...not from the very beginning. When you first came here, I didn't think you would make any better guardian for the girls than their aunt. But as I got to know you, it seemed you were the answer to my prayers."

"Your prayers?" Gideon infused the word with all the scorn he felt for his own foolish weakness. How could he have imagined a woman like her might take a fancy to a charmless old sea dog? To think he had fretted about injuring her reputation and her feelings, when her only interest in him had been to further her plans.

"So you believe the Lord and Master of the Universe dances to your tune, Miss Murray? I suppose you think He had a young man killed and my reputation dragged through the mud all for your convenience!" As if it wasn't daft enough of him to believe she might care for him, he had even begun to swallow all her moonshine about the power of prayer and God's personal interest in him.

"I think no such thing!" Her eyes blazed with violent indignation. "I do not believe God makes ill-fortune befall us. What happened on your ship was the doing of men who put their desire to dominate others ahead of anything else. But I *do* believe the Lord can bring good out of evil in answer to our prayers."

There was something dangerously appealing about that notion, but Gideon refused to surrender to it. Marian Murray had never cared for him except as a means to provide the sort of future she deemed best for his young cousins. "I fail to see how even God can answer both your prayers and mine when the things we want are so vastly opposed."

The hostile tension that had gripped Marian Murray seemed to let her go all at once. "I thought you would want to help Cissy and Dolly."

Those plaintive words posed a greater threat to Gideon's resolve than her earlier hostility. "I do, but I fail to see how my seeking guardianship would accomplish that."

"Why?" she challenged him again, but with less vigor, as if she knew it was hopeless. "Because you hold yourself partly to blame for what happened to that young midshipman? Because he was your responsibility and you feel you failed him?"

Hearing his deepest regrets laid bare that way shook Gideon to the core.

"Yes, if you must know." He turned and stalked toward the door. "Now I see nothing to be gained by discussing this matter any further. Your duty is to your pupils. Mine is to my ship and my crew."

"God forgives you," she called after him, her voice shrill with desperation. "Please do not punish the girls because you cannot forgive yourself!"

When he refused to rise to the bait, Miss Murray hurled one final accusation after him. "I thought you cared about Cissy and Dolly. Clearly you are capable of pretending greater feelings than you possess!"

Pretend *greater* feelings that he possessed? Absurd! When he recalled how it had taxed his self-possession to conceal the extent of his feelings for her, Gideon longed to turn back and set Miss Murray straight. But he knew he did not dare.

Chapter Fourteen

She'd had no right to accuse Gideon Radcliffe of pretending more affection than he felt.

In the week following his departure for London, Marian often recalled their final conversation with regret. It was not *his* fault she had come to care more for him than she had any right to. He had done nothing deliberate to encourage her. The fault was hers for reading more into his kind actions than he'd ever intended.

"I wish Cousin Gideon took us to London with him." The words burst out of Dolly one morning in the middle of their history lesson. "I miss him."

Marian stifled an almost overwhelming urge to agree. Finding she could not keep silent altogether, she offered a tepid reply. "Knightley Park does not seem quite the same without him."

Not the same at all. Indeed, it felt as if he had taken all the air and warmth and light away with him. Since his departure, Marian often caught herself listening for his footsteps or gazing out the window, hoping to glimpse him riding in the distance. More often than ever, she visited the library in the evenings. Not to borrow more books, but because it was there she felt a lingering echo of his presence most strongly.

"Perhaps Aunt Lavinia will take us to London when she comes," suggested Cissy, her nose buried in her book. Though she did not ask about Captain Radcliffe as incessantly as her sister, his going seemed to have left the child more subdued than ever.

The thought of Lady Villiers taking the girls anywhere sent a chill down Marian's back and loaded her with a crushing burden of guilt. God had presented her with an ideal means of delivering Cissy and Dolly from their aunt, but she had destroyed any hope of it. She should have persuaded Gideon gently rather than allowing his resistance to make her angry and spout hurtful words.

How could she blame him for his reluctance to take charge of his young cousins after his last effort to play a fatherly role had ended so disastrously? She'd mouthed glib platitudes about God's forgiveness, but would she ever be able to forgive herself for failing the girls in this most important task?

"I don't want to go with Aunt Lavinia." Dolly wriggled out of her seat and ran over to admire her toy boat. "She wouldn't take us anywhere interesting in London. I want to see all the ships on the River Thames."

With a sigh of impatience and regret, Marian went after the child. "You may play with your boat later. Now come back to the table and we'll have a geography lesson with your dissected puzzle."

"But this is the time for history," Cissy complained.

"Besides, we've put that silly old puzzle together so many times we could do it with our eyes closed."

"Well, I like it." Dolly stuck out her tongue at her sister.

Cissy glared back at her.

"Enough," Marian warned them both in a stern tone. "We'll do something different this time. I shall tell you a clue about the country and if you guess its name, I will give you the piece to add to the puzzle."

"That sounds like fun." Dolly skipped back to the table.

Cissy slammed her book shut.

Marian was about to speak sharply to her when she spied a film of unshed tears in the child's eyes. "Here's your first clue. It is a country on the North Sea and its capital city is Copenhagen."

As they proceeded with the game, using the Christmas gift Gideon had bought for Dolly, Marian knew she was right that the girls needed him far more than the Royal Navy did. She also believed they enriched his life beyond the measure of his naval duties. If only she had not allowed her secret feelings for him to interfere with the girls' interests, perhaps she could have made him see that, too.

She managed to get through the day by focusing her attention strictly on the children, trying to make up for how she had failed them. Once they were in bed she slipped down to the library for a half hour where she allowed herself to indulge in missing him, reliving the evenings they'd spent there discussing books and getting to know one another. But she did not choose a new book to read. Having read *Sense and Sensibility* through once, she'd already started on it again. Both the characters of Edward Ferrars and Colonel Brandon reminded her of Gideon. Reading about them made her feel a little closer to him.

As she slipped through the darkened nursery to her bedchamber, the sound of a sniffle stopped her. She held her breath, listening closely. Dolly's breath was coming in deep, slow gusts. Groping her way toward Cissy's bed, Marian perched on the edge.

"Are you feeling ill?" she whispered, reaching to lay her palm on the child's forehead. "Or did you have a bad dream?"

Cissy's face was a bit warm but not feverish. In answer to Marian's question, she shook her head.

"What's the matter, then?" Marian's hand trailed down to wipe a tear from the child's cheek. "Is it because of the captain going away? You don't talk about him all the time as Dolly does, but I believe you still miss him."

Cissy gulped for air as her small frame trembled with sobs. "It's m-my fault…he went away. Dolly said so. Be-because I wasn't…nice to him."

"Shh!" Marian gathered the child into her arms. "That isn't true at all. The captain had important business in London. I'm certain he misses you and Dolly as much as you miss him."

"Will he come ba-back?" The child's weeping quieted a little. "When he's taken care of that bus-business?"

Marian wished she could reassure Cissy that Gideon would return to Knightley Park. But she could not lie to the child. That would only make matters worse in the long run. "I'm not certain. We will have to hope and pray that he does. But if by chance he is not able to return soon, you must not think it is because of you."

If anyone was to blame, Marian knew it was her.

She sat with Cissy and rubbed her head until the child finally fell asleep. All the while, a silent prayer ran through her mind. "*Please, Heavenly Father, let Gideon Radcliffe have a change of heart. Bring him back to Knightley Park to seek guardianship of the girls. They need him and he needs them. Please, please make him see that.*"

Could Marian Murray seriously believe he would make a good guardian for Cissy and Dolly? That question and many others plagued Gideon on his long, cold journey to London. He knew he should be planning his defense for the upcoming inquiry, but somehow the future of those two dear girls seemed at least as important as his future in the Royal Navy.

As vigorously as he'd tried to deny the things Miss Murray had said, some of them rang uncomfortably true. He *did* feel responsible for Harry Watson's death, almost as much as if he'd committed the vile deed with his own hands. He hadn't protected the boy as he should. He'd placed too much trust in the wrong people and in his own authority. A distant, disinterested God might be able to forgive him, but his own conscience was a harsher tribunal.

As for showing more affection than he felt, that was patently absurd. Over the past weeks, he had fought against his reticent nature to demonstrate even a little of the feelings in his heart. He had not even admitted to himself how much the children...and their governess...had come to mean to him. Only when he reached London, with a hundred and twenty miles of frozen countryside between them, did he truly plumb the depths of his feelings.

An aching emptiness gnawed at him as if he had not eaten in days. Except that the void afflicted his chest rather than his stomach. The only remedy he could find was to reflect upon his memories of the time he'd spent with them—the evening at the pantomime, the concert they'd performed for him on Twelfth Night, even their Sunday morning attendance at church. Savoring such sweet memories helped fill the void, yet it made the ache of longing more acute.

As the days passed, he strove to distract himself by consulting with his counsel, reviewing his testimony for the inquiry, making contact with any retired naval officers who might testify to his character. Such activities helped to occupy his thoughts; but whenever his concentration lapsed, he found himself wondering if there had been more snow in Nottinghamshire. Had Dolly caught the cold? Had Marian read all the new books he'd purchased for the library?

With each day that passed, he grew sorrier for having reacted so angrily to her well-intended suggestion that he become the girls' guardian. He still felt like a fool that he'd misinterpreted her efforts to bring that about. But he no longer suspected she had deliberately sought to engage his affections to further her cause.

He knew he should be flattered that she considered him worthy to have charge of the children she loved so dearly. He wondered why she was so set against Lady

Villiers having the girls. The reasons she'd given him hardly sounded sufficient. Could it be that, having assumed a motherly role in the children's lives, she could not bear to step aside for another woman?

Gideon could understand such feelings. How would he take it, if Lady Villiers remarried and her new husband became a father figure to Cissy and Dolly? Though that man was nothing more than a shadowy abstraction who might not ever exist, he still roused Gideon's suspicion and hostility. How much more might the very real Lady Villiers loom as a threat to Marian Murray, who had no claim upon her young pupils except love?

At last the board of inquiry convened, and Gideon duly presented himself at the Admiralty to give evidence. As he entered the imposing Board Room, his gaze was drawn to an elaborate bay at the far end of the chamber. He could not help wondering what Dolly would think of the immense globe it held. No doubt Marian would be more interested in the tall, narrow bookcases that flanked the bay. Would Cissy ask why the big clock above it had only one hand rather than two? When he revealed that it was not a clock but a wind dial, Dolly would surely demand to know all about the workings of such an instrument.

One of the members of the inquiry board cleared his throat, reminding Gideon of his purpose there. "Now, Captain Radcliffe, if you would please give us an account of the events aboard HMS *Integrity* that led to your being suspended from command."

"Certainly." Gideon inhaled a deep breath and began to speak. To his relief, his earlier thoughts of Marian and the girls gave him confidence. He knew they had faith in him and would never believe the false accusations against him. "It began when the late Mister Watson was assigned to my crew as a midshipman...."

The officers and gentleman of the board listened gravely, a few nodding in agreement with some point he made. But others scowled as he spoke, their brows raised in dubious expressions. Gideon recalled how Marian had offered to pray that justice would be done in his case.

It appeared he would need all the prayers he could get.

Over a month had passed since Gideon Radcliffe left Knightley Park. Dolly no longer asked about him quite so often. Cissy never mentioned him at all. If Marian hadn't known better, she might have thought his visit was only a pleasant dream. Yet she found it hard to let go of that dream and the dwindling hope that Gideon might return before Lady Villiers arrived to collect the girls.

The clock in the library struck ten, jarring Marian from her concentration upon the newspaper. Every day she could get a copy of the paper, she brought it here to scan the pages, searching for any mention of Gideon's inquiry. Again today, she'd found nothing.

Folding up the newspaper with a sigh, Marian wished she had asked Gideon to write her with his news. Not that he would have been disposed to agree after the way they'd quarreled. But he might have sent a note to the girls at least.

Perhaps she had been right to claim that he pretended

to care for Cissy and Dolly more than he truly did. At the time, however, she'd been thinking more about his feelings for her.

Was it futile for her to keep searching the newspapers? For all she knew, the inquiry might have concluded days ago. If the press failed to report the fact, it could only be because Captain Radcliffe had been exonerated of all wrongdoing. Having been avid to publish every vile rumor against him, they would surely be embarrassed to be proven wrong.

Pausing behind the chair in which Gideon had sat so many evenings, Marian ran her hand over the upholstery where his head had once rested. If the men on that board of inquiry had any sense at all, they would have known at once that Captain Radcliffe was incapable of dishonorable conduct. As soon as they heard his testimony, they had likely found him *innocent* and dispatched him back to his ship. If he ever returned to Knightley Park in the future, she and the girls would be long gone.

Marian wrenched her hand away from the chair and marched out of the room. She must stop coming here so often to scrutinize the newspapers. Above all, she must stop pestering God with her incessant prayers to fetch Gideon back to Knightley Park. Either He was ignoring her prayers or He had given her an answer and that answer was no. All she could do now was ask for the strength to bear His will and pray that Lady Villiers would not separate her from the girls.

When she heard the front door open and shut, Marian thought it must be Mr. Culpepper checking that the house was well secured for the night. After an uncertain beginning, he and Captain Radcliffe had reached a point of mutual respect. With the captain gone, Mr. Culpepper seemed to have found fresh purpose in keeping Knightley Park running smoothly for his absent master.

The sound of footsteps behind her made Marian pause on the staircase and turn to bid the butler goodnight. So sure was her expectation of seeing Mr. Culpepper that for a moment she scarcely recognized the tall, tired-looking man standing there in his greatcoat.

When recognition finally dawned, it took her breath away. The newspaper she'd been holding fluttered to the floor as her hand flew to her chest.

"Gid—er…Captain, you're home!" Elation bubbled up within her until it felt as if she floated toward him. "Thank heaven you're back. I prayed you would change your mind!"

Somehow she managed to keep from throwing her arms around him. But she could not prevent her gaze from sinking deep into his. The shadow of anguish in his eyes shattered her fragile delight.

"What's wrong?" More than ever she yearned to take him in her arms. But that would only cause more trouble. "Are you ill?"

Gideon shook his head wearily and nodded toward the library door. "Only sick at heart."

Those words tore at her as if she had inflicted this suffering upon him. Had she? She'd prayed so fervently for his return, had she bullied God into granting her request, no matter what it cost Gideon?

"Did the board of inquiry hold you to blame for what happened on your ship?" Taking his arm, she led him into the library where they could talk without fear of interruption. "Then they must be a pack of fools!"

"They haven't...yet." Gideon followed her with ponderous steps. "But they will. I have no doubt. It will make no difference who else testifies or what other evidence is presented. Three members of the panel are related to the ones truly responsible. They will not want the taint of any wrongdoing to besmirch their family names."

"Are you certain?" She helped him out of his greatcoat and laid it over a nearby chair. "Perhaps it is not as bad as you think. If the board has not announced its findings yet, there may still be hope."

When she turned back toward him, she found that Gideon had sunk onto the chair he usually occupied— the one she had caressed only a few minutes ago, longing for his return. It went against his courteous nature to sit while she stood. That told Marian more about his state of despair than any words could.

Fearing he might try to rise, she knelt beside his chair. If only there was something she could do to relieve the sense of defeat she glimpsed in his eyes and in the bowing of his broad shoulders.

"I have seldom been more certain of anything in my life." He heaved an arid sigh. "My naval career is over, my reputation blackened beyond any hope of rehabilitation. I could tell by the tone of their questions, by the way they looked at me and each other. I am to be made a scapegoat for this whole unfortunate affair because I have no influence with those in power."

It was difficult to imagine a man of his integrity and strength being bullied, but that was how it sounded. The notion roused Marian's indignation. "If that's the way the Royal Navy is run, then perhaps you're better out of it."

His hands rested on the arms of the chair. Forgetting propriety, she covered one with hers, aching to offer him whatever comfort she could. "The people around here know what kind of man you really are. They won't take any notice of what some corrupt politicians in London have to say. Instead of being in command of a single ship, you'll have a whole estate. Just think what you can make of it. Perhaps this will turn out to be all the best for you."

If she'd hoped he might take consolation from her words, she was badly mistaken.

"It does not signify what is best for *me!*" He wrenched his hand out from beneath hers. "What about poor Watson? How is he to rest in peace when those responsible for his death are not brought to justice? What about the men and boys of my crew, serving under that ambitious villain and his pack of scoundrels? My return to command was their only hope of rescue!"

Conditions aboard that ship would be worse than the school of her youth with the strict, embittered teachers, the corrupt matron and the *great girls* who used their size and seniority to claim more than their share of what little food and warmth there was to be had. Only the solidarity of her circle of friends and the intervention of a kind headmistress had made existence bearable. What if someone had taken Miss Chapel away, for her own good and the benefit of a few others?

"I failed them." Gideon hunched forward, burying

his face in his hands. "First Harry Watson and now my whole crew."

Marian could almost feel the waves of misery rolling off him. This was not his fault. It was hers for misusing the power of prayer. Who was she to decide what was best for everyone? Had she used Cissy and Dolly's welfare as an excuse to keep Gideon around where she could pretend they were a happy family?

"You did not fail anyone." Instinctively she strove to comfort him as she would one of the children, wrapping her arms around him, drawing his head to rest against her shoulder, stroking his hair. "You tried your best to do what was right and protect those who needed it. I didn't understand. I am so sorry. I promised to pray you would get justice but…"

The whisper of his hair against her cheek and the lure of his fresh, briny scent overwhelmed her, making her forget what she meant to say. She turned her face toward his, grazing his cheek with her lips.

At the same instant, he tilted his head toward her. Their lips met.

At first, Marian could only think of her need to comfort him and to atone for what she'd done. Her lips moved against his, softly and slowly, offering a respite from his bitter regrets and feelings of failure. At the same time, her kiss implored his forgiveness. Though she had believed she cared for him, she had still been willing to disregard his needs and wishes to get what she wanted.

She cherished a flicker of satisfaction when Gideon stirred from his breathless stillness and began to return her kiss. His firm, daunting mouth relaxed, and his lips brushed against hers in a tender rhythm, accepting her consolation and granting forgiveness.

He brought his hands up to cradle her face. With a blissful sigh, Marian sank into the welcome warmth of their kiss. Her original motives of comfort and atonement melted away, exposing more vulnerable feelings beneath. She cared for Gideon Radcliffe in a way she had never expected to feel for any man, a way she'd never dared hope could be returned. She wanted nothing from him but the opportunity to share his company and provide him with whatever support and companionship he was willing to accept from her. As their kiss intensified, she opened her heart, laying it bare for him to claim.

A sudden, insistent rap on the library door made them spring apart with sharp gasps. Like a barrage of cannon fire, that sound heralded an invasion of the small, defenseless island of intimacy they'd created. The world crashed in on them with all its roles and expectations. Suddenly they were no longer simply two people sharing a tender moment. She was a hired servant who had no business embracing the master of the house.

"I'm sorry, Captain!" She pulled away and surged to her feet. "I did not mean to presume. I was only trying to make you feel better."

Her desperate apology collided with his. "Forgive me, Miss Murray. I should never have taken advantage of your kind gesture!"

Adding to the confusion, the butler called in, "Are you there, Captain? Is there anything you require, sir?"

Unable to bear the raw, inflamed feelings their kiss

had provoked, Marian flew to the door and flung it open. "The captain is here, Mr. Culpepper. He seemed quite exhausted when he arrived, so I helped him in. Now I must leave him to your capable ministrations and get back to the nursery."

She scarcely recognized her own voice, so shrill and breathless. The Scottish accent for which she'd often been ridiculed at school sounded more pronounced than ever.

"Thank you for your assistance, Miss Murray." Gideon Radcliffe's voice rang out behind her. Cold and sharp as the icicles hanging from the eaves of the house, each word pierced her.

It was clear he wanted to pretend their kiss had never taken place. No doubt he wished it hadn't. She had hurled herself upon him in a moment of weakness, tempting him to forget himself.

"Think nothing of it, Captain." She sought to assure him that she would not divulge their secret embrace. "I hope you are soon recovered from your journey. Good night."

With that, she slipped past the bewildered butler and fled.

How could he have exploited Marian Murray's kind attempt to console him?

For the next few days, as she made a determined effort to avoid him, Gideon rebuked himself repeatedly. It was clear he had upset her, perhaps frightened her with his show of unwelcome ardor. Was she also afraid that being discovered alone with him in the library might damage her reputation?

He longed to reassure her that he would do the honorable thing and make her an offer of marriage...if that was what she wanted. Under the circumstances, that course of action appealed to him intensely. Now that it appeared certain he would not be returning to command, the prospect of settling down at Knightley Park and taking a wife offered him a renewed sense of purpose.

As Marian had tried to tell him, it seemed the Lord might have provided an opportunity for something good to come out of the ruin of his naval career. He still regretted the circumstances in which he'd left his crew. But perhaps if he prayed upon the matter, he might receive some divine guidance on how to assist his men. In the meantime, it was quite possible his cousin's young daughters did need him more than the crew of the *Integrity*. Perhaps almost as much as he needed them.

He longed to see the girls again, yet he shrank from imposing his company upon their governess when it seemed clear she did not want it. Would she look upon a marriage proposal from him in the same light? Might she feel pressured to wed a man she did not love because he had damaged her reputation and because he might be willing to seek guardianship of the children she adored?

He would rather continue on as they had been than have her feel trapped in a marriage and gradually grow to resent him. He had failed too many people he cared about. He could not bear to fail her, too.

But what action should he take? During his naval career, Gideon had been accustomed to making swift, definite decisions, often under considerable pressure, with lives at stake. Whatever the outcome, he had been able to learn from it, live with it and move forward. Young Watson's death and the inquiry had changed that, making him second-guess his actions and bitterly regret his mistakes.

Staring out the great bow window of the Chinese drawing room, he contemplated the pristine beauty of the frozen lake and snow dusted trees. One day soon, the ice and snow would melt and new life would quicken according to an ageless plan. Perhaps the time had come to stop relying solely on his own all-too-fallible strength and judgment and instead seek divine guidance.

"Heavenly Father," he whispered, possessed by an unaccountable conviction that he was being heard. "Please help me do what is right for Marian and the children."

What would happen now, he wondered. Would the Lord provide some sort of sign? Or would he suddenly know beyond doubt what he should do? Neither of those things happened. He was still as confused as ever about whether he ought to propose to Marian Murray. Both choices before him seemed likely to end in the one way he could not bear—with her hating him.

Had his prayer gone unanswered because he had not used the proper form? Must he kneel and bow his head as if he were in church?

Church. He had been so lost in regrets and indecision that he had scarcely noticed what day of the week it was. Now he realized tomorrow would be Sunday. Was that a random thought of his own or a divine nudge in the right direction? He might never know for certain, but Gideon chose to believe the latter.

* * *

The next morning he lingered in the entry hall, waiting for the girls and their governess to appear. He had not been there long when he heard the approach of footsteps and the chatter of familiar voices. A moment later, they descended the stairs.

"Cousin Gideon!" Dolly leapt down the last three steps and charged toward him. "Martha told us you'd come back. We begged and begged to see you, but Miss Marian said you were very tired from your journey and needed to rest."

Her rapturous welcome buoyed his spirits. Leaning forward, Gideon caught the child in his arms and lifted her into a fond embrace. Dolly returned it so vigorously, she nearly throttled him.

"That was very considerate of her." Gideon set the child back on her feet and turned his attention to her sister. Cissy might not express her emotions as emphatically as Dolly, but that did not mean she felt them any less. "But I am quite well rested now and looking forward to escorting my favorite ladies to church."

He cast a fleeting glance toward Marian, hoping she would understand that he included her among his "favorite ladies." Then he knelt in front of Cissy, who stared at him with unsettling intensity. "I didn't think you would come back," she whispered. "But you did."

When Gideon opened his arms, she surprised him by hurling herself into his embrace. Her parents had gone to a place from which they could never return. He understood how important it was to her that he had come back. He pressed a kiss to the crown of her head.

Until he'd seen and held them again, Gideon did

not fully fathom how much he'd missed them and how deeply he had come to love them. He glanced up at Marian. Silently, he tried to tell her she had been right all along. He did need the girls, and it seemed they needed him. Perhaps when he told her he intended to seek guardianship, she might look more favorably upon him as a suitor.

As Dolly chattered away on the drive to church and Cissy gazed at him, her eyes shining with newfound trust, Gideon felt the awkwardness between him and Marian beginning to ease. It seemed she was willing to forgive and forget the inexcusable liberty he had taken, perhaps on the grounds of his distress over the inquiry. While he welcomed her forgiveness, he knew he would never be able to forget that wondrous moment of communion between them.

When they arrived at the church, the other parishioners offered Gideon a cordial welcome home. Perhaps Marian had been right to reassure him that the local people would not hold the inquiry's decision against him.

During his sailing days, Gideon had often been moved by the distant majesty of the Almighty and the grandeur of His Creation. On a clear night in the middle of the ocean, he had gazed up into the limitless firmament crowded with blazing stars. He had watched the sun rise in all its rosy splendor, on the vast eastern horizon of the Pacific. But never in his life, before that morning, had he felt the presence of God so warmly wrapped around him.

By the time they returned home after the service, his mind was bubbling with plans for Knightley Park, for the girls—and perhaps with God's help—for him and Marian.

Mr. Culpepper met them in the entry hall when they arrived home. Before Gideon could get the door closed, the butler announced. "A guest has arrived while you were at church, Captain. The late Mrs. Radcliffe's sister, Lady Villiers."

The girls accompanied them gladly back to the house and
Marian...

As Gideon feared that Marian might balk when they
returned to that same room and post to the hay-stack...
The room announced he chose the softest sofas, and
to all charmed Cissy and Lily. The have found it
give Gideon...

Chapter Fifteen

Mr. Culpepper's announcement struck Marian like a bolt of lightning. For months she had dreaded this moment, worked and planned to avoid its consequences. Now just when she had hope God might answer her desperate prayers, it had come. Worse yet, the girls seemed to welcome it—Cissy certainly did.

"Aunt Lavinia!" The child seized her sister by the hand and pulled Dolly off in search of their aunt.

And Gideon…what about him? He cast a furtive glance at Marian, then followed the girls.

Breathing a quick prayer for strength, she hurried after him.

"Aunt Lavinia!" she heard Cissy's voice from the Chinese drawing room, more animated than in a very long time. "It's so good to see you. We were afraid you might never come."

When Marian and Gideon entered the drawing room, they found the girls being petted and embraced by their aunt. "Oh, my dearest darlings, how good it is to see you both again! I was quite prostrate with grief when

I received the sad news about your poor, dear papa. I started for home just as soon as I was fit to travel, but I was in Naples, which is an excessively long way. And travel in the winter is such an ordeal. There were times I feared I might succumb to the elements!"

Her ladyship did not appear any the worse for her recent ordeal. At least not to Marian, who stood back quietly observing the scene. Lady Villiers's arrival had thrust her back into the role of servant after months of feeling like something more.

The girls' aunt was dressed and coiffed in the height of fashion. The rich peacock blue of her traveling gown set off her fine eyes and raven hair to perfection. She resembled her late sister in beauty, if little else, with fine features, luxurious eyelashes and a pert little mouth.

In contrast to such an elegant creature, Marian felt plainer and dowdier than ever. But that was nothing to the way her heart plunged when Lady Villiers paused in her gushing attentions to the girls and glanced up at Gideon. Her eyes fairly blazed with predatory interest, and her lips curved into a beguiling smile.

She rose gracefully and targeted Gideon with the full barrage of her considerable charm. "Bless me! Here I have been rattling on, so delighted to see you both again, that I am all sixes and sevens. Pray, my darlings, introduce me to this handsome gentleman."

"What handsome gentleman?" Dolly's nose wrinkled in a puzzled frown.

"She means Cousin Gideon, of course." Cissy shot the younger girl a glare of disdain. "Aunt Lavinia, this is Papa's cousin, Captain Radcliffe. He is the new master of Knightley Park. Cousin Gideon, this is Mama's sister, Lady Villiers."

The child delivered the introduction with impeccable decorum, just the way her governess had taught her. But Marian could take no pride in the accomplishment of her young pupil at the moment. Instead, she stood transfixed as Lady Villiers swept Gideon a flirtatious curtsy.

"It is a pleasure to make your acquaintance at last, Captain Radcliffe. To think you are dear Daniel's cousin and I am Emma's sister. That almost makes us family...though not *too* closely connected."

Not too closely connected for what? Marian's lips drew into a tight, disapproving line. Though they had met once before, the girls' aunt did not even flick a glance in her direction. It was as if she had been rendered invisible.

Lady Villiers extended her hand toward Gideon. It was too high and in quite the wrong position to shake. Clearly she expected a more gallant greeting.

"Welcome to Knightley Park, your ladyship." The warmth of Gideon's greeting was tempered with a certain endearing awkwardness. He bowed low over Lady Villiers's hand but did not raise it to his lips. "I understand you have been traveling on the Continent. I trust you enjoyed your tour."

"Immensely!" Her ladyship sank onto the settee and pulled Cissy and Dolly up on either side of her, an arm draped around each child. "Seeing all the sights for myself at last was such an adventure."

"Cousin Gideon has had lots of adventures," Dolly

boasted. "He has circum…circum…he's sailed around the world."

"Has he, indeed?" Her ladyship lavished the captain with an admiring smile. "How very fortunate I am to make the acquaintance of a bold adventurer! You must tell me about all the exotic places you have visited, Captain."

"Perhaps we can exchange accounts of our travels." Gideon started to take a seat, then recalled Marian's presence. "Come join us, Miss Murray."

Marian would rather have fled to the nursery to sort out her confused feelings and consider the consequences of Lady Villiers's arrival, but she was not at liberty to come and go as she pleased. She was hired to do her employers' bidding, and the master of Knightley Park had asked her to be seated.

At last Lady Villiers deigned to notice Marian, flicking a dismissive glance in her direction. "Oh, yes, the governess."

Edging around the perimeter of the room, Marian perched on the window seat. It was close enough to the others to satisfy the captain's invitation to join them while still being in keeping with her peripheral place in the household.

Once Marian had taken a seat, the captain sank onto his chair. "Miss Murray has been much more to your nieces than a governess in the past months. She has been mother, father, teacher and advocate. The girls were very fortunate to be in her care during this difficult time."

If Marian had needed anything to make her care for him more, his gallant tribute would have accomplished that. But she already cared for him far too much. The cruel stab of jealousy she felt watching Lady Villiers flirt with him warned Marian she must quash those dangerous feelings or risk worse misery than she had known since her school days.

"How commendable." Her ladyship sounded surprised that Marian could be capable of such conduct. "Emma and I had such horrible governesses when we were girls. I pleaded with Father to send us to school where we might have the advantage of many different teachers."

School. Marian barely stifled a whimper. Her worst fears about Lady Villiers had been right. The moment she took the girls from Knightley Park, their aunt would seek to place them in a school, all the while assuring herself it was in their best interests. And there was nothing Marian could do to prevent her. Any effort she made would seem like a selfish attempt to keep from losing her position.

"Did you enjoy your time at school, Captain?" Her ladyship seemed eager to turn the conversation back to him. "Which one did you attend, pray? You have the distinguished look of an Eton man to me."

"I received my education in the Royal Navy," Gideon replied. "If I'd had a choice, I would have preferred to remain at home with a governess or tutor."

Lady Villiers gave a trill of high-pitched laughter that pierced Marian like shards of glass under her skin. "I suppose we all hanker for whatever we have not had. Your naval training seems to have made a fine man of you."

Marian could not dispute that, though she resented

Lady Villiers for being free to flatter him so blatantly when she had been obliged to guard every word.

Gideon did not acknowledge her ladyship's praise. "Surely you must admit your nieces do credit to Miss Murray's tutelage."

"They are perfectly adorable!" Her ladyship hugged Cissy and Dolly close, attention the girls appeared to welcome. "So like their dear mama. I am certain they would flourish under any circumstances. But come, Captain, you promised me stories of your travels."

Gideon obliged her with an account of his visit to New Zealand, a story he had shared with Marian and the girls some weeks before. To Marian's admittedly biased ears, he did not sound as relaxed and animated as he had then. Dolly interrupted him often in an effort to enliven the tale.

Marian itched to remind the child to mind her manners, but bit her tongue for fear it would only rouse the veiled antagonism she sensed from Lady Villiers. The last thing Cissy and Dolly needed was for their aunt to have any excuse to dismiss her. She would speak to Dolly later in the privacy of the nursery.

As the afternoon progressed, Marian sat watching from the fringes while Lady Villiers usurped the place she had so recently enjoyed in their little family. Her thoughts turned to Gideon's inquiry and his misery at the prospect of losing his command and reputation. She could not help feeling that her prayers might have contributed to the situation. At the very least, she had failed to keep her original promise to pray that he would get justice.

She must find some way to make things right for

him. But how? If a man like him felt bullied, without influence or power, how could someone in her humble circumstances be of any assistance? She could appeal to God again, but would He pay any heed after she had changed her mind so often about what she wanted? It would be tantamount to taking the favor He'd granted her and throwing it back in His face. Gideon had been right—the Creator of the Universe was not a tailor to be bidden to make minute alterations to the garment of life.

It was up to her to help Gideon receive the justice he'd been denied. She could think of only one person who might possess the power to intervene on Gideon's behalf. Perhaps it would do no good, but she must try or she could never truly claim to care for him.

Lady Villiers did not appear to be in any hurry to leave Knightley Park. As the days began to lengthen and winter loosened its grip on the countryside, Gideon could not decide whether to be irritated or relieved. The latter, surely, for as long as her ladyship remained under his roof, Cissy and Dolly did, too. And so did Marian Murray.

Not that relations between him and the girls' governess had recovered since their kiss. It seemed to have transformed her back into the quiet, dour woman he recalled from the earliest days of their acquaintance. To see her now, no one would suspect Miss Murray was capable of chasing about with the children, laughing uproariously at a pantomime, or singing wistful Scottish love songs. No one would believe she could be such a sympathetic listener, such a dispenser of wise, compassionate advice. But he knew all those things and more. They made him yearn to have *that* woman back again.

He'd hoped by keeping his distance and treating her with temperate civility, he might coax her out again. But so far it had not worked. Miss Murray took every opportunity to remind him that she was an employee and not a member of the family, as she had once seemed. Was she trying to remind him that he had taken advantage of her position in his household to impose his unwanted attentions upon her? She need not have bothered, for he was well aware of how he had destroyed the fragile trust between them.

Much as he wished he could ask how to get it back, he feared any such overture would only make matters worse. Besides, when would he have an opportunity to broach the subject? She never visited the library in the evenings anymore. At least not during those rare occasions when he could escape Lady Villiers's company to seek refuge there, as he had this evening.

Or perhaps he had not escaped after all.

Without even the most cursory excuse for a knock, the library door opened—first a crack, then flung wide.

"There you are!" Lady Villiers invaded his sanctuary. "I declare, one would think we were playing hide-and-seek. Do you know, this is one room of the house where I've never been before."

She glanced around at the tall shelves of books, and her nose wrinkled in distaste. "Now I can see why. It is dreadfully gloomy. How do you abide it? And what is that odor?"

Stifling a sigh, Gideon rose from his chair. "I presume

you mean the aroma of old books. It is more pleasant to me than any perfume."

Her ladyship gave an indulgent chuckle. "My dear Captain, you are delightfully droll! You need someone in your life to draw you out—someone to take care of you."

Gideon could not dispute that. He did need such a person, but he already had her in his life. Not only had Marian Murray drawn him out and taken care of him, she'd slipped into his private sanctum and enriched it with her presence. She had also helped him draw close to the girls...and closer to God. Was it selfish of him to want more than that from her?

Yet the way Lady Villiers spoke of it made him uneasy. Since coming to Knightley Park, she had gone out of her way to be attentive and agreeable, but Gideon had not warmed to her. Though she had not mentioned any desire to take the girls away, it seemed to hang in the air like an unspoken threat. Perhaps the time had come to stop this game of cat and mouse and bring the subject out in the open to find out where they stood.

"That is very perceptive of you, Lady Villiers." He motioned her to take a seat. "I have come to realize I also need someone of whom I can take care. During my time at sea, I did my best to look after my crew. Since coming to Knightley Park, I have taken great satisfaction in helping to care for your nieces."

"And a splendid job you have made of it, dear Captain." Her ladyship perched on the edge of her seat, leaning toward him. "The girls both seem so well and happy, considering what they have been through, losing their papa. I believe they have found a most admirable substitute for their father in you."

Her words touched Gideon. Perhaps he had misjudged the lady. "That is most kind of you to say. I have become fonder of the girls than I ever expected. Their welfare and happiness have become among my chief concerns."

Lady Villiers nodded. "As they have long been of mine, ever since Daniel and Emma asked Huntley and me to be the girls' godparents. To think I am the only one of the four left to take charge of those dear children."

She heaved a poignant sigh. "It comforts me to discover I am not entirely alone in my affection for them."

"You are not." Gideon assured her. "The girls also have me and Miss Murray."

"Their governess?" Her ladyship's handsome features twisted into a most unattractive sneer. "I will concede she is a considerable improvement over the gargoyles who made my girlhood so miserable, but it is her job to care for the children. That scarcely compares to your admirable concern, which is motivated solely by kindness and family feeling."

Gideon supposed he must make allowances for her ladyship's coolness toward Marian Murray, given her past experience, yet it never failed to grate on him. He must give Lady Villiers credit for beginning to acknowledge Marian's worth. In time, he had faith Marian would win her over entirely.

"My concern for the girls leads me to believe it would not be in their best interests to remove them from Knightley Park." There, he had said it. Now, before her ladyship could object, he rushed on to bolster his argument. "They have been deprived of both their parents at a young age. They need the stability and continuity of the only home they have ever known."

Gideon realized he was repeating the plea Marian had made to him when he first came to Knightley Park. He was grateful he had heeded it. Now, if only Lady Villiers would.

His heart leapt when she met his suggestion with a brilliant smile. "I declare, Captain, you and I are of one mind! After seeing their situation for myself, I had come to the very same conclusion. Only I did not know quite how to raise the matter."

A powerful wave of relief swept Gideon out of his chair to kneel before the lady, seize her hand and press it to his lips. "My dear Lady Villiers, words can scarcely convey my gratitude to you. I vow I will do everything within my power to see that your nieces are given the best possible upbringing. Of course, you will always be welcome to visit the girls at Knightley Park whenever you wish."

"Visit?" Her ladyship laughed in a way that made Gideon think of a chandelier tinkling as it crashed to the floor. "Oh, Captain, you are jesting again, aren't you?"

Her fingers gripped his with astonishing power for such a dainty creature. "Not only do the girls need to remain in familiar surroundings, they also need a new mother and father to replace those they lost. Since you are in possession of Knightley Park and I am the girls' godmother, is it not obvious we should marry and raise them together?"

Her ladyship's proposition struck Gideon dumb. Perhaps it should have been obvious what direction she'd been going all along. With his thoughts fixed on Marian and his worry that the girls might be taken from him, he had been blind to where it all might lead. He had taken no evasive action whatsoever. Instead he had sailed into an ambush.

"It is the perfect solution, don't you agree?" Lady Villiers took advantage of his stunned silence to rattle on. "We both adore the girls and it can be no secret what a great fancy I have taken to you. In spite of your diffidence, I believe you are not indifferent to me. Ours will be a match made in heaven!"

With that, the lady abruptly released his hands to seize him around the neck and pull his face toward hers, as her lips puckered for a kiss.

A match made in heaven? Hardly!

As Lady Villiers's declaration drifted through the half open library door, Marian stood frozen, staring into the room at Gideon on his knees in front of her ladyship. As she watched, they sealed their betrothal with a kiss. Her gorge rose and her heart plummeted.

Ever since Lady Villiers's arrival, Marian had been torn over whether to speak or keep silent. Now it was too late.

Concern for Cissy and Dolly had urged her to tell Gideon all the reasons her ladyship would not be a suitable guardian for the girls. Her lavish style of living and the debts that went with it. Her constant travel in search of a rich husband. Her unsavory set of friends known for gambling and loose living. Marian had overheard Mr. Radcliffe complain of those things when his sister-in-law had written to him for money. She'd been reluctant to reveal what she knew for fear Lady Villiers would learn of it and immediately remove the girls from her care.

At first, her ladyship's flirtatious manner toward Gideon had roused Marian's jealousy, yet she had assumed it was how the woman behaved around every new man she encountered. But as the days passed, Marian began to suspect Lady Villiers had set her cap for Gideon. But how could she put him on guard without appearing like a spiteful woman scorned, which perhaps she was.

Not that Gideon had scorned her, exactly. He was far too kind a gentleman for that. But the way he'd reacted to their kiss made it clear he regretted succumbing to an unfortunate impulse with a woman in her position. He was too honorable to lay the blame on her, where it belonged. Instead, he chose to pretend it had never happened. Though her reasonable, cautious side agreed that might be for the best, another part of her wished he had acknowledged her feelings and gently explained why he could not return them.

Seeing him in an embrace with another woman set a cruel black beast to maul her heart.

Marian clapped a hand over her mouth to stifle a whimper of pain that might draw attention to her presence. Then she turned and fled back to the nursery. Her battered, aching heart wanted nothing more than for her to pack a bag and slip away from this house, never to return. Practicality and duty forbade it. She could not afford to leave without another position in place, and for that she would need a satisfactory reference from someone at Knightley Park. Besides, she asked herself as she slipped into the dark, quiet nursery, how could she think of leaving Cissy and Dolly after all the losses they'd experienced in their young lives?

As she changed into her nightclothes, Marian began to tremble, though not from the cold, to which she was accustomed. Once she was swathed in her nightgown and wrapper with a nightcap over her braided hair, she knelt by her bed, seeking comfort and strength in prayer.

"Heavenly Father, please…" What should she ask— that God intervene to prevent Gideon from marrying Lady Villiers? But what might the consequences be? What if her ladyship became so vexed, she took the girls away at once? "I want what is best for all of us, the girls especially. But I cannot be certain what that is. Only You can."

She'd convinced herself that Gideon's coming to Knightley Park might be part of God's plan. What if Lady Villiers had a role to play in that plan, too? Was it possible she had misjudged the woman, just as she'd initially misjudged Gideon Radcliffe? Perhaps being married to such a good man and serving as a mother to the girls might make her ladyship a better person, give purpose and meaning to her shallow, aimless life.

"I see now that I haven't always trusted You as I should, Father. There have been so many times when I thought You weren't responding to my prayers because You didn't give me exactly what I wanted. Please forgive me for that. I didn't understand."

She should have, though. Perhaps not when she was

a child, but lately when she'd been responsible for the care of the Radcliffe girls. Much as she loved Dolly, she would never give the child everything she asked for. The result would be indigestion, ill-humor from being up too late, perhaps broken bones from sliding down the banisters. Nor could she always indulge Dolly at Cissy's expense—that would not be fair. A headstrong, young child like Dolly had no way of knowing what was best for her.

Compared to the eternal wisdom of the Lord, Marian realized she must seem even less than a child. How could she expect a loving God to give her everything she prayed for when those things might not be best for her and others? Once she acknowledged that, there was only one prayer she could lift to Heaven.

"Father, thank You for all the blessings You have given me. Wonderful friends and a good education to enable me to earn a living. A comfortable life at Knightley Park with a family who always treated me well."

And Gideon. She must not forget him. Even though they could not be as close as she would like, his presence in her life was a blessing she would always cherish.

It wasn't easy for her to surrender control after all those years at school fighting for what she and her friends needed to survive. Yet Marian sensed she must learn to trust in God's love and care for everyone involved...even her ladyship.

"Thank You, Lord, for bringing Gideon into my life. Even if nothing can ever come of my feelings for him, our acquaintance has enriched my life beyond measure.

As for what will happen between him and Lady Villiers, I leave that in Your hands. All I ask is that You grant me the patience and strength to play my part. Amen."

With that she crawled into bed and tried to sleep. She would need her rest to face what tomorrow might bring.

Chapter Sixteen

"You wanted to see me, Captain?" When Marian Murray entered the dining room the following evening, her brow furrowed and her gaze moved restlessly.

Was she alarmed to find him alone there, without Lady Villiers or even any of the servants?

"I did." Gideon rose and gestured toward a chair he had pulled up near his end of the table. "Thank you for joining me, Miss Murray. I have a rather important decision to make, and there is no one whose counsel I value more than yours."

"Thank you, sir." She caught her lower lip between her teeth as she moved toward the table. "I hope you know I wish the very best for you, always."

Gideon nodded as she took her seat. Now that the time had come, he was not altogether certain how to begin. There was no use beating about the bush, he decided. Better to have out with it. "Lady Villiers and I have been discussing the girls' future."

A soft sigh escaped Marian's lips. "And what have you decided?"

"Nothing yet for certain." That was not altogether true. He might not know precisely what he meant to do, but he knew what he would *not* do. He hoped the advice Marian offered him would give a clue to her feelings. Lady Villiers's disconcerting kiss had given him a hopeful insight. Now he needed to find further evidence to support the conclusion he yearned to believe.

"Her ladyship suggested she and I should marry so we could raise Cissy and Dolly together."

Marian showed no sign of surprise at his announcement. Her luminous brown eyes did not widen. Her dark brows did not rise. Her soft, generous lips did not fall open or tighten into a disapproving line. It was as if she had expected this all along.

Faced with her disappointing silence, Gideon was obliged to continue. "I know the girls' well-being has always been of the utmost importance to you."

"Indeed it has, Captain," she murmured.

It was a priority he had come to share, but surely there must be a limit to what they were willing to sacrifice for the children's sake.

"I would like your opinion of her ladyship's plan." As he watched her trying to decide his future, Gideon found himself picturing her glare of outrage when Dolly had barreled into him. Her uncertainty when they'd first encountered one another in the library and discovered their mutual love of books. Her sitting with him and the girls in church, head reverently bowed in prayer.

He did not want to lose her or be responsible for the girls losing her. That was why he must be quite certain of her feeling before he dared to reveal his.

Marian sat tall on her chair and squared her shoulders. Gideon could picture her as a child, gamely sticking up for her school friends. "I think it would be good for the girls to be raised by two loving parents, Captain."

Her answer took the breath out of him, like a hard blow deep in the belly. It was all he could do to keep from flinching. When he finally had command of his voice again, he ventured, "I am surprised to hear you say that. As I recall, you had grave reservations about her ladyship's suitability to bring up Cissy and Dolly."

"If you'll recall, sir, my objections were to her way of living. I believe marriage to you would have a steadying influence upon her ladyship. It would also mean the girls could stay at Knightley Park with you."

It sounded as if she'd already given the matter a great deal of thought. Had she foreseen Lady Villiers's intentions all along? Then why had she not warned him? Did she truly want to see him with another woman?

"There is only one thing I would ask of you, Captain." Marian's skittish gaze calmed and focused directly upon him, pleading for agreement.

"What is that, pray?"

"That you will not send the girls away to school." One of her hands came to rest upon the table reaching toward him. Before Gideon could take her hand, she pulled it back again. "That is what I have been trying to prevent ever since you came to Knightley Park. I swear I am not asking because I fear to lose my position."

"Of course not." Gideon wished she had permitted him to hold her hand, so he could give her fingers a reassuring squeeze. "I would never suspect it of you."

Apparently his words accomplished his aim. The tension that had gripped her features eased. "Thank you, Captain. I appreciate your faith in me. I know not all schools are as bad as the one I attended, yet I still do not believe any school would provide the girls with a better education than they can receive here at home."

She seemed ready with many more arguments. Much as he enjoyed listening to the sound of her voice, Gideon could not bear to keep her in suspense. "Let me assure you, I have no intention of sending the girls away from Knightley Park until they are ready and wish to go."

Marian let out a slow, shaky breath. "I am vastly relieved to hear it, sir. Will that be all, Captain?"

Preoccupied with his bitter disappointment that she had urged him to marry another woman, Gideon muttered, "I beg your pardon?"

"Was there anything else you wished to say to me, sir? If not, I should get back to the nursery."

Of course there was more he wanted to say to her, but did he dare? If he kept silent, they could go back to their previous arrangement, pretending to be a family. But that was no longer enough to satisfy him. Yet, if he spoke, it might frighten Marian away. He cared too much for Cissy and Dolly to want to be responsible for that.

Not trusting himself to speak, he replied with a brief nod.

Marian rose and turned to go, but at the last moment, she paused and looked back. "I wish you joy in your marriage, Captain."

Was it his imagination, or did her voice catch on the word *marriage?*

Torn by conflicting desires, Gideon raised a silent prayer. *Lord, please help me do what is right and true.*

True—what had made him add that? A verse from the Bible flitted through his mind. *"Know ye the truth and the truth shall set ye free."* He had concealed his feelings from the woman he cared for, giving himself all manner of noble excuses for his silence. But his true motive had been fear that she could not return his feelings. That fear had built a stout bastion to protect his heart. But lately it had become more like a prison.

Expecting Marian to set him free, by declaring her feelings without knowing his, was cowardly, and not at all fair to her.

By the time all that passed through his mind, she had gone through the door and was just closing it behind her.

"Wait!" Gideon forced the word out past the lump in his throat.

Marian peeped back in, her brows raised in a wordless question.

Trusting that the truth would set him free, he willed himself to continue. "There is one other thing I would like to discuss with you, if I may?"

Could he not let her get away before her composure deserted her entirely? Marian strove to stifle her impatience with Gideon. It was not fair to expect him to realize how difficult this was for her, when he had no idea how much she cared for him. Had she not just wished him joy in his marriage to another woman?

Determined not to embarrass herself with an emotional outburst, she inhaled a deep breath and headed back into the dining room. "What else did you want to talk about, sir?"

She closed the door behind her but refused to approach him any closer, for fear he might glimpse a suspicious trace of moisture in her eyes.

"To begin with, I wanted to thank you."

"For what, Captain?" For not creating any obstacles to his marriage, perhaps, by threatening to tell Lady Villiers about the tender kiss they'd shared? Surely he could not believe her capable of such conduct?

"For helping me get to know Cissy and Dolly. They have brought joy and purpose to my life that I would never have discovered without your help. I have come to believe you may be right about God caring for me enough to give me what I truly need rather than what I thought I wanted."

A sense of bittersweet joy welled up in Marian to think she had helped Gideon find faith and love...even if it could not be with her. Her self-control was too fragile to permit her to speak. She acknowledged his thanks with a nod and a tremulous smile.

That seemed to be enough for Gideon. "There is almost nothing I would not do for the girls. But even for their sakes and in spite of your kind advice, I cannot wed a woman I do not love."

Gideon was not going to marry Lady Villiers after all? Marian clamped her lips together to contain a cheer. She was not certain how she could have watched the man she cared for wed to another woman—especially one she could not abide.

But that happy thought soon gave way to an alarming one. "But what about the girls? Lady Villiers will take them from you now! I fear she may put them in a school somewhere, then go live off their money."

Gideon took several steps toward her, then stopped abruptly a short distance away. "I was afraid of that, too, but you need not fret. I was able to persuade her ladyship to sign over guardianship of the girls to me."

Had she heard right or was this all a dream? "H-how did you manage that?"

Gideon gave a self-deprecating shrug. "It was not as difficult as you might think. I may not have a great deal of experience with women, but I have known enough grasping, unscrupulous people to recognize one. I offered Lady Villiers a very generous sum to appoint me as guardian to her nieces. We went into Newark today to have a solicitor draw up the papers."

It *was* true! From the nursery window, Marian had glimpsed them driving off toward town. She'd assumed they must be going to purchase a wedding ring.

Gideon gave a soft chuckle. "Her ladyship was all too eager to accept my money without having to endure marriage to a dry old stick like me."

"In that case, Lady Villiers is very foolish." Joy and relief loosened Marian's guard on her tongue. "No amount of money would be worth giving up the honor and pleasure of being married to such a wonderful man."

She bowed her head to avoid his gaze and clenched her lips tightly together to keep any more unwelcome revelations from slipping out. But that was rather like shutting the stable door after the horse had bolted.

Perhaps she need not worry, though. Gideon had shown himself willing to ignore worse lapses in propriety than that.

But not this time.

"Do you mean that?" he asked in an anxious tone. "Or were you only trying to spare my feelings?"

It would be prudent to seize upon the convenient excuse he'd offered her. But Marian could not bring herself to deny her feelings for him so blatantly.

"Of course I meant it," she snapped, half angry with him for making her admit it. "Now, if that is all, I will beg you excuse me."

"There is just one more thing."

What now? Marian wanted to make as dignified an exit as possible under the circumstances and try to forget her latest gaffe. She glanced up to find that Gideon had drawn closer to her. If she extended her hand, she could touch him.

"There is one point upon which I agree with her ladyship." Gideon's deep mellow voice seemed to penetrate to her heart and caress it. "I reckon it would be good for Cissy and Dolly to have two loving parents again. As excellent a governess as you have been to them, I believe you would make an even better mother."

Could Gideon possibly mean what her hopeful heart suspected? Surely not, cautious reason protested. For a penniless governess like her to secure a husband with wealth and property was like something out of a nursery tale.

She was too much accustomed to difficulties and disappointments to trust this unaccountable good fortune. "B-but you said that even for the girls' sake, you could not wed."

"I beg you quote me correctly." His strong, warm hand clasped her icy fingers. "What I said was that I could not marry a woman *I did not love.* I assure you, there will be no risk of that if you consent to be my wife."

Marian's mouth opened and closed, but she could not coax any words out. Her heart seemed to swell in her chest, so full of love and happiness that she feared it would burst. This was a blessing far beyond any she would have dared to pray for, yet here it was—hers for the taking. All her past hurts and deprivations made her treasure it that much more.

But Gideon could not tell all that was going on inside her. Instead, he saw only her hesitation to accept his proposal and perhaps the glint of a tear in her eye. "If I have mistaken your feelings and you cannot return mine, I beg you not to feel obliged to accept my proposal for the sake of the children. Whatever your answer, I would never think of parting you from them."

The look of bitter disappointment was etched so clearly upon his features that Marian could not doubt the sincerity of his offer.

When he tried to release her hand, she clung to his and refused to let go. Concern for his feelings shattered the doubts that had frozen her tongue. "Please, Gideon, you mistake me. I have no intention of refusing you. My feelings are quite the opposite of her ladyship's. I would be just as honored and happy to wed you if you had no fortune whatsoever."

"Are you quite certain?" He seemed to have as much

difficulty believing her answer as she had his proposal. "I am no Galahad or Romeo."

"Perhaps not." Marian recalled the conversation they'd once had about marriage. "But in every respect, you are still the answer to *this* maiden's prayer."

Once she'd said that, what was there for him to do but kiss her?

Slowly he pulled her into his arms and bent to claim her lips. She sensed a slight hesitation in his approach, but now she knew it did not spring from reluctance or lack of feeling. Instead it mirrored her own sense of disbelief that such a deeply desired blessing had been bestowed on her. She could not quite escape the nagging fear that she did not deserve such happiness.

If that was how Gideon felt, she was determined to reassure him. Reaching up to caress his cheek, she surged onto her toes to close the last inch between her lips and his.

Her eyes closed instinctively, the better to savor the multitude of sensations and emotions this sweet intimacy provoked. The velvety warmth of Gideon's kiss told a wordless tale of slowly growing love that had put down roots deep in his heart. It whispered of steadfast devotion that would be hers for all time, asking nothing in return.

A month after his proposal, Gideon set out on horseback for the village church, where he would await the arrival of Marian and the girls. As he rode, he recalled the first time he'd accompanied them to worship. The countryside had been dull, barren and chilled by frost, not unlike his heart. Now, wherever he looked, fresh, vigorous new life was springing forth. His heart quickened in response.

A tiny voice in the back of his mind cautioned against drinking too deeply from the cup of happiness, for the dregs might be bitter indeed. Gideon dismissed such forebodings as wedding nerves, though he could not imagine why he should have those. He had no misgivings about wedding Marian...except perhaps whether he could make her happy. Even those had begun to fade during their brief engagement as he'd witnessed her transparent delight in their wedding preparations.

When he reached the church, he tethered his horse, then hurried inside where the vicar was waiting for him. Most of the guests were already assembled, and the rest soon arrived.

The bride did not keep them waiting. When the organist struck up the processional, Gideon turned to see Cissy and Dolly walking down the aisle strewing flower petals. Their radiant smiles were the crowning delight to his happiest of days. He and Marian had worried the girls might be upset by their aunt's abrupt departure. Cissy had been a little at first, but when she and Dolly learned that Gideon intended to marry their beloved governess and become their guardian, the girls could scarcely contain their elation. Dolly wore a purple dress with a bright yellow sash, while her sister wore a yellow dress with a purple sash. He wondered at the unusual choice of colors until he looked past the girls to catch his first glimpse of Marian carrying a nosegay of purple and yellow crocuses, those bright, hardy little heralds of springtime.

For her wedding march, she clung to the arm of Mr. Culpepper. The butler beamed with pride over being chosen for this honor.

Gideon could scarcely take his eyes off his lovely bride. Having only seen her wearing dark colors, he marveled at how well she looked in her creamy white wedding dress. It brightened her complexion and brought out the gold and copper highlights in her dark brown hair. But no dress could account for the luminous glow in her dark eyes or the sweet radiance of her wide smile. Those could only come from a source of joy within her heart. That sweet certainty banished Gideon's last lurking shadows of doubt. He savored the realization that their union brought her as much happiness as it brought him.

When Marian reached his side, he returned her loving gaze and lavished her with a doting smile.

"Dearly beloved..." The opening words of the marriage ceremony drew their attention to the vicar. "We are gathered together here in the sight of God and in the face of his congregation to join together this man and this woman in holy matrimony."

An instant of breathless tension gripped Gideon when the vicar asked if there were objections to the marriage. Some tiny part of him still feared Marian might change her mind at the last moment. But she responded to the vicar's charge with serene silence, and the service moved on.

So intense was Gideon's relief that he was only vaguely aware of the vicar addressing him. Then came a moment of expectant silence in which he realized he was supposed to reply.

Fortunately, Dolly came to his rescue. In a loud whisper she prompted him, "You're supposed to say, *'I will.'*"

Gideon's response was nearly drowned out by a soft ripple of laughter that ran through the congregation.

Fortunately, Marian did not seem to take his hesitation amiss. After the vicar asked her the same question about loving, honoring and keeping Gideon, she needed no help from the girls to reply with fond resolve, "I will."

Determined to make up for his earlier lapse, Gideon concentrated very hard on repeating his vows to Marian clearly and sincerely. "I, Gideon, take thee, Marian, to be my wedded wife, to have and to hold from this day forward, for better, for worse, for richer, for poorer, in sickness and in health, to love and to cherish, till death us do part."

Soon it was time to slip the gold ring onto his bride's finger and pledge himself and all he owned to her.

As the vicar prayed for God's blessing upon their marriage, and late winter sunshine filtered into the sanctuary, Gideon could feel the divine presence surrounding them and stirring within them. Deep in his heart there pulsed a prayer of thanksgiving for two of the most precious blessings in all of creation—family and love.

Epilogue

Nottinghamshire, England
1815

Would Gideon ever come home? That question ran through Marian's thoughts as she sat in the nursery reading a story to Cissy and Dolly.

The blissful happiness of her wedding day had quietly shattered a fortnight later when Gideon received word from the Admiralty that he had been absolved of any wrongdoing and was being returned to the command of HMS *Integrity*.

"I don't understand," she recalled him saying as he stared at the letter in bewilderment. "I was certain the board meant to make me their scapegoat."

"Do you suppose they changed their minds after Napoleon returned to power?" Marian suggested. "In time of war the Admiralty must know they need strong leadership, not men who are only concerned with advancing their careers."

Though her heart quailed at the thought of Gideon

returning to sea, she could not be sorry he had gotten the justice he deserved at last. Besides the possible explanation she'd offered for his acquittal, Marian wondered if perhaps her friend Rebecca had persuaded Lord Benedict to look into the matter.

"You do realize what this means?" he asked, clearly torn between devotion to his family and duty to his crew and country.

"Of course." Much as she hated to see him go, Marian could not bear to add to his conflict. "You'll be able to return to your ship and protect your crew from those horrible bullies."

Though he hadn't spoken of it since the night he'd returned from London, Marian could tell that concern for his crew had weighed upon him.

Gideon gave a grim nod. "So I shall. But once this war is over, I intend to retire from the Royal Navy and return home to Knightley Park to stay."

Marian pretended to believe it would happen, though a streak of fatalism in her character insisted that any happiness she found in life would always be snatched away.

"This is something I must do," he murmured as he held her close and stroked her hair. "For my men and for my country. Before I returned to Knightley Park last autumn, my country was only a vague abstraction. Now it means so much more. It is you and the girls, our household, all the people of the parish, those school friends of yours whom I hope to meet someday. Everything I do as captain of the *Integrity* will be in your service."

The girls had reacted to his going in the way Marian

expected. Dolly wanted desperately to go along and share his adventures at sea while Cissy seemed to feel abandoned by yet another parental figure. Gideon assured the girls he would write to them as often as possible and begged them to write him about all their doings. He promised when the fighting was over and he returned to Knightley Park to stay, he would bring them presents from London.

On the night before his departure, after tucking the girls in with a kiss, he confided in Marian. "Thank heaven we were able to secure guardianship of the children. If any harm should befall me, I shall have the comfort of knowing you will love and care for them always."

"Please do not speak of harm coming to you, my love." She clasped his arm tighter, wishing she never had to let go. "I cannot bear to think of that."

But it was not her only worry. She also feared what might happen when he was reunited with his first and greatest love—the sea. Could he give up a life of adventure and gallant service for the quiet existence of a country squire?

The morning he left for London, she sensed their parting was as difficult for Gideon as for her and the girls. For all their sakes, Marian strove to appear cheerfully resigned, pretending to believe her husband would soon return. It was only after his carriage disappeared from view down the elm-lined lane and the girls had gone to play in the garden that she indulged in a few tears.

As the days turned to weeks and weeks to months, life at Knightley Park returned to its old familiar rhythm, with a few important differences. Marian was now the lady of the house, a role in which she was not altogether comfortable. But, for the sake of Gideon, the girls and the tenants, she gradually rose to the challenge. Whenever she was inclined to feel sorry for herself, she tried to remember that she now had everything for which she'd once prayed…and so much more. With that thought in mind, she concentrated on treasuring her blessings rather than yearning for the one thing she no longer had.

Whenever the longing for Gideon overwhelmed her, she wrote him another letter or prayed for his safety and happiness. Somehow, that helped her feel close to him again.

Now, several weeks after Napoleon's defeat at Waterloo, Marian rejoiced that the war was over, but grieved that she had not received a letter from her husband in some time. Clearly, his other life had reclaimed him. Perhaps this was his way of indicating he would rather she did not pester him with mail.

Her voice caught on the words she was reading. She could not make out the next passage through the haze of tears that rose in her eyes.

"Is something the matter?" Cissy leaned closer to Marian and ran a hand down her arm in a comforting caress.

When Marian could not master her emotions to reply, Dolly heaved a great sigh. "You miss him, too, don't you?"

Swallowing her tears, Marian gave a shaky smile and nodded.

"Don't fret," advised Dolly as if their roles were suddenly reversed and she was now the adult. "He'll be home soon, you'll see, and he'll bring us presents from London."

The sound of rushing footsteps made all three of them look up as Martha burst in. "It's him, ma'am— Captain Radcliffe, driving up the lane!"

The book Marian had been reading to the girls slid from her fingers to land on the carpet with a soft thud. The moment she'd hoped for all these weeks had arrived at last...in answer to her fervent prayers.

"Are you certain it's him?" demanded Cissy, clearly reluctant to get her hopes up.

"Of course it's him." Dolly seized her sister by the hand and pulled her toward the door. "Didn't I tell you he'd be coming home soon?"

In a daze of happiness, Marian rose and followed the children. The tears of longing she'd suppressed welled up again from a deep spring of joy.

No long line of servants waited under the portico to greet the captain this time, only his family.

When the carriage came to a halt, he did not wait for the footman, but thrust the door open himself and sprang out.

Dolly and Cissy ran toward him, crying, "Welcome home!"

His face alight with happiness, Gideon caught the girls each in one arm and pulled them into a warm embrace.

He looked rather gaunt and weary, but Marian relished the opportunity to fuss over him, making sure he got plenty of food and rest.

Gideon pressed a kiss on each of the girls' foreheads.

"That is the finest welcome I've ever received. But there is one other lady I have been longing to see."

When he looked up at Marian, his smile froze and his eyes widened. Striding toward his wife, he took her in his arms with restrained eagerness and kissed her tenderly.

"Why did you not tell me?" he whispered, lowering one hand to caress her swelling belly.

"I didn't want you coming back only for the sake of the child. I was afraid that once you returned to your ship, you would want to stay at sea."

"Never." Gideon shook his head vehemently. "In fact, there were times I got so homesick for you and the girls that I wanted to desert. Every evening in my cabin I read your letters and imagined myself back in the library at Knightley Park. Now that the war is over for good, and I have settled matters aboard the *Integrity,* I consider myself blessed to have such a fine family to come home to."

Feeling a familiar tug on his coat, which he had missed so keenly, Gideon glanced down at his darling Dolly.

"Did you bring us presents?" she demanded. "You promised you would when you went away, remember?"

"He came back." Sweet Cissy looked up at him with such love and faith that it made his throat tighten. "That's better than any present."

Gideon glanced at his beloved wife, whose eyes were shining with unshed tears of joy.

"It certainly is the best possible gift for me." He reached for Cissy's hand and gave it a warm squeeze. "But Dolly is right. A promise is a promise. I had great fun scouring the shops of London for things you might enjoy."

"Frederick," he called out to one of the footmen unloading his baggage. "Bring that small trunk into the Chinese drawing room."

A short while later, the whole family crowded together on the window seat as Gideon prepared to dispense the gifts he had bought. He could hardly wait to see Marian's face when he presented her with a gold locket in which he planned to put miniature portraits of the girls. Soon he would need to get her another one to hold the likeness of the child she was carrying.

"So tell me," he asked her as the girls opened the first of their presents, "when can we expect the newest member of our family to make an appearance?"

His question brought a gentle, brooding smile to her lips that made him catch his breath. "The midwife says the baby will likely arrive by mid-December."

As he recalled the Christmas that had made them a family and looked forward to many equally joyous in the years ahead, Gideon heaved a sigh of blessed happiness. "What better Christmas gift could we ask for?"

* * * * *

Dear Reader,

This story holds a special place in my heart. It came to me at a time when I was under contract to write another series. To keep the characters from taking too much of my attention away from those books, I wrote down a loose outline and bits of scenes, then stuck them away in a file.

By the time I was free to work on the story again, Love Inspired Books had launched its Historical line which I read and loved. I wondered if my governess story might be a good fit for the line. Taking out the old file, I began writing Gideon and Marian's story as an inspirational and found it worked so much better.

I had originally imagined the story taking place in the English countryside during the summer months, but when I checked the time frame of Napoleon's return to power after Elba, I realized that wouldn't work. Instead, the story would have to take place over the autumn and winter. Writing it as a Christmas story made all the pieces fall into place.

I hope you will enjoy this story of two lonely people, a pair of orphaned children and the Christmas that made them a family!

Wishing you the joy and peace of Christmas,
Deborah Hale

Questions for Discussion

1. At the beginning of the story, Marian hears that Captain Radcliffe has arrived at Knightley Park in spite of her prayers. Have you ever felt God was ignoring your prayers? How did that make you feel? Looking back, do you still see it that way or has time given you a new perspective?

2. Faced with his two young cousins, Gideon fears he cannot provide what they might need emotionally. Have you ever felt you weren't equipped to help someone who might have needed you? What did you do?

3. Marian allows rumors and gossip about the captain to color her initial opinion of him. Do you find it hard to keep an open mind about someone when you've heard bad things about them? Can you think of ways you might try to counter the effects of gossip?

4. When Marian asks if he will mind hearing the girls practice their piano lessons, Gideon says, "It is difficult to learn anything of value without making mistakes." How do you think that statement applies to Gideon in this story?

5. Gideon doesn't believe that God knows or cares about his "trivial concerns any more than the vast ocean cares for one insignificant ship that floats

upon it." What kind of answer would you have given Gideon if you had been in Marian's place?

6. When Marian decides it would be good for Gideon to seek custody of Dolly and Cissy, she thinks it is "too important a task to leave up to the power of prayer alone." What do you think about that? In what ways might our prayers and actions work together for good?

7. How did the events of Gideon's childhood shape his doubts about the power of prayer? Have painful events in your life affected your ability to trust or believe? Were you able to overcome them and, if so, how?

8. Gideon thinks that Marian's painful memories might trouble her more at Christmastime, in contrast to the pervading happiness of the season. Do you know anyone for whom Christmas is a sad or lonely time? Can you think of any ways you might help?

9. When she hears the carolers singing, Marian is touched by the wonder of Christmas. What is your favorite Christmas carol? Why does it have special significance for you?

10. When Gideon slips on a patch of ice while running after Cissy in Newark, it seems like a disaster, yet his fall brings the child back to him. Have you ever

had something bad happen to you that turned out to be a blessing in disguise?

11. Cissy tells Gideon she thinks God hasn't answered her prayers because she hasn't been good enough. How would you respond to a child who felt that way?

12. Gideon, Marian and the girls exchange small Christmas gifts that carry a great deal of care and love. What other precious, intangible gifts do they give each other through the course of the story?

INSPIRATIONAL

Wholesome romances that touch the heart and soul.

Love Inspired.
HISTORICAL

COMING NEXT MONTH
AVAILABLE JANUARY 10, 2012

THE COWBOY TUTOR
Three Brides for Three Cowboys
Linda Ford

AN INCONVENIENT MATCH
Janet Dean

ALL ROADS LEAD HOME
Christine Johnson

THE UNLIKELY WIFE
Debra Ullrick

Look for these and other Love Inspired books wherever books are sold, including most bookstores, supermarkets, discount stores and drugstores.

LIHCNM1211

In the exciting new FITZGERALD BAY *series
from Love Inspired Suspense, law enforcement siblings
fight for justice and family when one of their own
is accused of murder.*

Read on for a sneak preview of the first book,
THE LAWMAN'S LEGACY *by Shirlee McCoy.*

Police captain Douglas Fitzgerald stepped into his father's house. The entire Fitzgerald clan had gathered, and he was the last to arrive. Not a problem. He had a foolproof excuse. Duty first. That's the way his father had raised him. It was the only way he knew how to be.

Voices carried from the dining room. With his boisterous family around, his life could never be empty.

But there *were* moments when he felt that something was missing.

Some*one* was missing.

Before he could dwell on his thoughts, his radio crackled and the dispatcher came on.

"Captain? We have a situation on our hands. A body has been found near the lighthouse."

"Where?"

"At the base of the cliffs. The caller believes the deceased may be Olivia Henry."

"It can't be Olivia." Douglas's brother Charles spoke. The custodial parent to his twin toddlers, he employed Olivia as their nanny.

"I'll be there in ten minutes." He jogged back outside and jumped into his vehicle.

Douglas flew down Main Street and out onto the rural road that led to the bluff. Two police cars followed. His brothers and his father. Douglas was sure of it. Together, they'd piece together what had happened.

The lighthouse loomed in the distance, growing closer with every passing mile. A beat-up station wagon sat in the driveway.

Douglas got out and made his way along the path to the cliff.

Up ahead, a woman stood near the edge.

Meredith O'Leary.

There was no mistaking her strawberry-blond hair, her feminine curves, or the way his stomach clenched, his senses springing to life when he saw her.

"Merry!"

"Captain Fitzgerald! Olivia is…"

"Stay here. I'll take a look."

He approached the cliff's edge. Even from a distance, Douglas recognized the small frame.

His father stepped up beside him. "It's her."

"I'm afraid so."

"We need to be the first to examine the body. If she fell, fine. If she didn't, we need to know what happened."

If she fell.

The words seemed to hang in the air, the other possibilities hovering with them.

Can Merry work together with Douglas to find justice for Olivia…without giving up her own deadly secrets?
To find out, pick up
THE LAWMAN'S LEGACY *by Shirlee McCoy,*
on sale January 10, 2012.

REQUEST YOUR FREE BOOKS!

2 FREE INSPIRATIONAL NOVELS
PLUS 2
FREE
MYSTERY GIFTS

Love Inspired

HISTORICAL
INSPIRATIONAL HISTORICAL ROMANCE

YES! Please send me 2 FREE Love Inspired® Historical novels and my 2 FREE mystery gifts (gifts are worth about $10). After receiving them, if I don't wish to receive any more books, I can return the shipping statement marked "cancel". If I don't cancel, I will receive 4 brand-new novels every month and be billed just $4.49 per book in the U.S. or $4.99 per book in Canada. That's a saving of at least 22% off the cover price. It's quite a bargain! Shipping and handling is just 50¢ per book in the U.S. and 75¢ per book in Canada.* I understand that accepting the 2 free books and gifts places me under no obligation to buy anything. I can always return a shipment and cancel at any time. Even if I never buy another book, the two free books and gifts are mine to keep forever.

102/302 IDN FEHF

Name	(PLEASE PRINT)	
Address		Apt. #
City	State/Prov.	Zip/Postal Code

Signature (if under 18, a parent or guardian must sign)

Mail to the **Reader Service:**
IN U.S.A.: P.O. Box 1867, Buffalo, NY 14240-1867
IN CANADA: P.O. Box 609, Fort Erie, Ontario L2A 5X3

Not valid for current subscribers to Love Inspired Historical books.

Want to try two free books from another series?
Call 1-800-873-8635 or visit www.ReaderService.com.

---

* Terms and prices subject to change without notice. Prices do not include applicable taxes. Sales tax applicable in N.Y. Canadian residents will be charged applicable taxes. Offer not valid in Quebec. This offer is limited to one order per household. All orders subject to credit approval. Credit or debit balances in a customer's account(s) may be offset by any other outstanding balance owed by or to the customer. Please allow 4 to 6 weeks for delivery. Offer available while quantities last.

Your Privacy—The Reader Service is committed to protecting your privacy. Our Privacy Policy is available online at www.ReaderService.com or upon request from the Reader Service.

We make a portion of our mailing list available to reputable third parties that offer products we believe may interest you. If you prefer that we not exchange your name with third parties, or if you wish to clarify or modify your communication preferences, please visit us at www.ReaderService.com/consumerchoice or write to us at Reader Service Preference Service, P.O. Box 9062, Buffalo, NY 14269. Include your complete name and address.

LIH11B

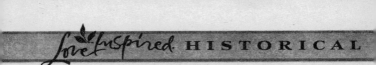

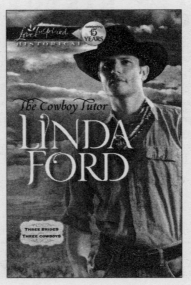

LIH82899

ReaderService.com has a new look!

We have refreshed our website and we want to share our new look with you. Head over to ReaderService.com and check it out!

On ReaderService.com, you can:

- Try 2 free books from any series
- Access risk-free special offers
- View your account history & manage payments
- Browse the latest Bonus Bucks catalog

Don't miss out!

If you want to stay up-to-date on the latest at the Reader Service and enjoy more Harlequin content, make sure you've signed up for our monthly News & Notes email newsletter. Sign up online at ReaderService.com.